The *Ganzfield* Series

Minder
Adversary
Legacy (January 2011)
Accused (Summer 2011)

Praise for *Minder*

"Absolutely flawless!" - Reading Teen
A Reading Teen "What to Read This Summer" Pick for 2010

"*Minder* is dynamic, original, thoughtful, and entrancing... nothing short of brilliant." - Book Crazy

"Suspenseful, enchanting, and romantic, *Minder* is a great start to an exciting new series." - Ellz Readz

"*It*. Some books have *it*, some don't. *It* is simply what makes you keep reading, what pulls you forward, what keeps a book niggling in your mind until you simply have to reread it...or pick up the sequel. *Minder* has *it*. I was completely hooked by the premise, and *Minder* definitely delivered." - Elephants on Trapezes

"Clever and creative...this book sucked me in and would not let me go—not that I would have wanted it to." - Escape Between The Pages

"This book snatches your attention from the first paragraph and doesn't let go." - Critique this WIP

"I love this book! The author creates a world in *Minder* that is so easy to get lost in that I had to remind myself that there really isn't a Ganzfield. But then again, would we really know if there was? *Minder* is a very fun read!" – Books Complete Me

"This is a must read. Kaynak brings plenty of action, unique story telling, and lots of romance...be prepared for lots of swooning. " – Cari's Book Blog

"*Minder* is an engaging psychological thriller with a streak of science fiction for good measure. The world Kate Kaynak creates is dark and twisted, full of intense young adult issues as well as looming supernatural threats. A mesmerizing and heart-pounding race against time. " – The Bookish Type

Spencer Hill Press

Please visit our website at spencerhillpress.com

First Edition August 2010

Kaynak, Kate, 1971—
Adversary : a novel / by Kate Kaynak – 1st ed.
p. cm.
Summary:
The story of telepathic teenager Maddie Dunn continues as she and her friends train to protect the people at Ganzfield. But things are more dangerous than they know, and not everyone will survive.

Cover design by K. Kaynak

ISBN 978-0-9845311-2-7 (paperback)
ISBN 978-0-9845311-3-4 (e-book)

Printed in the United States of America

ADVERSARY

A GANZFIELD NOVEL BY

KATE

KAYNAK

For Alex,
Your request to read
this made me glow green.

SPENCER HILL PRESS

Kate Kaynak

Dear Reader,

Adversary is the second book of the Ganzfield series. I hope you've read *Minder*, the first Ganzfield book, before reading this one. Otherwise, you're entering Maddie's world of minders, sparks, charms, and RVs without knowing what these things are, and that will confuse the heck out of you.

Some TV shows have a little montage at the beginning that says, "Previously, on…" and gives you a quick summary of the stuff that happened earlier. So, this little intro is the "Previously, at Ganzfield…" montage that reminds you who people are and what they can do. Here's what you need to know:

GANZFIELD

Ganzfield is a secret training facility that occupies a couple hundred acres near North Conway, New Hampshire. Inside the walls, there's a lake, two big, rambling farmhouses (the main building and Blake House), and an old red barn between them. The smaller houses at the old crossroads now serve as dorms for students and housing for some of the instructors. Maddie and Trevor live in the old church that sits back in the woods. The sparks sleep in a cluster of fireproof cottages at the edge of the lake. A few isolated cabins lie scattered around the rest of the wooded property, and some wind generators sit atop one of the hills.

G-POSITIVES and DODECAMINE

The people of Ganzfield have a recessive genetic trait that they call "G-positive." People with this trait naturally have flashes of an extra ability—like telepathy—from time to time. However, if G-positives receive regular doses of the synthetic neurotransmitter dodecamine, they can develop into minders, telekinetics, sparks, charms, healers, or RVs. G-positives need to keep taking dodecamine every few weeks or they lose their abilities. Most people at Ganzfield are teenagers who've been on the meds for less than two years and are still learning to use their abilities.

MINDERS

Minders are mind-readers, a.k.a. telepaths. Sixteen-year-old Maddie Dunn came to Ganzfield last October after three guys from her high school dragged her into a van and tried to do things that still haunt her nightmares. She ended up frying their brains and killing them. Now that she takes dodecamine, she can hear people's thoughts when they're near her and block her own thoughts from other minders with a mental shield. Maddie accidentally projects her dreams to others when she's asleep, so she tries not to do that around most people. She also can blast people's brains with different intensities of energy, sort of like setting herself from "stun" to "kill." Only one other G-positive has ever had this lethal ability: Isaiah Lerner—and he's not nearly as dead as he's made people think.

Two other minders live at Ganzfield. Dr. Jon Williamson runs the place. He can hear everyone's thoughts and shield his own from other minders. He's been telepathic for decades, starting when he was part of Project Star Gate (by the way, this was a *real* U.S. Government project. Really. You can Google it). Dr. Williamson funds Ganzfield by reading the minds of investment bankers and playing the stock market. His niece, Ann, used to be a minder, but she left shortly after Maddie arrived.

The other minder, Seth Black, can't project his thoughts to non-telepaths, although he has the strongest receptive telepathy of all of the minders. This makes people's thoughts very loud for him, so he usually keeps his distance from others, especially the other minders, since their thoughts sound even louder to him.

TELEKINETICS

Telekinesis is the ability to move things mentally, and Trevor Laurence is Ganzfield's only telekinetic. He's also Maddie's boyfriend—even more than that, he's her "soulmate." The two of them have an amazing way of connecting as pure energy. They also share dreams in which he uses lucid dreaming techniques to change their imagined environment—and to help Maddie with her nightmares. Trevor controls two extra-strong mental hands with his ability. He can extend them about fifteen feet from him or widen them to cover large areas. In *Minder,* he shielded Maddie from being shot. Trevor needs to sleep in a large, open place, since his telekinetic ability comes out during his dreams... and it's strong enough to knock down walls.

SPARKS

Sparks can control fire, and they also have telekinesis with burning objects. There are two known families of people with this pyrokinetic ability. The McFees—a big clan of Irish firefighters— include Trevor's best friend, Drew, his brother, Harrison, and a bunch of burly, red-headed cousins. The Underwoods are descended from William Underwood, who was a real person and the first "documented" pyrokinetic. There are about twenty sparks at Ganzfield.

CHARMS

Charms can control other people's actions with verbal commands. When they use their ability, it's like strong hypnosis or the "Jedi mind trick," and only minders are immune to them. Some charms become sociopathic with their ability, using it to take advantage of others. Charm compulsion usually doesn't wear off with time, although charms can remove each other's commands. A few charms, like Cecelia Mitchell, have started using charming to help people—and to keep the other charms in line. About thirty charms live at Ganzfield; this is the most common G-positive ability.

REMOTE VIEWERS (RVs)

RVs can see people, objects, or locations that are far away from them. Rachel Fontaine used this ability to find Trevor after he'd been abducted, although they arrived too late to save her Uncle Charlie, another RV, who'd been vivisected by a scientist trying to find out more about G-positive abilities. About a dozen RVs live at Ganzfield.

HEALERS

Healers use their ability to rev up the body's natural healing and instantly mend cuts, burns, broken bones, etc. Matilda and Morris Taylor, a brother and sister originally from Liberia, do most of the healing at Ganzfield. They also train the two teenage healers: Hannah Washington and Lester Gale.

And now, back to the show…

Kate Kaynak
New Hampshire, January 2010

For Yaya

CHAPTER 1

Were we too late? Sick fear twisted my gut as we ran, and the dark hall seemed to lengthen with each echoing step. I tried to type the code into the keypad by the door but my shaking fingers wouldn't cooperate. Drew started burning around the lock. The sudden blare of an alarm jarred my frayed nerves to the shattering point. I felt telepathically behind the door for a familiar mind, but all that I could get were fractured images of nightmarish tortures. Tears streaked down my face; I felt so useless.

So stupid.

I hugged my arms around my waist tightly, as though I could keep myself together through sheer, blunt will.

We were too late. I just knew we were too late.

Drew kicked the door open and it disappeared into the dark. A little ball of flame rose above his hand and a macabre scene floated out of the firelight. People I knew lay strapped to gurneys with metal rings screwed around their heads. Their skin was grey in death; their eyes filmed white. Bloody head wounds shone slickly black.

The world tilted when I recognized the cold mask of anguish in front of me.

Trevor.

Oh, God. No, no, no, no, no! My mind exploded in pain. I fell to the floor, racked with sobs.

Too late…

"This one again?" A familiar voice came from behind me.

After a flash of confusion, light flooded back into the world as I recognized Trevor's voice. It didn't come from the unmoving body on the operating table. Trevor knelt next to me, beautifully whole and alive, wrapping his arms around me. I clung to him, a fairly useless mass of quivering relief, as he pulled me up to stand. His eyes fell on the corpse on the operating table next to us. It was his own mangled corpse.

Okay, that makes no sense.

Was this just a dream? Trevor and I must be sharing dreams again. I exhaled with a half-sob. The sickening nightmare landscape faded away. Thanks to Trevor's lucid-dreaming skills, he and I now stood in a high mountain meadow in mid-summer. A glittering river, white with little waterfalls, danced below us. The air felt like it cleansed my lungs with every breath. Wild-flowers overflowed around us—gold, white, and purple—rippling with a gentle push from the wind.

I met his warm, chocolate-brown eyes, feeling gratitude on many levels.

"You couldn't dream about kittens, could you?" Trevor smiled with mock exasperation. "Oh, no. No cute little puppies for you."

I pulled closer to him, shut my eyes, and rested my cheek against his chest as I felt my heart unclench. "Thanks."

"Have you considered looking at pictures of bunnies before going to bed?" His hand stroked my hair. "Maybe baby chicks, all yellow and fluffy?"

I laughed shakily, tilting up to meet his gaze again, warmed by the light within his eyes. "In my twisted subconscious, those baby chicks would become vicious monsters that would peck our brains out."

Trevor laughed. "Probably." He gave me a quick, sweet kiss. "You do have a dark side. You know what we could do—"

The sound of a gunshot cut him off. Hot agony ripped through me and I cried out. I was suddenly horribly awake—and back in the real world. Trevor was no longer beside me. I curled into the fetal position, overwhelmed by the excruciating, screaming pain.

CHAPTER 2

In the pre-dawn dark, Trevor vaulted up to my loft in the old church. His hands gripped my face. "Maddie! What happened? What's wrong?"

"It's not me," I hissed through clenched teeth. "Drew's outside. He's shot."

Trevor took a couple of sleep-muddled seconds to process that I wasn't injured. Once everything clicked, he jumped back down to the main floor of the church and stuffed his feet into boots. Outside our front door, his best friend lay bleeding in the fresh snow, swearing and feeling stupid.

Trevor picked up Drew and quickly started off toward the infirmary. Drew was about the size and build of a bear, so it was a good thing Trevor could carry several hundred pounds telekinetically. As they left my mental range, my face muscles unlocked from their grimace. I took a deep breath.

Feeling other people's pain was definitely one of the downsides of telepathy, and the sensation of a fresh bullet wound was probably the worst wake-up call ever. I'd sensed that Drew had gotten himself in the leg—a long, angry injury that ripped from the top of his outer thigh nearly to his knee. From the location, I assumed the gun had been holstered. I rolled my eyes; Drew should know better than to carry a loaded gun around. As a spark, he accidentally ignited things all the time.

On the plus side, he never needed to carry matches.

No stress—Drew's wound was nasty, but it would be gone in a few minutes. I needed to give the healers a head start since I didn't want to share his pain again. I used the bathroom, brushed my teeth, and pulled on some clothes. Grabbing Trevor's coat along with my own, I headed out to the infirmary, flashlight in hand.

Drew looked up from the exam table as I came in. His red-haired, freckled bulk dwarfed tiny Matilda, who was just finishing with the bullet wound. I could feel the vicarious electric tingles from her healing ability working through Drew's leg. She and I smiled a silent hi at each other, her white teeth flashing in bright contrast to her mahogany complexion.

"Sorry, Maddie." Drew gave me a sheepish look.

I laughed. "Only in a weird place like Ganzfield would someone accidentally shoot himself, and then apologize to someone else."

Trevor had carried Drew all the way from our church to Blake House in ten-degree weather wearing just a long-sleeved t-shirt and flannel PJ-pants, and his lanky frame still shivered. I hung his coat over a chair then slid my arms around him and rubbed his back. He sighed and leaned against me. Since he's about ten inches taller than my little five-foot-three frame, we nearly toppled over, but his invisible hands steadied us.

"So, Drew, why were you coming over so early?"

He slid his feet to the floor, experimentally testing his leg as he put his linebacker-like weight on it. "It's a go."

Excitement flashed through me. "Today?"

"Yup. Williamson okayed it…*if* we get Frank and Greg to sign off. But here's the catch." I unfolded the sheet of paper he handed me and scanned it quickly. My eyebrows crawled up my face as I read.

I let out a long breath and handed the paper to Trevor. "I'll go up and wake the rest of the team."

"Give me ten minutes." Hannah jumped out of bed.

"Give me coffee," groaned Rachel. A few strands of her hair formed a static halo around her head as she lifted it from the pillow.

"Dining hall. Let's make it twenty minutes." I went down the hall and knocked on Grace's door.

"Go away." The voice dripped with charm resonance.

Save it for someone who'll do what you say, I thought directly into her mind. The unexpected mental contact shocked her awake. *Bring your documents. Team's meeting in the dining hall in twenty.*

"Documents?" She flung open the door. "You mean—?"

"We've got to pass Frank and Greg's latest test, but when we do, it's a go."

Grace grinned. It was the first time I'd seen her smile in a while.

Drew was the last to join us; he'd needed to go to his locker down by the spark houses to find a pair of jeans without rips and bloodstains. Trevor finished reading Dr. Williamson's note aloud to the others.

Prove that you are ready to leave Ganzfield as a team. Frank has the first piece of information. Get it from him without raising his suspicions. Follow the steps until you have what you need. Good luck.

"Another scavenger hunt?" Grace scowled. "What's the point?"

Rachel rolled her eyes. "Don't start."

"We've been training for over a month now, and all we do is—"

"That's training." I cut her off. "And now, if we do this, we get a reward. C'mon. We all want to go, right?"

"This stuff just seems pointless," Grace sulked.

"It wouldn't seem pointless to you if you'd been at Eden Imaging that night." Drew was tired of her whining, as well.

"I'm sick of hearing about Eden Imaging all the time." I saw deep red flecks of irritation rising from her—an aura of annoyance. "I'm *this* close to charming you all to shut up about it!"

Grace, DON'T threaten them with your ability. My voice filled her head—dead-serious and cold. *Ever.*

Grace paled and met my eyes as she realized what she'd said. "I wouldn't really. You know that, Maddie."

I nodded, but Rachel looked at Grace with loathing and even Drew leaned away from her. Refocus—we needed to work together. But the continual bickering, particularly between Grace and Rachel, made my head ache. "Okay, forget it. Let's do this. I'm thinking Rachel finds Frank, and then Grace and I go talk to him."

"He's in his room." Rachel wore her straight, blonde hair pulled back tightly from her face, making her look older and serious. She could pass for twenty-something, even though she wasn't going to be eighteen for a few more months. I could see the RV connection in her mind; it looked like a golden thread of light to me. Rachel could locate things just about anywhere. She'd effortlessly found Frank in his home here at Ganzfield.

I gave Trevor's hand a squeeze as Grace and I stood up. "We'll be right back."

"You want backup?" Something twitched in Trevor at the thought of separation.

"The fewer people he can charm, the better." I would've preferred to do this solo, but I'd need Grace's help if Frank noticed me in his head.

"What's the plan?" she asked, once we'd left the main building. It was later than it looked; reluctant grey light filtered through the trees as we walked to one of the smaller houses surrounding the old crossroads. *I can't believe I said that—about charming them— after what Victor tried to make me do in the basement. But I'm so sick of being treated like an outsider…and no one likes me anyway.*

Grace hadn't meant for me to hear her thoughts. I closed my eyes for a moment, wishing I could stop feeling so much from everyone—just for a little while. I'd had the contents of so many people's heads dumped into mine over the past few months. Most of the time, it was more than I wanted to know, I'd gotten better at pretending I didn't sense what people were really thinking, so I responded to what she'd said aloud.

"I'll see if I can get the intel without him knowing I'm there. But there's a good chance he'll figure out what I'm doing—he'll be expecting me. I'll signal you if I need help."

We skirted around the newly-built access ramp at the back of the house. I could now hear Frank's thoughts, bitter and familiar. He pulled on his second prosthetic leg, adjusting the support straps above his knee. Pain painted his memories purple. He flashed back to his last day with military intelligence in Baghdad when his second tour had been cut short by the explosion of a roadside IED. The injuries no longer hurt him physically—Morris had seen to that the day Frank had returned to Ganzfield. He'd come straight from the military hospital at the end of December—more than a month ago. Frank paused, refrained from throwing the prosthetic across the room, and then tightened the strap across his thigh and reached for his crutches.

Get close to the window, I thought to Grace. Snow muffled our footsteps.

What does the team need to know for today's training mission? I floated the thought lightly into Frank's head.

Frank stiffened. "Nice try, Maddie." His head filled with images of a brick wall and an old Pink Floyd song.

Crap.

Okay, Plan B. *Grace, charm him to think about what we need to know.*

"Franklin Summers! Don't say another word to us. Think about what we need to know!" she charm-yelled at the window. Quick surprise flashed through Frank—he'd assumed I'd come alone. He hadn't even tried to charm me, since he knew I was immune to his ability. Now the image of a cloth bag hanging from a tree filled his thoughts. *Where is it?* I thought strongly into his mind. No need for stealth anymore. I recognized the path near the front gate.

We were never here, I thought to Grace.

"Forget we were ever here, Frank!" she yelled. Frank's thoughts returned to the pain of that last day in Baghdad. I bit my lip. Should we give him a happier train of thought? No. Pleasant emotions might make Frank suspicious. We left him with his memories.

Okay, This wasn't as elegantly executed as I would've liked, but at least we had the next step. I touched Trevor's mind with mine as we returned—our special connection gave me a larger range with him than with other people. *Time for a walk in the woods.*

Rachel's ability took us into the maze of grey, leafless trunks and dark evergreens. We moved without talking; when we trained, I used my ability to relay instructions to everyone. The team knew how to frame thoughts into words so I could read them clearly, although most still felt uncomfortable with me in their heads.

The sky had lightened further by the time I sensed the two charms in a hunter's blind. I recognized their minds: Alex and Josh. The cold of inactivity seeped through both of them, giving me sympathy shivers. I wondered what they'd been offered to undertake guard duty. Most people at Ganzfield refused to train against us anymore.

I smiled. In a way, that was a huge compliment—we'd gotten that good.

Rachel's ability cast an invisible golden halo around the little bag high above the little shelter, impaled to the trunk with an arrow.

Two guards. Charms, I silently told the team.

Trevor met my eyes. *I'm ready to try it.*

I nodded. We watched as he moved in behind the blind with careful steps. My heart pounded faster, but it was with excitement, not fear. Actually, with no real threat present, training was kinda fun. It was like playing an unusual sport where the rules could change if we thought of another way to do things. We'd come up with new ways to use our abilities to gather intel, scale walls, and disarm or disable our opponents. To think that a few months ago, my biggest challenges had been exams in Mr. Storrs' A.P. history class.

Trevor threw out his telekinetic hands as he slid around the side of the shelter. The startled charms didn't have time to react before Trevor's invisible grip covered their mouths and pushed them back in their seats. Their shock flashed sunrise colors brightly through their minds.

It worked! Trevor's yellow-green thrill of joy brought a smile to my lips. I jumped up to join him, trailed by the rest of the team.

Trevor frowned at the little bag that hung high above us. "I could climb up on the shelter roof and reach it." He gauged the distance with his fifteen-foot telekinetic range in mind. *But then I'd need to let go of these two.*

"Don't bother." Drew focused and the wood around the arrowhead began to smoke. Flames licked along the arrow as Drew pulled the fire to him. The bag landed in his hand.

"A map." Drew unfolded the paper sealed in plastic.

Grace groaned.

"X marks the spot." Rachel sent little golden rays to the location, seeing it in her mind. "The car."

"Josh. Alex. Stay where you are for the next hour. Don't say anything." Grace's voice filled with charm resonance.

Trevor released his hold on them and Hannah touched each of them briefly, using her ability to make sure Trevor hadn't caused any damage. My lips twitched slightly—she'd finally agreed to join the team to keep people safe from *me*. But I hadn't caused a single injury to anyone since we'd started training. She'd gradually relaxed about the whole "killer telepath" thing. Now she only looked at me like I was a dangerous monster a couple of times a week.

"Forget you saw us out here," Grace added.

Our breath formed little clouds as we followed a single set of tire tracks through the snow. The brick wall to our left formed the barrier between Ganzfield and the rest of the world, while the quiet thoughts of birds and chipmunks filled the trees. I felt like our walled compound was an uncharted island in the middle of a sea of trees and winter.

The silver sedan blocked the narrow trail. Drew frowned. "Hey, where are the keys?"

Rachel threw golden tendrils out from her mind once more. "Greg's house."

"Anyone there?" I asked. She widened her view, searching through the house, and then shook her head.

"Let's go." Trevor took my hand in his. Rachel followed.

Think he's set booby-traps again? I asked silently. It'd taken most of a week to get all of the paint out of my hair from the last time.

Probably, but we're not going in through the door.

I grinned as I followed his thoughts.

Trevor had been doing his physical instruction with Greg, Dr. Williamson's driver and a former Navy SEAL, for more than a year. When Dr. Williamson asked him to train our team, Greg threw himself into it with gruff enthusiasm. His brother Kurt had been an archeologist who'd used his remote viewing ability to make some extraordinary finds in his early career. Dr. Williamson had told me about them.

Greg accidentally discovered Kurt's ability six years ago.

Why didn't you send a charm to talk to him? I'd asked. That was Dr. Williamson's usual M.O. in cases like this.

Isaiah killed Kurt. Greg witnessed it. We did send a charm to talk to Greg—twice. But he kept looking for answers in his brother's disappearance. Finally, we simply took off the charm commands, let him remember what he'd seen, and explained the rest to him. He's not a G-positive, but he wanted to help protect Ganzfield. Felt that he owed it to Kurt.

I scanned for Greg's mind as we approached the house. If he'd set traps, I could float thoughts into his head and figure out what he'd done. This time, though, he was far enough away that I couldn't read him.

"Second floor," said Rachel.

"I'm on it." Trevor unlatched the upstairs window with his ability and slid both the storm glass and the inner panes open. *Ready?* he thought to me.

I nodded. *Ready.*

Trevor's invisible hands gripped my waist, boosting me through the open window. I used my connection to Rachel's mind, following the golden thread across the orderly bedroom to the small bathroom.

Rachel's vision led to a plastic bag sunk in the back of the toilet. The keys weighted it down to the bottom. I flushed and watched the water level drop, grabbing the exposed plastic bag before the tank filled again.

Got them! I thought to the waiting team below, returning to the window. Trevor lifted me back down, catching me in his arms, and then closed and re-locked the window.

"Let's go!" Rachel was already headed toward the car.

The others waited for us. I tossed the keys to Drew. The sedan only had five seats, but we needed this car today—we'd practiced with it. Drew and Rachel sat up front; Grace, Hannah, and Trevor got in back. Trevor pulled me into his lap, wrapping me in two sets of long arms: one visible, one invisible. I leaned against his chest, turning my head to fit against his neck, and his heartbeat tapped soothingly against my cheek. He snapped the seatbelt around us both as the car bumped across the frozen trail.

Gravel crunched under the tires as we left the Ganzfield property for the first time in nearly two months. We knew that the real tests still lay ahead of us.

At the New Hampshire DMV.

I did a paranoid mental sweep as we left the safety of Ganzfield. Did anyone recognize us? Was anyone targeting us? As far as I could tell, no one was. I relaxed once we hit the main road and joined the flow of morning traffic. A few months ago, I'd caught a mental whiff of someone surveilling us but hadn't known enough to understand the danger. Then the people I'd sensed had kidnapped Trevor. They'd wanted to experiment on him. The memory still made my gut twist with sick dread. We'd stopped them and I'd even killed some of them.

We arrived at the Conway Town Hall just as they opened, piling out of the car like clowns out of a circus Volkswagen.

Ready for this, Grace? I asked.

Absolutely! It's my first chance to charm a real person.

I nearly gave her some grief about that. We were "real" people out at Ganzfield—just "gifted," as Dr. Williamson called it. However, I decided not to rattle her. We found the town clerk's office and Grace had a few words with her. Soon, we were back in the car with four signed letters of residency.

Grace grinned smugly. "That was too easy."

Rachel rolled her eyes and Grace's pleasure evaporated with her smile.

Over the past month, I'd enjoyed training with Grace, but as a minder, I was immune to her "Jedi mind trick." Grace's presence reminded Rachel of unpleasant memories and the others still felt uneasy around her. Still, I wished they'd just get over it.

The closest DMV was nearly an hour away in Berlin. The name of Berlin, New Hampshire, was pronounced with the emphasis on the first syllable: "BURL-in." I'd been told this had started with a burst of patriotism during the First World War and they'd never bothered to change it back.

We'd been throwing the idea of this trip around since mid-December. I'd asked my mom to bring my birth certificate and passport when she'd come at Christmas so I'd be prepared for today. My mom's Christmas visit had been memorable—literally. She had taken the information about G-positives well, which meant Dr. Williamson hadn't been forced to have someone charm her to forget before she'd gone home. She'd even gotten the healers to test her—she was a G-positive, too.

She'd smiled at the news. "That explains a lot." She'd become a psychologist, after all. People paid her to have insights into their mental states.

My mom on dodecamine? Yikes. People who first started using the drug as adults usually developed weaker abilities, but Dr. Williamson had been over thirty for his first dose, and he was a very strong telepath. There was no way to tell how strong my mom's ability would be—if she was a telepath at all. It was a good bet; relatives often had the same abilities. The best example was Drew's family; the McFees accounted for more than half of the known sparks.

The thought made me a bit uncomfortable. I really didn't want my mom to hear all of the things I was thinking and feeling—particularly when it came to Trevor. She'd met him at Christmastime and all had gone well for the first few hours. She's a good judge of character and Trevor had been eager to make a good impression.

Then she'd found out that we were living together in the old church.

I winced at the memory. She'd glared at me, up at Trevor,

and around the sanctuary in turns. I'd felt like I had when I was five years old and she'd caught me coloring the dining room wallpaper with crayons. Her fists had balled on her plump hips and her green eyes had flashed with as much anger and dismay as her mind. With her round face and dark-brown hair wisping out around her, she'd looked like a fairy godmother in a tizzy. *I know those separate beds are just a ruse—a rather obvious and pathetic one.*

Her feelings about Trevor had shifted in that moment. *The crush Maddie has on this boy is too intense. It's a distraction that could keep her from getting into a good college.* She still hadn't accepted that a traditional college experience was no longer a real option for me. She believed that I was giving up on that dream in order to be with my boyfriend. *But if I make an issue of it, she'll just hold onto him harder.*

Ugh. I'd suspected that hearing my mom's thoughts might be disturbing. At least everything at Ganzfield had looked pretty, all covered in snow. It meant that the frosty attitude my mom now had for Trevor fit right in with the scenery.

Completely unfair.

Trevor was so eager to please, and his relationship with his own family was so strained and complicated. He didn't want to cause problems between my mom and me. And the main thing she held against Trevor was false—we *weren't* having sex. Trevor had given Dr. Williamson his word on that and had been adamant about keeping it.

The "no sex" thing was not that big a deal—honestly. We had other things we could do. In fact, I was pretty sure that soulmating was better than sex. We could intertwine our mental energies in a way that was all-encompassing, passionate, and overwhelming. Each time we did it, our mental and emotional connection grew stronger—we became more aware, more attuned to each other. It affected us physically, of course, but our thoughts and emotions also blended together like a single consciousness. And I didn't have to think about projecting thoughts to Trevor anymore—it just happened.

Right now, Trevor was daydreaming about kissing me. I closed my eyes, focused in, and could almost feel his lips against mine. In his mind, he trailed down and started kissing the hollow of my neck. My heart hammered and a buzzing red energy danced over my skin. *Oh, yes.* I let Trevor feel the effect he was having on me. His breathing quickened—mine did, too. The thoughts of the others in the car faded away and we drifted together in his daydream.

"What on earth are you two doing?" Drew's voice broke into our little reverie.

Crap.

My eyes flew open. Everyone in the car had stopped talking—they were all staring at us. Hannah's dismay and embarrassment flowed hot-pink as she inched away on the seat. Trevor and I were both flushed and breathing hard, although we weren't physically doing anything. Is it a P.D.A. if you're just *thinking* about kissing each other? I felt the deepening blush creep up both of our faces.

"Oops." We were usually more discrete. "Sorry."

"Sorry." Trevor dipped his head, embarrassed.

"Geez, you two." A smirk played across Drew's face. "Get a church."

Trevor, can you think of something else?

Not at the moment.

Me neither..

He chuckled and kissed the top of my head.

DMV! I thought at him. *We're going to the DMV. The DMV is definitely not sexy. Let's think about that.*

Trevor pictured us making out in the DMV.

I rolled my eyes, feeling the red energy begin to trace along my skin again. *That's not helping!*

Can't stop. I think I'm addicted to you.

I grinned. *The first step is admitting you have a problem.*

CHAPTER 3

The actual DMV was definitely not sexy. After the four of us successfully completed the eye exams and written tests, only Hannah and I did well enough on the road tests to pass. I finally had a real driver's license. I pulled it out and looked at it again, still amazed. The picture was mug-shot horrible. I guess that made it all the more real.

Grace said a few charmed words to the tester, a heavyset, middle-aged man who smelled like bacon. He then "forgot" about the mistakes she'd made parallel parking.

Rachel scowled to cover her embarrassment.

Grace can talk to him about—

"No!" she said, cutting me off. Her outburst startled a few people waiting in the purgatorial check-in line. *No charm stuff from her.*

She doesn't want you to, I thought to Grace, heading off her intervention. Now Grace was offended and upset, too. I rolled my eyes. *Great*—more drama.

Grace confronted Rachel as soon as the car door slammed

shut. "What was that about?"

"I didn't want to get it that way," she replied after a cold second.

"Well, now you're going to have to come all the way back again for the retest," said Grace.

"You don't have to come with me," Rachel snapped.

"Hey! Who's hungry?" Drew tried to change the subject. We'd all been starving a few minutes earlier, but now my appetite was gone.

Grace exhaled angrily. "That's it. I'm done. Find yourself another charm for this little 'superfriends' thing you have here."

I was amazed at how quickly the situation had devolved into this. "Grace, you don't have to—"

"Maddie, I'm sick of it. I stayed for the license run. Now I'm out."

Ah, hell. I'd known she was unhappy. I frowned—there was no obvious way to talk her out of this decision. It didn't seem right; she'd been good about not charming the team members. *Arrgh!* I wanted to yell at everyone to just cut it out and get along.

The uncomfortable car ride back seemed to take much longer than an hour. For the rest of them, it was just awkwardly quiet. I, on the other hand, got to listen to everyone's mental fuming.

Oh, joy.

Rachel was full of dark-red, angry snarls; Grace felt unappreciated and put-upon; Hannah, as usual, just wished herself elsewhere.

Replacing Grace probably wasn't going to be difficult—Ganzfield had plenty of charms. But Grace's decision made me worry about Hannah. She wasn't comfortable with the training we'd started. Hannah was a gentle, quiet person with a strong Christian faith. The quasi-military exercises and legally-grey nature of some of the things we practiced upset her. Healers were rarer than charms—there was only one other one besides Hannah in training, and Lester kept mentally undressing me when we were in the same room. I didn't want him on the team.

I needed to find a way to make Hannah happier with the training, but I didn't know how. And all this drama gave me a headache.

Trevor, their thoughts are driving me crazy. Please distract me!

An invisible hand started rubbing my neck, soothing me. *Something like this?*

I closed my eyes, trying to block out the tension emanating from the rest of them. It didn't work; it never did. If I was close enough, thoughts hit me whether I wanted to hear them or not. Fortunately, Trevor's presence buffered their intensity for me.

Why did we wait until now? Why didn't someone tell me we could drive at sixteen in New Hampshire? Back in New Jersey, the driving age is seventeen. I could've taken the driver's test here months ago. We'd waited until today, my seventeenth birthday, for no reason.

I got mine in Michigan. I didn't know about New Hampshire. And Drew's had his for a while now. Besides, you're a minder so we never think we have to tell you anything.

I pouted. *Someone should have thought it.*

Trevor chuckled. His laughter always did something wonderful to me. His joy amplified as it came into my mind, filling me with warmth.

A few minutes out from Ganzfield, I felt the touch of two new minds. Fear and hatred flowed blood-hot through the two strangers. *Here come some of them now!*

My head shot up and every muscle tensed. *Dead*—they wanted us all dead.

"We're being watched," I said aloud.

I felt Trevor's invisible arms wrap around me. He'd stopped bullets with those arms in the past to protect me. He was ready to do it again.

Drew filled with energy, ready to fight. I suddenly hoped he didn't accidentally spark anything near the car's gas lines.

The watchers head-counted us. *"Too many. Wait until we can catch one or two of them alone."* They had flame-retardant clothing and white-noise-generating earpieces, which meant that they knew what sparks and charms could do. Cold washed down my neck and arms.

The strangers also had friends; one grabbed a cell phone. *"Six of them in the grey sedan, heading back in,"* he reported as we moved out of range.

The gate clanged shut behind the car and I started breathing again. "I need to talk to Dr. Williamson."

I spent a lot of time in Dr. Williamson's office on the third floor of the main building. Since I'd started training with the team, I'd stopped attending regular classes but my workload had only gotten heavier. Dr. Williamson had me studying neurology—how to find and differentiate the areas of the brain—fine-tuning my ability to incapacitate.

We worked together to figure out what I was capable of with my ability. If I overloaded the visual cortex, could I blind someone?

Possibly.

Could I overload Broca's area in someone's brain? If I did that to a charm, it would render the charm unable to speak for a while. Painless, too—they might not even know what'd happened to them until they tried to talk. It was like a little seizure—just zapping a little extra energy into one part of the brain. No pain. No problem.

Theoretically, at least—it wasn't as though I could practice brain blasts on volunteers or anything. Who'd volunteer for *that*?

Dr. Williamson and I had a practical one-on-one nearly every day. Between these lessons, training with the team, and my connection with Trevor, telepathy had become second nature to me. My mental range had gradually increased, too; I could now hear people's thoughts from nearly eighty feet away. However, this still gave me the shortest range of all the minders. Dr. Williamson's was nearly two-hundred feet, and Seth could feel someone's presence more than half a mile away, although he had to be closer to get a clear read on their thoughts.

Climbing the stairs of the rambling, old farmhouse that had become Ganzfield's main building, I mentally touched in with Dr. Williamson so he knew I was coming. It's hard to surprise a minder, so it was more of a courtesy than anything.

Dr. Williamson had developed an informal code of "telepath etiquette" that he thought we all should follow. That little "mental knock" was part of it. So was speaking aloud when discussing things with non-telepaths present. He also avoided using the term "minder"—the short form of "mind-reader"—used at Ganzfield. He didn't like the secondary meaning—those who watched over the others and kept them in line. It was a little too close to being uncomfortably true.

A middle-aged black man who radiated authority, Dr. Williamson was always impeccably groomed, even when casually dressed in a cashmere sweater, like today. *What did you see?* His thoughts boiled with brooding contemplation. He'd been like this for the past two months—ever since he'd learned Isaiah Lerner was alive.

I'd never met Isaiah. What I knew of him came from Dr. Williamson. He'd shown me his own memories from years ago, before Isaiah had faked his own death and hidden under the new name. I knew from those memories that we were up against a powerful predator—Isaiah was one of two telepaths who could send enough energy into another person's brain to kill them.

I was the other.

But he had a larger telepathic range than I did—hundreds of feet, at least. And he didn't need visual contact to "fry" someone, like I did. If he got close enough, he could kill someone with a thought. That was how Isaiah had murdered Elise, Dr. Williamson's wife and soulmate. Dr. Williamson wasn't going to know peace until he was *sure* Isaiah was no longer in the world.

Minders usually just framed thoughts to each other to communicate. I'd never heard Seth speak—or even seen him face-to-face. Not only was my mind abrasively loud to him when I got too close, but we also annoyed each other.

That annoyance was mostly due to Seth's personality.

Now I showed Dr. Williamson what I'd sensed outside the gate. *Think they're Sons of Adam?* The Sons of Adam were like the K.K.K. to G-positives like us. Luckily, most people didn't know about us and couldn't comprehend the extent of our abilities, so their numbers remained small. If our existence became public knowledge, it might be enough to bring thousands of pitchfork-and-torch-wielding villagers down on us—or their shotgun-and-flashlight-wielding descendents, at least.

Sometimes, I felt they had a point. Charms could be the ultimate sociopaths—able to talk people into doing anything. And I really wasn't one to judge—my own telepathic ability could be intrusive, dangerous, and predatory. I had to be very careful how I used it if I didn't want to wake up some morning and discover I'd become a monster; at times, I thought I already had.

Possibly.

I startled, but then realized that Dr. Williamson hadn't been paying attention to my existential ambivalence. He was concerned about the men who'd been watching us. *You saw the earpieces and the fire-resistant gear. Anything else?*

I shook my head. *Just that there were more than these two and they know we're here. They recognized the car and are waiting to catch one or two of us alone.*

Dr. Williamson pondered that behind a mental shield.

Think they'll try to hurt us?

Dr. Williamson didn't respond, which said it all.

What's the plan?

I'll send some charms to have a talk with them — if it's safe, he added unintentionally. Dr. Williamson didn't let things slip often—things must be worse than I knew. If these men were prepared with earpieces and the like, it might be too risky to send our people out to charm them.

Speaking of charms, we need a new one for the team. Grace wants out.

Who do you want? Dr. Williamson felt comfortable with the topic change.

Not sure. Any suggestions?

Try John Samuels.

I nodded, trying to remember which one he was.

Now, let's see how you're shielding today.

John lasted two days. He kept mentally undressing Hannah,

Rachel, and me, even after I'd warned him to control himself. When he charm-voiced Rachel to "start acting sweeter toward him," I'd snapped a blast of pain through his brain. After he was able to stand again, he'd left and hadn't returned.

Okay, I *might've* overreacted.

The thing is, I could've killed him. I'd already killed five people and I got jumpy when it came to a charm with inappropriately sexual thoughts in his head, especially for Rachel's sake.

Sarah worked out for nearly two weeks.

Devon lasted three hours.

Sonja quit after four days.

Intellectually, we knew a charm was a very useful addition to the team. We just couldn't stand being around most of them.

CHAPTER 4

February fifteenth—Trevor's eighteenth birthday. At the end of the afternoon, I found Trevor and Drew on the new shooting range down near the sparks' houses. Hannah shivered unhappily behind a protective cinderblock barrier, giving me a half-wave as I came near. She wore a bulky set of bright blue ear protectors as she tried to read.

My stomach fell as Drew emptied an entire clip directly at Trevor. Rapid-fire shots cracked the air, leaving my ears ringing and freezing a piece of my soul.

Intellectually, I knew Trevor needed to practice stopping bullets. But I still had to suppress the sudden impulse to *make him stop!* Drew wasn't trying to hurt Trevor. They both wore Kevlar vests and riot helmets with clear visors that covered their faces. Hannah was there to deal with any injuries. And Trevor could handle it. The bullets hung suspended in front of him like a scene from the *Matrix*.

I waited until Drew lowered the gun before I tried to get their attention. Then I forced a cheerful smile over my taut nerves.

"Hey guys. Party time!"

Drew's grin turned predatory as Trevor blanched.

I snorted. *So you're cool with Drew SHOOTING at you, but not with him throwing you a birthday party?*

Trevor shrugged. "Some things are scarier than others."

February is cold and grey in New Hampshire. People draw into themselves, becoming cold and grey as well in response to the long, dark winter. Ganzfield's sparks seemed to enjoy the season more than most other people, though. Maybe it was because it was easier for pyrokinetics to stay warm; maybe it was because the early sunsets made their games of Fireball more dramatic. In the winter, the sparks played out on the thick ice of the lake, which brightened the game further. It also added the risk of sliding into open water through the goal-holes cut in the ice. So far this winter, only Harrison and Ellen had been dunked. Each was quickly fished out and warmed by the collective flames of both teams.

Some huge blocks of ice had appeared in the middle of their little community in early January. Most were several feet high—the tallest towered over the little cinderblock buildings. I never found out how they'd been acquired, but over the next weeks, a few sparks carved them with projected flames. The resulting ice sculptures—mostly smooth, clear abstracts—were eerily beautiful.

Drew had decided to use Trevor's birthday as an excuse for the latest party. He didn't need much of an excuse—two weeks ago, Drew had organized a celebration of "Groundhog's Day Eve." Tonight, a huge bonfire lit the narrow beach where the circle of damp sand held a couple dozen people. Fireball was played like soccer, only the three-foot-wide ball remained suspended above the ground by a flame-reactive form of telekinesis. The blazing sphere lit the ice beneath it, reflecting a mirror image against the dark surface. A sizzling hiss and a plume of steam accompanied each scored goal.

After the game, the sparks took turns sculpting the bonfire in a kind of performance art. It ranged from the simplicity of shadow puppets to more artistic and complex forms. The evening's activities then turned into a contest of fire-walking. The sparks stepped through the fire, using their ability to bend the flames around themselves. Other sparks called out encouragement, advice, or trash-talk.

Katie Underwood made the blaze twirl around her like an elegant ball gown that nearly kissed her skin. She received exuberant applause for her efforts.

A chunk of Grant McFee's jeans blackened before he could think out the flames, resulting in good-natured boos and laughter. Considering the sparks could still get burns, and an inhaled breath at the wrong time could pull superheated air right into their lungs, this was not a pastime for the meek. So, of course, it was exciting to watch. We had a great time. Finally, Drew brought out Trevor's cake, lighting the excessive display of candles with a magician's flourish.

The icy air seemed to bite us as Trevor and I headed back to the old church. We walked on the familiar path through the skeletal, winter woods. Thousands of stars sparkled like spilled glitter through the empty branches above us.

The new heating system had transformed the church into our warm, private sanctuary. We took our turns in the bathroom, both dressed in unsexy, flannel PJs and thick socks against the eddies of cold that haunted the corners of the old building. Trevor flipped off the lights, and then joined me up in my loft by vaulting up over the rail, the same way other guys might jump over a waist-high fence. He ducked in under the metalwork canopy and we pulled close under my quilt, lying face to face on my shared pillow.

I felt a sudden twist of hesitation in my gut. *Trevor?* I lightly stroked his cheek with my fingertip. *About this no sex thing…* His mind flared with wary, yet excited interest. This was a sensitive topic for us. Trevor was the unplanned child of a teen mom; he worried that a similar experience would ruin our lives. And Dr. Williamson had gotten Trevor's word that we wouldn't. It was the main reason I was allowed to stay here in the church with him. *I've been thinking—*

We can't.

I know, but—

But?

What about in the lucid dreams?

I felt his pulse bounce up as his eyes widened. The pros and cons flashed through his mind. There really weren't any cons—no risk of pregnancy, at least, which was his main issue. Did it break his word to Dr. Williamson? He wasn't sure. I felt the matter was grey enough that we could argue our way out of an accusation, if it came to that.

You want to? He filled with a combination of nervous, lusty hopefulness, feelings of unworthiness, and fear of rejection.

Yes. I leaned forward and kissed him deeply, opening my mind to him, letting my intense love for him wash away his insecurities. His anxieties trickled into nothingness as his tongue traced lightly along my upper lip. I moaned. One of his hands cradled my neck while an invisible arm encircled my body, pulling me closer. His unseen touch caressed me as though I was wearing nothing at all.

Hot, buzzing-red energy tingled across my skin. I could feel Trevor's mind fill with tender, yet primal impulses; ideas that made me quiver and melt. I opened my thoughts further to his, letting my passion flow over him. The church went dim and the world fell away. Suddenly, we were two beings of energy, merging in an explosive series of waves that tumbled us together until we shattered into a thousand fizzy little fireworks that seemed to linger in the trembling of our newly-returned bodies.

And we were still two fully-dressed virgins.

Each time we soulmated, our mental and emotional connection became more perfect. Trevor and I still lay face to face on the pillow. My right hand still rested on his cheek. I could feel his skin, covered with sandy-textured, end-of-day stubble beneath the pads of my fingers. Simultaneously, I also experienced that same contact from Trevor's perspective—my hand on his cheek, the fingers warmer against his skin than the surrounding air. The physical effects of soulmating on his body—as well as my own—filled me, and I knew he felt what I did. Our thoughts sped between us without a need for words; there was just an instant *knowing*.

I loved him so much: his quiet strength, his goodness, his openness. There were no boundaries between us—we even shared each other's dreams. Trevor and I could simply be together and we felt whole—complete. There was a joy and peace to it that I'd never known before I'd met him.

Amazingly, he felt the same way about me.

The thought occurred to me that we might someday have difficulty with the actual sex part. We were so open to each other's minds that we connected as energy before we ever did anything too controversial.

Without realizing it, we drifted to sleep in each other's arms.

That was a mistake.

The floor smacked against me, jarring me awake. My mind felt stupidly fuzzy.

Dark. Someone pushing me.

Trevor lay dreaming in my bed, batting invisible arms at nebulous things. I made the connection as I was thrown hard against the wrought-iron railing of the loft, which creaked a whiny, metallic protest.

Crap! Get down the ladder. Fast!

The unseen push came as I was halfway to the ground. My socks slipped from the narrow metal steps. I held on for a fraction of a second before I went down, landing hard on my left leg. Something made an audible snap above my ankle. The pain lanced through me as the leg collapsed and I fell hard against the wooden floor.

My scream woke Trevor. "Maddie? Maddie!"

I managed a whimper. He was down beside me in a second.

It's my leg. I couldn't speak. *I think it's broken.* I tried to keep the pain from leaking through the connection between us, but I felt a lot of it bouncing back from him, as though we were caught in a feedback loop of agony.

Trevor gathered me in his arms, using his ability to hold the broken limb steady. Even so, his every step sent another jolt of excruciating pain from my ankle up to my hip. I squeezed my eyes shut and balled my fists. The frigid walk to the infirmary left me shaking badly, although that also could've been from shock. Tears that felt like ice left trails on my cheeks. In this weather, maybe they actually had frozen.

Matilda looked up from her book as we came in. Trevor carefully placed me on the exam table. Every movement hurt with a terrible sense of wrongness, like shards of broken ceramic grating under my skin.

"What happened?" Matilda pulled up the leg of my PJ-pants and peeled off my sock. The edges of the shattered bone scraped roughly against each other as she put her hands on my calf. I moaned and gritted my teeth. Swelling had already turned my leg an ugly red and purple, and seeing the unnatural angle of my foot made my stomach heave.

"I …fell off…the ladder…of the loft." Pain pulsed through my mind, blotting out most of the dorm resident's dreams, although a few of them gently pushed on the edges of my consciousness.

Matilda concentrated on the leg, sending little feelers of energy into the damaged portion. After nearly a minute, she said, "Broken in two places. We'll need to set the bones properly before I can heal them."

She looked at Trevor, considering how his ability could help. Trevor clasped one of my clenched fists against his chest. He stroked my hair as his muddy-yellow guilt and nausea bombarded me. *Did I do this to her? Oh, God. Did I hurt Maddie like I hurt Reed? I'm dangerous. I shouldn't be around people.*

He didn't hear Matilda the first time.

"Trevor," she repeated in her softly-accented voice. "I asked if you could use telekinesis to move the bones back into place. You can work through solid matter, isn't that correct?"

Trevor nodded. He didn't trust himself to speak.

"It would go much faster and cause Maddie less pain if we work together. I'll focus in as you pull the bones back into position. When I tell you they are in alignment, you hold them in place while I heal them."

The next bit hurt like liquid hell. Matilda held my foot. Trevor pushed his emotional turmoil down so he could concentrate on helping me. I subdued my scream into a high-pitched whimper.

"That's it. Hold it there." Matilda, shot electric tendrils through my calf, speeding the knitting bones then repairing the soft tissue and reducing the swelling.

I felt my lungs inflate to full capacity as the pain subsided. The tension ebbed. My leg felt hot and it pulsed with tiny, electric aftershocks.

"I want you to stay in the infirmary for the rest of the night. Don't put any weight on that leg until I have a chance to check it in a few hours," Matilda said.

"It feels healed." I'd thought Trevor and I would be free to leave. His emotions twisted painfully, wringing his soul. I needed to help him.

Sudden awareness of the pain in his feet distracted me—I hadn't noticed it over the scream from my leg. "Matilda, could you take a look at Trevor's feet, please?" Trevor looked down, noting with surprise that he was wearing only wet socks. Matilda treated his feet before frostbite could set in.

You've been carting a lot of people with leg injuries to the infirmary lately. I tried to joke with him. *You'd think grabbing your boots would be second-nature by now.*

He wasn't in a laughing mood. Trevor gathered me carefully in his arms again and carried me into the next room—the one-story annex off the infirmary that held a half-dozen cots in a long row. In the last bed, someone pretended to sleep.

Trevor? Are you all right?

I have to get away from her, he thought to himself. *As far away as possible.*

I forced down a bubble of hurt and panic.

"I can't stay here." Raspy desperation filled his words.

Trevor, I can't stay here, either. Please don't leave me. I needed to talk with him, to be with him, to take the pain and guilt and horror from his mind. I gripped his hand harder when he tried to pull away. His eyes met mine; they were filled with anguish. *Please,* I pleaded.

He paused for a second, and then nodded. "Wait here for a few minutes. I'll be back." Trevor planned to use his ability to lift himself from the snow, walking with invisible hands under his bare feet, almost like those cups-on-strings stilts that kids use. He'd get our boots and coats from the church and return for me.

As Trevor moved away, the cloud of his emotions cleared from my head. I was able to breathe a little better without them. We'd gotten careless. We wouldn't do it again. We just needed to talk about it and he'd understand it was okay. Once I'd worked that through, I relaxed and finally noticed the intense confusion of the other person in the little annex. He must be new.

"So, why are you pretending to be asleep?"

Oh, so she CAN talk. His head came up. In the light coming through the infirmary door, I saw that he was a good-looking guy with black hair and vivid blue eyes. Back before I'd met Trevor, I might've been attracted to him. "How could you tell?"

"Telepath."

"No joke?"

"No joke."

"Zack Greyson."

"Maddie Dunn."

"That guy's your boyfriend?" He meant Trevor.

"Uh huh."

"Lucky guy." He smiled.

My eyebrows shot up in surprise and I gave a startled laugh.

Flirting? Really? People at Ganzfield didn't flirt with me. I was a *minder*. The guys who'd been here a while knew better. At least Zack seemed sincere, although I had to question his taste—I probably looked a mess. And his thoughts weren't overly raunchy—I'd heard enough adolescent guys' minds to know how bad they could get.

"That's funny?"

"You're new." In a few days he'd look back in horror at this conversation.

He glanced at the clock; it was just after 2 a.m. "My third day here."

"You on dodecamine yet?"

"The shot? Got it yesterday."

"Any time now, then."

"That's what they tell me."

"They say what they think you are?"

He gave a small laugh. "They think…they think I'm going to be charming…or something." The term confused him. Why didn't the Ganzfield people give better information to the new arrivals? Maybe we should make up a pamphlet. I could see it now—*Dick and Jane's New Superpowers.*

See Dick charm. Charm, Dick, charm. See Jane Remote View. View, Jane, view.

"Jedi mind trick."

"Huh?"

"Star Wars? You know the Jedi mind trick? 'These aren't the droids you're looking for?'"

His confusion turned to excitement. "Seriously? I'm going to be able to do that?"

"Yeah, if you're a charm." My voice turned serious. "Don't hurt anyone with it, though."

He understood that I'd just given him a warning, but his thoughts twisted in defiance. "Or what? What can they do to me?"

I got seriously annoyed. *The last guy here who used his charming ability to force girls to have sex with him is now dead.* I left out that I'd been the one who'd killed him and I'd done it when he'd made someone shoot at us.

Zack paled. I guess it was the first time someone had spoken inside his head. Suddenly, he was genuinely worried about misusing his ability.

I smiled. *My work here is done.*

With excellent timing, I could feel the tide of emotional turmoil roll in as Trevor returned. Wordlessly, he helped me with my coat and boots, taking extra care not to jostle my left leg.

"Nice talking with you, Zack," I said, as Trevor gathered me up in his arms. "Welcome to Ganzfield."

Trevor carried me back to the church without speaking. I took the time to fill myself in on the details of his anguish, which swirled through my head like a hurricane of self-recrimination.

He lifted me to my loft and deposited me on the bed. I held onto his hand, pulling him back as he started to leave. *Trevor, please talk to me.*

His face reflected the pain in his mind. *I did this to you, didn't I?*

At that moment, I really, really wanted to lie to Trevor, but I couldn't. Deceiving him—even to protect his feelings—felt *wrong*. And we were so closely connected, he'd probably be able to tell if I were less than truthful anyway.

My silence answered the question for him and his eyes crumpled shut against the newest wave of guilt, pain, and self-loathing. How could I get him to stop? His anguish was killing me. I couldn't stand having him in pain—his pain was my pain.

Trevor. TREVOR! I needed to get through to him. Words weren't enough. I tried connecting emotionally, on a deeper level. The impact of his feelings made my tears well up. *Please. Please, stop.*

Stop?

Stop beating yourself up over an accident. IT WAS AN ACCIDENT. We're so close…I'm getting swamped with all of this pain and guilt.

His solution was to get far enough away from me that he couldn't hurt me physically *or* mentally.

Please don't go! I felt an unfamiliar frustration. Usually, talking to Trevor was so easy!

I need you. I need you to hold me. Please, don't pull away.

But I hurt you. I…I feel sick about it.

I know. Trevor, it was an accident. I'd forgive you, but there's nothing to forgive.

I put my hands on his face, pulling his reluctant eyes to mine. *It's okay. I'm okay. I'm not in pain.* I pulsed my feelings to him, showing him. *See? Pain free.*

Trevor pulled me close, burying his face in my hair. *If anything ever happened to you…*

I know. I feel the same way about you. The tension slid from him—and from me—leaving a relief that felt cool and calm.

Then my brain floated up a random comment about how, when Trevor and I had kids someday, labor might be harder on him than on me.

He pulled back, looking me in the eyes. He'd heard that? *Crap.* I hadn't meant to send that thought to him. It hadn't been very loud, even in my own mind.

You think about us having kids together?

I bit my lip and nodded. *Eventually. No rush.*

The same sense of sureness filled him and I felt my heart

expand. We'd only known each other for half a year, but we'd be together forever. We might be young, but he knew I was the love of his life—just as I knew he was the love of mine.

You know I'm going to ask you to marry me someday.

I smiled, feeling like my soul had grown wings.

And you know I'll say yes.

CHAPTER 5

"It hasn't healed quite right." Matilda's West African accent became more pronounced when something upset her. Not being able to fix an injury definitely fell into that category.

A quivering ache deep within my leg made me feel unsteady on my feet, like the bone might simply snap beneath me if I put too much weight on it. It was now Monday morning. I'd broken it Saturday night. By Ganzfield standards, I should be back to normal by now. Trevor's grip on my hand tightened in silent apology.

Matilda examined the break again. She couldn't pinpoint the damage.

"Don't worry, Maddie." Morris smirked. "I can fix my sister's mistakes."

Matilda covered her hurt feelings with an outer calm so Morris didn't realize the sting she felt. His own lack of success deflated his teasing mood, though.

"I'm going to send you for an MRI," said Matilda. "We have someone at Dartmouth-Hitchcock in Hanover who'll get you in tonight. She's a former student of ours. Dr. Williamson wants to send the new charm over for a head CT, as well."

"Zack?" I'd seen him on my daily check-ups. His thoughts were always light and pleasant when I noticed them. Zack wasn't in the infirmary at the moment. Apparently, he had gone to one of the smaller houses that served as boys' dorms to shower and change clothes.

"We'll send your whole team, anyway. It's not safe to go out in small groups these days. One more in the van shouldn't be a problem."

I wondered what they thought was wrong with Zack. Was he okay? Most of us hadn't needed CT scans. Trevor had gotten a few, since they were interested in what caused his telekinesis. Was Zack also different in some way?

Yes, he is. Dr. Williamson's mind touched mine as he approached the infirmary. *Can't you tell, Maddie? He's shielding.*

What? I felt my eyes widen. *But he's a charm!*

A charm who could block minders? That wasn't good. What was he thinking that I couldn't hear? What else could he do?

Dr. Williamson handed some cash, a print-out map, and a set of keys to Trevor. "They're to a house we own near Hanover," he explained aloud, politely including the others in our conversation. "I thought I'd check in on you before I left this morning."

"Recruiting or fundraising?" I intentionally spoke aloud—and highlighted that fact to him in my thoughts. *Ta-da!*

He acknowledged my efforts with a "humph." "Fundraising. I need to see if some quarterly results are going to meet forecasts." I understood what that meant—Dr. Williamson had been training me on the financial stuff. He'd read a few minds at the right companies to get their quarterly results in advance of their public announcement. He'd buy the stocks that were going to beat earnings projections or short the ones that were going to miss them. If the stocks didn't perform as the experts expected, he'd make hundreds of thousands of dollars—or more.

I was glad Dr. Williamson was focusing on something other than his darker, nearly obsessive thoughts about Isaiah. I felt a pang of annoyance, though—I wanted to try the stock market stuff myself. If my leg had been okay, I could've asked to go with him.

A thought occurred to me. *Are YOU safe going out alone?*

"Greg will drive. He knows how to take care of himself." Since Greg was a former Navy SEAL, that was an understatement. "And I can hear them coming. Seth will be in charge here and we've beefed up the electronic security on the perimeter wall. Everyone should be okay."

I nodded. "Have a good trip."

"You, too."

We left at 3 p.m. for the two-and-a-half hour drive. Hanover was on the other side of the state, on the Vermont border. Sean gave Rachel a shy kiss goodbye—the first public display of their new status as a couple. Drew stared openly at them, his jaw practically touching his chest. He hadn't known that his cousin was seeing Rachel, whom he considered a "major hottie" with an "ice queen" personality. The oxymoron inherent in this assessment escaped him. Sean flushed red enough to drown his freckles when he noticed Drew's reaction.

Personally, I was relieved. One less secret I had to pretend I didn't know.

About a mile outside the main gate, four men sat in a parked car on the side of the road. I felt a chill creep from my gut when I recognized the people in the grainy grey pictures in their hands.

Drew. Hannah. Rachel. Me.

They appeared to be from the night we'd rescued Trevor, so they must've come from the security cameras at Eden Imaging.

"Bad guys," I said. The entire group startled. "Four of them." Trevor's invisible embrace pulled me protectively close. I focused in as I felt them recognize Drew and Rachel up front. My heart thudded against my ribs as they grabbed for weapons and gear. "Crap. They're arming. They plan to take us out."

Drew braked suddenly—the tires scraped the asphalt with a squeal. He threw the van into reverse, flinging us along the edge of the road so the van's bumper nearly kissed the front of the green sedan. No houses in sight—no witnesses—probably why the men had picked this spot for their ambush.

I felt the metal in their hands. *Guns!* I thought at Drew.

"None that will work." Drew grinned, not looking in my direction. He had them in range and his focus was strong enough to keep them from firing. "Their car won't start, either." He'd suppressed the spark plugs, as well.

I smiled. *You read my mind.*

He chuckled. This was one of the scenarios we'd trained for over the past months—dealing with a car full of hostiles. Greg and Frank had given us some pointers and we'd developed ways to utilize our abilities in just this situation. I felt a surge of adrenalin, but it wasn't from fear. We knew how to handle this.

Drew's got the guns and the car. We need the earpieces out, I thought to Trevor. "Zack." I said, suddenly realizing that, with no training, he had no idea he had to do something here.

"'These aren't the droids you're looking for?'"

I nodded. At least he was quick on the uptake. "You got it. C'mon." Trevor opened the sliding side door, and then reached for me.

Any way I can be upright for this? I thought to Trevor. *I don't want to look weak.* He placed me on my feet in front of him. His arm wrapped around my waist, steadying me as I balanced on my uninjured leg. His face looked serious, hard and cold—his game face. I adopted a similar visage.

The four watchers pointed guns at us. One tried to fire at us through the windshield. A man in the back opened the car door. Trevor slammed it shut without visibly moving then hit the button for the door locks, sealing them in. The earpieces dropped from their ears one by one, crushed between his invisible fingers.

I worked to keep the smile off my face as we approached the front passenger window. Trevor hit the button to lower the glass. One of the men screamed. Two others tried to fire their guns at us, but they only clicked impotently.

The driver scrambled with the handle of the locked door. When he realized it wouldn't open, he tried to start the car. The front passenger threw his gun at us. It bounced off the invisible shield Trevor held in place and fell back into the car. Their fear and anger screamed louder than their voices.

—I don't want to die. Please, God help us—

—the monsters have us trapped—

—at least want to take some of them with me—

—kill them all! Not human, don't deserve to live—

"Tell them to be quiet and sit still," I said to Zack. Would my mental voice work when he shielded? Now wasn't the time to find out. He'd heard it the first night in the infirmary, but the dodecamine had kicked in since then.

At that moment, I really missed Grace. She'd have enjoyed intimidating a car full of hostiles. There was something within me—like a twisted feminism—that reveled in the image of a short, Eurasian woman from New York City cowing a bunch of dangerous men out in the middle of the woods. Was it wrong to be actually enjoying this a little? After all, they'd threatened us first—and they wanted to kill us. We just wanted them to go away and leave us alone.

Still, what we were doing wasn't…*nice*.

"Be quiet and sit still." Charm resonance permeated Zack's words. The four men slumped into instant, silent obedience, although their panicked minds still shrieked into mine.

I scanned through them. The front passenger was in charge: Gordon. "Who do you work for?" He remained silent, out of obstinacy and fear.

It didn't matter—I got the information from his mind. *Sons of Adam—the guardians of True Humanity.*

I asked several questions about their organization—how they contacted each other, what their plan was. We now had names, addresses, and other information. I mentally relayed these to Hannah in the van so she could write them down.

Gordon remained stubbornly silent. He actually thought he was being strong—that he was resisting me. He thought I was a charm. These guys really didn't know much—basically just foot soldiers. Most of the information they had concerned neutralizing our abilities.

How to kill us.

Crap. They knew about Trevor. Their only defense against him was keeping their distance…or shooting him. They didn't know he could stop bullets. Gordon and his crew were prepared for sparks and charms, though. But they didn't seem to know about telepaths.

Strange.

Were the Sons of Adam working with Isaiah? It was a good

bet. How else would they have images from Eden Imaging security cameras?

"Where did the pictures of us come from?" I asked.

Gordon didn't know.

Were we targets because I'd killed Michael and Dr. Hanson? I'd overloaded their minds with massive strokes. Did that mean Isaiah didn't know which of us had that ability? Was he interested because it was like his own?

Isaiah. *Oh.* That's why there was no information about how to neutralize telepaths. Isaiah wouldn't have told these people anything about his own ability. In fact, he might've downplayed or even denied the existence of telepathy in order to avoid detection. And these men had hoped to kill us from a distance. They hadn't counted on us reacting before they could come up behind our vehicle, shoot out a tire, and then slaughter us as we got out to assess the damage. Their ignorance of telepathy had been their weak link.

Hate and fear boiled within them. They honestly believed we were monsters—too dangerous and evil to be allowed to live. To them, we were like vampires—creatures of destruction masquerading in human form.

I felt my brow furrow and bit my lip then shot a thought to the team. *What does everyone think? Should we wipe their memories or should we let them think they killed us?*

Let them think we're dead, thought Drew.

Let's program them to open fire at the next Sons of Adam meeting, Rachel thought.

My gut heaved. *Too much.* I caught her reflection in the side-view mirror and shook my head. *I only kill people in self-defense.*

This would be self-defense, Rachel thought back to me. Her eyes were fierce. *Get them before they get us.* A memory of Uncle Charlie flashed through her mind.

Why don't we just wipe any traces of their contact with us from their minds? asked Hannah. *That way, no one gets hurt.*

If they think we're dead, they won't target us anymore, Trevor thought.

I couldn't read an opinion from Zack. Dr. Williamson was right—he shielded his thoughts pretty cleanly. The consensus of the rest of the group seemed to be faking our deaths. It appealed to me for its efficacy and its symmetry—Isaiah had, after all, faked his own death years ago. He didn't have an RV to track us down. How long would we be off his radar? I held back my smile.

This could totally work.

"Zack, tell them to remember how they followed our van, shot out the tires, and then picked us all off from a safe distance as we tried to run into the woods." He relayed this to the men in his charm-voice. "They loaded our bodies into the van, and then drove it down a hunter's trail and left it. All the people they were looking for—all their targets—were in the van. Once they've reported this, they'll feel sick about the killing. They'll leave the Sons of Adam and forget they ever knew anything about it or us."

"Anything else?"

"Tell them to teach their kids tolerance," I added, impulsively.

Trevor cracked a tiny smile. *Nice one.*

"You heard the lady—teach your kids tolerance. Respect for diversity, that sort of thing."

It almost felt like we'd made the world a better place. Camaraderie filled the van as we drove off, tainted with a hint of smugness.

I twisted around in my seat to face Zack. "You did well for your first time out." If I could read him, I'd ask him to be our team's new charm. For a newbie, he was a natural.

He grinned back. "Thanks." A little thought seeped out from behind his shield. *He liked being on the winning team—and on my team.*

I flitted from one mental contact to another for about a half-hour before I accepted that we weren't being followed. I pulled my focus back into the van.

Slanting afternoon light flashed into Drew's eyes between the leafless trees as he drove, lessening his enthusiasm for the experience. *Why is everyone getting into couples all of a sudden? First Trevor and Maddie. Now Sean and Rachel.* His new awareness of Sean and Rachel's status had sent him into a soul-searching mood. Since he was a person with more width than depth of character, this didn't take long. *I'm pretty much the same kind of guy as Sean. Guess that means I'll be able to date hot blondes, too. Cool!*

Rachel rode shotgun again, her normal spot as our human GPS, although her ability wasn't necessary on this trip. She was pretty good at warning us of speed traps, though, since she could RV any police cars on the road ahead of us well before I'd hear their minds. The giddy, warm glow of new love filled her thoughts, along with flashes of annoyance at my clumsiness. *If Maddie hadn't broken her leg, I wouldn't have to be away from Sean. I don't see why I had to come along.*

I leaned against Trevor's shoulder and watched the ocean of trees roll by in the fading afternoon light. I'd been off my leg for nearly three days now and I still hadn't used crutches—not that a place with G-positive healers had a pair lying around. I didn't want to be a burden, but Trevor viewed carrying me as a form of penance.

Behind us, Zack tried to start a conversation with Hannah. They quickly ran out of things to say. Hannah's thoughts focused on the upcoming tests. Now that I knew what to look for, Zack's thoughts seemed strangely empty. I didn't detect the block, only the absence of thought that should've been there. He shielded as well as Dr. Williamson did and it made me uncomfortable. *Jealous.* I'd been trying for months to do what Zack was doing, yet he seemed to be able to do it effortlessly.

We went through a fast-food drive-thru in Hanover for an early dinner, although the early dusk made it feel later. Trevor took a turn at the wheel while Drew ate—it was easier for Trevor to eat and drive with his extra set of hands. I scanned quickly for Sons of Adam people as we pulled up at Dartmouth-Hitchcock, a sprawling medical complex south of town.

I felt my shoulders relax. No one wanted to kill us here.

What a nice change.

The medical center's parking lot held only a few lonely vehicles among the enormous piles of plowed snow at the end of each row. People didn't spend the night in this part of the medical center. Good thing. I suddenly realized that if I went into a regular hospital, I'd feel the pain of every sick and injured person within my range.

Yeah, I wasn't going to be doing that.

Heather McFee, M.D. had the standard-issue McFee red hair and freckles, as well as a subversive streak that she hid from the G-negatives in her daily life. A rare smile lit Hannah's face. She didn't meet other healers often, and Matilda and Morris both spoke highly of this particular former student. Drew greeted his cousin Heather with a hug.

We trooped through the darkened corridors of the medical imaging building. Trevor carried me in his arms as if looking for a threshold to cross. The rest followed along behind us. Our echoing footsteps and the swishing of our clothing seemed to invade the silence.

I considered Heather as she led the way. How did she end up as a healer instead of a spark? I wondered, not for the first time, at the sheer number of McFee G-positives. There were so many of them! How did a recessive trait like the G-positive genotype end up being expressed so frequently in one family? Was it from some kind of...of inbreeding?

Ick.

Zack had to wait a few minutes after drinking a can of milkshake-like, radioactive goo before doing his test so we did mine first. My MRI showed a lesion within the bone marrow of my newly-mended leg. Did that mean that Matilda and Morris's diagnostic abilities were imperfect through solid bone?

Hannah studied the images for several minutes, frowning in concentration. "I think I can get it. Now that I know what I'm looking for, I think I can get it through the bone."

I gestured to my leg. "Go for it."

Hannah said a quick, silent prayer then laid her hands on my calf. I had a sudden, possibly blasphemous thought—could Jesus have been a G-positive healer? It wouldn't endear me to Hannah to share this insight. She loved her ability and she did feel a connection to Jesus as a result of it, but the relationship was one of emulation, not of equivalence. It would deeply offend her if I offered a non-divine explanation for such a central part of her beliefs, so I kept my thoughts to myself as the pins-and-needles sensation sank deep within my leg. An aching pain grew in intensity and then gradually subsided, leaving the area tingling and hot.

I stood up tentatively, testing it out. "Pretty sure you got it.

Thanks." My leg felt strong again—back to normal. I turned to Trevor and grinned. *Now I need to find a different reason to get you to carry me around everywhere.*

You know I will. He smiled back into my eyes. *Any excuse to hold you in my arms.* I felt his relief as the guilt that'd twisted within him lightened. Good—I hated being the cause of those feelings. The emotions between us seemed to get caught in feedback loops so often these days. Now that he no longer felt guilty, the positive cycle started. Silver light flickered playfully between us.

Hannah cleared her throat loudly. The intensity between Trevor and me made something within her squirm. "Maddie, I need you to help with one of Zack's scans."

I reluctantly pulled myself out of the sensual cocoon Trevor and I were beginning to weave. "What do you need me to do?"

She hesitated, and then framed a thought. *I need you to try to read Zack so we can see what he's doing when he blocks minders.*

Her seriousness sobered me. *This needs to be kept quiet?*

Hannah nodded.

"Say when."

Trevor looked at me curiously, but didn't ask directly.

We went down the hall to the machine that did a combination CT and PET scan. From studying neurology as part of my minder training, I knew that the CT showed the structures of the brain, including the changes in the basal ganglion that all G-positives experienced when exposed to dodecamine. The PET scan showed activity within the specific parts because the radioactive dye followed the blood flow. More blood flowed to active regions and to newly developed cells, so the images lit up more brightly in those areas.

Don't do anything with him right now, Hannah told me. *We'll start with a baseline reading.*

I nodded. I shielded my mind as much as possible and stood back. I figured that blocking couldn't hurt, and it might actually lessen any mental energy I might be leaking into the situation. It really didn't change my experience of his thoughts—or, rather, of the silence that stood in their place. However, telepaths were louder to other telepaths. If Zack had an ability related to telepathy, he might be sensitive to the same types of energy.

I frowned. It was as though his ability was the opposite of a projective telepath's.

Whoa.

Wait a minute. The only telepaths who could block were Dr. Williamson and me, and we were the only ones who could project thoughts to others. Were the abilities related? Could Zack become a projective telepath, even if he couldn't hear thoughts? In a way, it would be like a deaf person learning to speak verbally. And if Zack could learn to project thoughts—could he learn to *charm* that way?

Silent mind-control. Yikes. No wonder Dr. Williamson was interested—and no wonder he wanted things kept quiet. With an ability like that, Zack could be the most dangerous G-positive at Ganzfield.

Well, the *second* most dangerous, at least.

When the first scan was complete, Hannah signaled me with a silent, "*Okay, now,*" and I focused on trying to read as much as I could from Zack's mind. I pushed for information—dropping subtle thoughts into the narrow strip of consciousness I could hear from him—a trick I'd picked up from Dr. Williamson. If I did it right, he'd think the thoughts were his own.

How did Dr. Williamson discover I was a G-positive?

I saw the memory that this evoked—a confrontation with several football players in his high school, all much larger than

Zack. One had shoved him and Zack had snapped. He had told the guy to drop dead and had punched him. The jock had fallen hard and not gotten up. Most times, such an event would've resulted in Zack getting his butt kicked by the guy's friends, but he'd told them to "Just leave me alone!" They had.

What's my worst memory? Zack frowned and glanced at me, suspicious. His thoughts slammed shut. I pushed at his mental shield, amazed at the subtlety of it. If I hadn't known what I was looking for, I would've missed it. Like a spiderweb, it was gently yielding—nearly invisible—yet stronger than it looked. Now that I'd seen it, I thought I could duplicate it.

I smiled. This little field trip had been very educational.

"We're done." Hannah gathered up the external hard drive that held the digital records of the scan and returned it to her bag.

"Maddie, were you doing something just now?" Zack asked, still frowning.

"Just part of the test."

Dr. Williamson's map led north through Hanover then out a winding country road. The surrounding, night-shadowed pastures overflowed with the simple, ruminating thoughts of hundreds of sheep.

We stopped in front of a dark farmhouse. Faded, once-yellow paint flaked off the clapboards, revealing weather-greyed wood. Plywood covered the windows and a black vinyl sign nailed to the front door warned: "PRIVATE PROPERTY: KEEP OUT."

The place looked decidedly creepy. Was this really the right house?

Drew looked around skeptically. "Does anyone else feel like we're on the set of a horror movie?"

"Teenagers stay in an old house overnight on a dare?" Zack gave a mirthless laugh. "I think I saw that one…and its four sequels."

We piled out of the van, surreptitiously checking for someone running amok with a chainsaw or a machete. Our headlights cast the only light across the undisturbed snow.

"Relax, everyone. Superpowers, remember?" Drew threw a little fireball up from his palm as demonstration. The tension broke as we cracked up.

Trevor unlocked the front door, and then grabbed his gear and mine from the back of the van. The others could sleep in the house, but Drew, Trevor, and I had to use the outbuildings so we'd packed extra sleeping bags, inflatable mattresses, and battery-operated lanterns. The barn would provide adequate open space for Trevor, and it was far enough from the house that the others would be out of my mental range overnight.

Drew ended up in the "sugar shack"—a free-standing, closet-sized room made from sheets of corrugated metal. Inside, a cast iron stove supported the remains of the boiling apparatus used for making maple syrup and maple sugar. A lean-to nearby held a decent supply of dry firewood, which Drew eyed with the experience of a connoisseur as he gathered up a night's supply. Within minutes, a warm, yellow glow brightened the panes of the shack's tiny window.

The dusty smell of old hay and disuse filled the barn. I felt the scurrying thoughts of small animals—mostly mice—so I sent out a strong image of prowling cats that sent them running. Trevor and I set up our air mattresses and sleeping bags, and then headed to the house to use the bathrooms before settling in.

The cold barn instantly lost its feeble charm for us. Modern plumbing? Central heat? *Internet access?* The house's dilapidated exterior must be an intentional choice to keep away unwanted attention. Rachel and Zack watched a big, flat-screen TV from opposite ends of the living room couch. I frowned. I almost wished I hadn't seen the inside of the house. I'd have been more comfortable out in the barn if I'd thought the others were shivering in clammy creepiness.

"Why aren't you three staying in the house, Maddie?" asked Zack.

I kept forgetting how new this was for him. "Well, sparks sometimes start fires in their sleep, and Trevor might knock down the ceiling telekinetically."

"And you?"

"I…" I hesitated. My sleeping issue suddenly seemed private. *Personal.*

"Well, I throw nightmares when people are in range."

"Oh. You could stay here anyway. We can deal with a nightmare or two. It's too cold to be out there tonight."

He seemed sincere, but now I could feel the spiderweb over his thoughts, invisibly keeping things hidden. Something seemed… off.

"Stay," he said, and I found I really wanted to.

I started to nod, but then recognized what it was that seemed off—the gentle, fogging feeling. A cold lump sank in my gut.

Zack was charming me.

Charming me! Oh, crap.

I pushed back hard and felt a stabbing pain behind my eyes. I tried to make my voice light. "No, thanks." I forced myself to keep breathing normally, even though I wanted to run. *Fight-or-flight.* I didn't want to tip him off that I knew he'd tried to charm me. And I *really* didn't want him to know how close he'd come to being successful.

Zack scowled for a few seconds then his face became as blank as his mind. He returned his attention to the TV.

I waited by the front door for Trevor. Outside, the cold made my lungs ache. *Trevor, Zack can charm minders.*

WHAT?

Don't tell anyone. I'm not even sure Zack knows he can do it.

Are you okay? What did he make you do? Trevor's shaking had nothing to do with the temperature.

*Nothing. I resisted, but it hurt. If I hadn't recognized what he was doing, though…*My mind shied away from the thought as we closed the barn door.

You need to stay away from him. He could make you— Jealousy pinged yellow flecks of energy within Trevor. *I think he likes you.*

What? I was about to contradict him, but instead I frowned, considering it. With Zack shielding, how would I really know? Trevor picked up on things like body language more intuitively than I did. What about Zack's flirting that night in the infirmary? And he liked being on my team. Trevor could be right. *Oh, crap.*

I swallowed hard. Good thing I could resist charms—even shielding charms.

Well, even if that's the case, he's outta luck. I put my arms around Trevor's neck, drawing him into a deep kiss, reaffirming our connection.

He returned my kiss fervently, possessively. We slid under his sleeping bag together. The layers of clothing between us were no barrier to his invisible touch, which trailed electrically down my neck…and then lower. Scarlet energy made my skin hum and my heart blaze. Our breath mingled in little clouds as his unseen hands—

Oh, yes.

Our kisses became more urgent. My hands moved under his

shirt, sliding across the bare skin at his waist. With that contact, we could no longer hold back the explosive energy. The world fell away and we connected as souls.

Our bodies trembled against each other when we returned to them. *I love you*, one of us thought; I couldn't tell whether it came from Trevor or from me. It didn't matter. In the aftermath of soulmating, there was no distinction.

Leaving Trevor's embrace for the cold, lonely sleeping bag against the back wall made me want to whimper, but we couldn't risk another injury. I crawled in, fully dressed with a coat, hat, and gloves, and then pulled a second sleeping bag over me as a quilt. Still mentally connected, Trevor and I drifted together in the dreamlike, floatingly-peaceful state that comes before sleep.

In the morning, I woke up with the Beyoncé song "Halo" in my head. Being with Trevor gave me new appreciation for love songs. They now resonated with me in a way they never had before, capturing aspects of how I felt. And lyrics about being surrounded in an embrace took on a whole new meaning when the man I loved used his invisible arms to protect me from bullets.

I located my boots in the still-dark barn and stepped lightly as I left. Trevor's sleeping bag revealed only the top of his knit wool hat, pulled low against the cold. Dawn colored the eastern edge of the sky a pale, pearl-grey as I went to the house. I took a shower, feeling the warmth of the water loosen the hold that the cold barn had on me. I blow-dried my hair and dressed.

Dreams filled the house. Rachel dreamed that she and Sean— *Whoa!*

Explicit. *Ick.* I winced away from her mind and wished I could block out the images. Quick. I needed to focus on someone else.

Hannah swam through a giant circulatory system. I felt a tiny laugh escape me—that was just...weird. Actually, though, who was I to judge the weirdness of other people's dreams? In mine, I saw dead people so often I was like the little blond kid from that movie.

Zack wasn't dreaming or, if he was, he was somehow blocking me from seeing it. I scowled in concentration. How did that shield work, anyway? Was it unconscious or did he have control of it? What was he hiding? Was he dangerous? He seemed like a nice enough guy, but what if that was just an act? *Scary.* For me, trying to read people's external cues was like trying to communicate with smoke signals.

I made coffee in the kitchen then took a cup with me into the living room and quietly watched TV until everyone else got up. The kitchen was stocked with non-perishable essentials like the coffee, sugar, and powdered creamer that I'd used, but there was little actual food. Once everyone was ready, we cleaned up, packed up, locked up, and hit the road. We grabbed McBreakfast at the first drive-thru we found.

The sun sidled sideways as it rose ahead of us, tracing an arc to the south. Clouds rolled in and cast everything in diffuse, grey light—there might be more snow on the way. As we came closer to Ganzfield, I listened for hostile mental contacts. Did anyone recognize us? Did anyone want to hurt us? Nothing. No one was waiting for us after the turn-off onto the Ganzfield road from North Conway. *Strange.* I'd expected another ambush party, or at least a scout.

Drew keyed in the code at the main gate. Something seemed odd as we pulled up the crunching gravel drive. Unease flickered in the back of my mind.

Rachel tried to RV Sean. *Where is he? Why isn't he in Blake House?*

He'd normally be in class at this time. She widened her search as we drove through the woods toward the main buildings.

"Wait," I said. "Something's wrong." I couldn't hear thoughts from anyone outside the van.

Usually, I could feel the collection of people in the buildings ahead, even though I couldn't hear any specific thoughts. Like a crowded party, the noise and sense of people together carried beyond the building, making it seem fuller than a simple structure.

But there was no one. Ganzfield was empty.

Deserted.

Hannah saw the first body.

Oh, my God in Heaven.

Ice flashed through me. I recognized her through Hannah's mind and whipped my head around to see her with my eyes. She was a charm. *Alexis.* Her name was—had been—Alexis. She lay on her back like a discarded doll, wearing only a short nightgown. Her eyes stared sightlessly to the side. Blood from a wound in her abdomen stained the snow around her nearly black.

I felt Rachel's twisting panic as she tried to locate Sean with new desperation. *Where is he? Sean!* Her terror overloaded her ability. It seemed to fizzle and crackle in her head, leading nowhere…as though there might not be anywhere to lead. A hoarse sob escaped her.

There were more bodies in front of the main buildings—dozens of them. I felt like I'd been punched in the gut. I couldn't breathe.

A massacre.

The Ganzfield people had been collected in front of Blake House, and then gunned down. Contorted corpses sprawled in the snow. Many of the bullet wounds seemed small compared to the terrible final damage they'd caused. Others had exit wounds that had exploded from their bodies, spraying the trampled snow with blood and ripped pieces of flesh.

The van kept rolling forward. Drew seemed to have forgotten that he was driving. Trevor's invisible embrace tightened around me, a futile attempt to keep the horror from me. Hannah moved to open the van door; she wanted to try to save someone.

But I didn't think there was anyone left to save.

Seth! SETH! I made my mental call as loud as possible, throwing as much energy behind it as I could. If Seth were still at Ganzfield, he'd hear me. He had a huge telepathic range and I was particularly loud to him.

I got no answer. Was he one of the bodies scattered in the snow? I had no idea what he looked like. I'd never met him face to face.

Rachel tentatively touched Sean with her ability. *Alive!* The huge weight pressing her chest dissolved, letting her breathe again. She rested her forehead against the dashboard and sobbed. *Thank you, thank you, thank you, God!*

Through her vision, I saw several other people with Sean. They were fuzzy and indistinct; Rachel focused only on her boyfriend. Her golden thread seemed infused with her love for him, surrounding him and making him glow in her mind—an aura of sunlight breaking through the darkness.

As Rachel concentrated, more of the vision expanded and cleared. I saw Harrison and Ellen McFee. They both stared blankly into a huge fireplace in a large, high-ceilinged room. Their faces carried the marks of shock.

Survivors.

There were survivors. Rachel's golden connection to Sean headed south.

Drew's sudden, horrified thought for his brother jolted him

into full panic. "Harrison!" He flung open the front door and jumped out. Trevor stomped on the brake pedal with his ability, then shifted the gear back into park and shut off the ignition. Drew raced across the field toward the sparks' buildings, nearly tripping over several more bodies in the snow.

"Drew!" I called to him. "Drew! Harrison's okay! He's with Sean!"

It took Drew several steps to register what I'd said and several more for him to slow down. The rest of us climbed out of the van. *He's with Sean,* I repeated. *Rachel's seen them. I don't know where. Somewhere south of here.*

More corpses lay between the field of bodies and the lake. They wore strange, metallic, hooded coveralls, like spacesuits from a 1950s sci-fi movie. These weren't Ganzfield people. Wispy grey plumes of smoke filtered out of the seams by the hood and at the wrists and ankles where the gloves and boots had come loose. I felt Drew connect to the still-smoldering fires, sensing the damage they'd caused to the bodies within the metallic suits. Apparently, they'd been less fireproof in practice than their wearers might've hoped.

No wonder all of the survivors Rachel had envisioned seemed to be sparks.

I still couldn't hear anyone beyond our little group, which now seemed pitiful and small. My chin began to quiver and I glanced quickly at the treeline. My telepathic range was so short! If anyone tried to ambush us now, I'd be able to give almost no warning.

Hannah bent to check for signs of life from some of the people lying in the snow, slaughtered in the place I thought of as home. Whoever the killers were, they'd attacked at night. The Ganzfield people all wore sleep clothes. No coats. No boots. The attackers must've been immune to charms. I recalled the earpieces that Trevor had crushed in the car yesterday. The healers could knock someone out with a touch—would the metallic suits have worked against the healers, as well? I took a shuddering breath and looked for them. Matilda. Morris. Lester.

Lester was dead. Hannah cried out when she recognized him. Zack started a body count. Forty. Forty G-positives lay dead on the grounds, with another fourteen corpses in metallic suits. Rachel still focused on Sean; she tried to identify the other people around him. They were almost all sparks. Except for the ones who'd been with us, all of the charms and RVs of Ganzfield lay dead at our feet.

My brain didn't seem to be working right. Between my own shock and the overflow from the group, I couldn't focus. I felt a rolling hollowness within me that might turn into a scream. The thoughts of the others barreled into my mind and back out, unprocessed. I tried to detach myself from it all—to rise above it and see it as a problem to be solved. We needed to figure out what to do next.

Oh, my God. There's Grace!

A sob escaped as I covered my mouth with my hand and fell to my knees. *Oh, Grace. No!* Her eyes were closed, as though she was sleeping. It looked like she'd seen her killer take aim and, knowing she couldn't stop it, had simply shut her eyes and hoped it was a bad dream. She'd been a strong person, a fighter. Somehow, I'd expected her to look angrier. I felt a hot tear escape my eye, leaving a wet trail down my cheek that quickly turned cold.

Frank. Oh, no. Not Frank.

Bullet holes riddled our trainer's once-white t-shirt. Three metallic-suited corpses lay around him. Despite the fact he was missing his prosthetics, Frank had gone down fighting. They hadn't expected a man without legs to fight back as fiercely as he must have.

Dammit, Frank. What are we supposed to do now?

Frank would've expected us to handle this crisis the way he'd taught us: figure out the problem then generate ways to solve it. I squeezed my eyes shut. I had to stop letting my emotions—and the emotions of the others—cloud my ability to think.

Easier thought than done.

Next to me, shock and pain emanated from Trevor's turbulent thoughts. *Their families—the people who loved them—they'll never see them again. They'll never know why—never know what happened.* Ganzfield—our home—had been attacked. *Violated.* It was a primal association, as though our nest had been disturbed or someone had declared war on our tribe. This was wrong. Deeply, viscerally wrong.

Evil.

I forced myself to focus. We needed to clean this up and we needed to keep the police out of this. A secretive enclave—which many locals thought was a cult—filled with the massacred bodies of dozens of teenagers would draw media attention on an unbelievably massive scale. We had to keep this from going public. We were obviously vulnerable, and now half of Ganzfield had been wiped out. Where were the rest? Where were the older G-positives who no longer lived and trained here? We needed to find the living, go to them, find out what had happened, and see what we could do next.

Regroup. That would work for now.

Let's clean this up, and then go find Sean and the other survivors. I still couldn't make my voice work. *Rachel, do you know where they are? How to get there?*

Rachel nodded silently. Her expression had turned stony and her mind seethed with anger and the desire for revenge.

Tears traced down Hannah's face. She did the only thing she could for the dead—filling line after line on a sheet of white paper. Names. How did she know all of their names? I'd always considered her shy and not very social. *Please, Jesus, help me to be strong,* she thought, over and over. *Please, give me strength.*

Drew started dragging the scattered corpses together, dislodging them from the mix of blood and partially-melted snow that'd iced up beneath their bodies. He brought them away from the houses and out into the field that led down to the now-frozen lake. The bloodstained corpses screamed out their obscene presence in vivid contrast to the peaceful white and grey of the wintry world. As he worked, Drew stripped off the metallic suits from those wearing them. He placed the dead in a pile—a pyre. Trevor joined him, moving the bodies with his ability. The lifeless shapes seemed to float, two at a time, in a macabre dance.

Do we need wood?

Drew shook his head at me. The flames burned white-hot and the bodies turned to ash and charred bones after less than an hour. I thought it normally took much longer—Drew must've burned them at an extremely high temperature. I'd known he was strong, but I hadn't known he had that kind of power. Heated air pushed against us as the snow melted in the surrounding area leaving a circle of bare earth, scorched black near the flames. The foul smell, sizzle of flesh, and popping cracks of bone added to the sickening ambiance.

We'd known these people. They were *our* people. This should *not* have happened. This could *never* happen again.

The pain, the anger, and the nauseating horror of the others mixed with my own as we watched the fire swirl like a fiery tornado, twisting toward the sky. The black plume of smoke tilted toward the lake, thinning and dispersing as it rolled away from us. A few flakes of snow began to fall, as though the entire sky was turning to ash.

Hannah said an enormous silent prayer as we stood there, unspeaking observers to the destruction of our little world. After the flames had turned the remains to grey cinders, Trevor's unseen hands dug a pit in the newly-thawed earth next to the pyre. He swept the ashes in, and then covered them with freshly-turned dirt. The remains of the metallic suits filled a second pit. Trevor's thoughts were steel-grey with cold anger.

Ugly work.

We scavenged for supplies from the infirmary and the kitchen. Little remained; the survivors must've done the same. Cabinets hung open and empty drawers lay scattered on the infirmary floor. The electricity was off and the main building seemed especially dark in the tepid light that came though the windows.

Trevor and I went to our church. The front door creaked on its hinges as we approached. Our private sanctuary had been violated. My jaw quivered as I stumbled on the path.

If we'd been here last night…

Trevor and I silently gathered up our belongings and clothing. We didn't know when—or if—we'd be coming back. Trevor's mind churned—sick, grief-filled, and angry in turns. *What if we'd been here? What if we hadn't let the four men go yesterday? Did their report of killing us trigger this attack?*

I felt a hot flush wash up through my chest and into my head. I couldn't swallow. *Oh, no.* Had this been our fault? Had we set this massacre in motion?

No. We couldn't start thinking like that. The Sons of Adam had to've been planning this for a while. What had happened to our security systems? What had knocked out the power? We were off the grid here; our wind turbines occupied one of the hills above the valley. Could that have been the weakness in our defenses?

As we looked back from the double doors into our now-empty home, Trevor gathered me close. I wrapped my arms around him and we stood there in the dark, cold church, comforting each other—drawing strength from each other—as a torrent of emotions passed between us. A primal protectiveness built within Trevor, but I was feeling uncomfortably weak. I kept seeing lifeless eyes staring up from the snow. How frightened had the victims been as faceless, armed intruders herded them from their beds? Had they felt much pain when they died?

Oh, God.

I felt like curling up somewhere, making myself as small as possible, as though I could avoid the overwhelming emotions by making myself too insignificant to hold them. I'd never felt this powerless before—this helpless. I wanted to get angry, to feel a sense of energy, of purpose.

Righteous wrath.

I knew it was there, but it was like Trevor and I had switched reactions—he felt the anger that I usually did.

Trevor carried our bags as we returned to the van. The snow fell more steadily now, swathing the world in a grey-white silence, covering the frozen bloodstains in the snow with a pure layer of white. The others also held bags filled with their belongings. We silently piled into the van. The intense emotions washing into me from everyone else made me want to scream.

It was time to go.

CHAPTER 6

Rachel's mental connection to Sean led south, a golden thread stretching past the horizon. Drew drove us down through Massachusetts, crossing into Connecticut. We stopped for gas at one point, and Hannah made us eat something from the gas station mini-mart.

More than five hours later, as the last of the light ebbed from the sky, we pulled onto a winding, narrow road that Drew recognized. "My uncles have a property near here. It used to be a summer camp."

I curled against Trevor and clenched my hands to my forehead as though they would somehow hold everything in place and keep my silent scream from coming out. I had everyone else's pain, fear, and anger inside my head along with my own. It felt like my brain was going to either melt or explode.

A makeshift wooden barricade blocked the road. Flames blazed up from large metal drums on either side. Two people moved cautiously in the dark places beyond the fires. One of them slid off to the side, staying out of view. I recognized the sound of his mind from Ganzfield—Drew's cousin, Grant. We'd come to the right place.

The other man came toward us around the barricade. Flames reflected off the metal of his shotgun as he approached with slow, wary steps. Firelight back-lit his red hair and wide-set shoulders. *Must be a McFee.* He looked older, perhaps in his forties. I felt the bright recognition in Drew's mind. He threw open the driver's door to jump out, and then froze with his hand half-extended. He'd needed to stop the gun from firing.

"Geez! Uncle Jim, don't shoot!"

Jim McFee's face mirrored the horror in his mind. "Drew? Is that really you?"

"Yeah, it's me! You gonna lower that shotgun now?"

Jim pointed the weapon at the ground as he pulled his nephew into a tight, one-armed hug. The rest of us piled out of the van. "The minder said you were dead."

"Dr. Williamson said we were dead?" I asked, surprised. *Why would he—?*

"Not Williamson. The other one, just a kid, really..."

"Seth?" I asked.

"Yeah." Uncle Jim nodded. "Williamson was killed. Ambushed outside of North Conway."

The world tilted sickeningly.

No, no, no.

That couldn't be true. *Dr. Williamson was dead?* I'd thought—I'd assumed—he'd have come here. He'd be in charge. He'd know what to do.

And everything would be okay...

The horror of the entire day came to a terrible head. I'd just lost the closest thing I'd known to a father. My whole body shook uncontrollably and couldn't seem to get enough air. A strangled sob escaped from me and my hands flew up to cover my mouth. Trevor caught me as my legs gave out.

Grant and Uncle Jim pulled the barricade aside. Drew rolled the van between the flaming barrels into the inky blackness beyond. When the paved road ran out, we pulled to a stop next to the other two Ganzfield vans in front of a large, barn-like building. Silhouettes appeared at the lighted windows, drawn by the sound of our engine.

The door of the lodge flung open with a high-pitched cry. I recognized Drew's mother—a McFee-sized blonde woman—as she ran to the driver's door of the van and yanked Drew into a hug. Drew's brother, Harrison, descended on us, as well. The brightness of their joy shone in contrast to the emotional tone of the others here. I closed my eyes and took a shuddering breath.

You're not dead. I felt the familiar mental voice distantly in my mind—Seth.

I never said I was. Why did you? We usually picked at each other like siblings but we were both too traumatized to make much more of an effort at it tonight.

One of the guys we captured said his people had killed you on the road to town. Something that felt like a tortured scream filled Seth's mind.

False memory. The new charm's good at it. A sliver of hope stabbed through my consciousness. *Wait—did these same guys tell you they got Dr. Williamson, too?*

Yeah. The same thought occurred to him. *That RV still with you?*

I was already on it. "Rachel!" My shout interrupted a rather demonstrative reunion with Sean. He poured a series of exuberant, passionate kisses on her that she ardently returned. "Rachel! RACHEL!" *Geez. RACHEL!* Calling her name directly into her skull finally got her attention. "We need you to find Dr. Williamson. Right now!"

Please, God. I really hoped I wasn't about to give her a head full of images of his mangled corpse.

Her golden threads found Dr. Williamson, pacing in some kind of holding cell.

Thank you, God!

I started crying again as I saw the vision in her mind.

Seth saw it, too. A small sense of order fell across his thoughts with this new piece of welcome data. *It looks official. Good.*

Official? Why does that matter? Dr. Williamson's alive!

"He's alive?" asked Trevor. Was I leaking thoughts to him again?

I met his eyes through my tears and nodded.

"Who's alive?" asked Hannah.

"Dr. Williamson," Rachel answered. Nearly thirty people had gathered around us. Most were sparks from Ganzfield. A few older McFees filled out the group. People began to badger Rachel—as the only RV—for information about the whereabouts and welfare of people who were missing.

Hannah went to the lodge to treat the wounded. No other healers had made it out and five people had sustained gunshot wounds that would've drawn unwanted attention at an emergency room. Word spread that Hannah had a list of the dead and people approached her somberly as she moved between patients.

At the far end of a low stone bench, a brown-haired woman watched silently. The light from the windows caught the edges of the tears that streaked her cheeks, and something in her earnest thoughts held my attention. *Dear Lord, deliver us from evil. May your protecting hand be over us. Father, send your angels to keep watch over us. Yea, though we walk through the valley of death, we will fear no evil, for you are with us—*

Mel touched her arm. "Aunt Leah? My mom's looking for you."

Trevor and I moved away from the others. Their thoughts filled my head with taut emotions and urgent babble, and the pain of the injured ate at the edges of my mind. I couldn't deal with it all.

Overload.

Our feet crunched through the crusty snow as we left the shoveled walk and took the path that seemed to lead in Seth's direction, away from other people. Around the field's edge, small cottages formed three sides of a square. Shoveled paths linked them together like beads strung on a necklace. The night closed around us, swallowing the noise of all those jangling thoughts.

Seth, what happened? I didn't want to know the details but I had to ask. Next to me, Trevor sensed the connection. I'd broadcast to him again without thinking about it. Through Seth's thoughts, I saw his little campsite in the woods. He'd pitched a small tent next to a bright fire, as far as he could get from the other people on the property. Was it far enough to keep their thoughts from pressing in on him?

Helicopters. Seth's mind filled with vivid images and suddenly it was as though I was there.

Four helicopters swept over the hills just after midnight. The sound of their rotors chopped into the night. They dropped something on the little power station up by the wind turbines. A bright flash then the lights had all gone out as a low, rolling boom—like thunder—came across the lake.

I'd just finished bedcheck among the sparks. I'd...I was just about to go home. Rotor wash kicked up a hiss of snow that stung his face. *They...they...so much hate. They wanted to kill us all. I...I couldn't warn them.* Seth had been the only minder at Ganzfield and he couldn't project his thoughts to non-telepaths. He'd had no way to use his ability to alert the people in the houses.

He started yelling.

The helicopters landed in front of the main building. Silver-hooded attackers immediately spread out to the various dormitories, pulling the people out of bed at gunpoint, herding them out into the cold night. Seth felt each person wake. He sensed their confusion—their fear. Each time one of the charms tried to stop them, their abilities had been useless.

Seth's yells woke the sparks. Several started across the field to join the fight. Someone opened the weapons locker at the firing range so they were doubly armed.

Then the first shots rang out. Frank grabbed the two invaders who'd dragged him out of his room. He bashed their heads together and they collapsed in a pile. A man hauled Frank out by the neck. Frank gripped his arm and flipped him so he took the first shot intended for Frank. Then two of the silver-suits emptied several rounds into Frank's chest, killing him.

The invaders opened fire on the assembled crowd and Seth, with his strong telepathic ability and huge range, felt the pain of every shot as it ripped into them.

No!

—pray for us sinners, now and at the hour of—

Stop them!

This isn't happening. This can't be happ—

Oh, God. I don't want to die!

Someone help me!

He experienced their sick horror of watching their friends die around them. Screams and sobs burned into his brain, followed by the cold that seeped into the wounded as their lives drained away.

As I experienced Seth's memories, I felt what he'd felt.

Oh, God.

Trevor held me close, giving me some of his strength. Several images leaked through to him, enough to for him piece together the bigger picture.

Grant McFee took down the first invader. He dropped to one knee and aimed for the heart. The crack of his rifle was covered by the attacker's gunshots as they moved from body to body in the snow, shooting those who were still alive after the first volley. Grant's second shot wounded another attacker. His strangled howl alerted the others to the sparks' attack.

By that point, Katie Underwood and her cousin, Jonah Parker, had gotten close enough to use their abilities. They threw themselves flat in the snow and focused on the guns. Between the two of them, they suppressed more than half of the invaders' weapons. Melanie cried out as a shot clipped her shoulder and the pain tore through her—and through Seth. Two more injured sparks screamed as bullets slammed into them. Seth fell to his knees in proximity to such intense agony. He curled his arms around his head as though the motion might block out his ability.

More shots. More pain.

Tom McFee's voice cut through the confusion. "Burn 'em! From the inside out!"

Seth felt him focus within the silver suit of one attacker, heating a spot of clothing that suddenly caught and spread. The screams weren't loud through the helmet, but the pain of burning flesh seared into Seth's mind. A bullet caught Tom in the chest, knocking his suddenly lifeless body back into the snow.

Invaders shrieked as they roasted alive within their gear. Ellen and Harrison added their efforts to suppress the guns. The silver-suits began a panicked retreat to the helicopters. The pilots took off while men still tried to scramble aboard, flying away from the sparks and out of their range in a rush to escape. The invaders' fears of being left to the mercy of the freaks and monsters tasted bitter through the filter of Seth's memories.

They were the brutal killers of dozens of unarmed teenagers, but *we* were the monsters?

The attackers who'd been left behind tried to run. Seth staggered forward and grabbed Sean's arm. With the contact, Sean's thoughts kicked Seth in the head. "Keep…them alive…for questioning," Seth gasped, and then dropped his hand.

Sean nodded and passed the word, but seven sparks had been shot and two of them were dead. *Family.* Several more silver-suited men burned alive before the order to take prisoners took effect. The two survivors were now tied up in one of the outbuildings here at this old summer camp.

Back at Ganzfield, Seth hadn't needed the men to answer his questions—he'd only needed them to *think* about the answers. "The people that left here this afternoon…what happened to them?"

Dead. They'd truly believed we were dead. Zack had charmed the watchers into believing that they'd killed all of their targets—Dr. Williamson must've been on the target list, as well. Seth's questions had filtered through the men's thoughts. He'd seen their connection to the Sons of Adam and to their leader, Jonas Pike.

Holy crap.

Jonas Pike was *Isaiah's* alias. Isaiah Lerner, probably the most dangerous G-positive on the planet, now controlled the group dedicated to the destruction of G-positives, supposedly because *we* were dangerous.

If I hadn't been so sick at heart, I might've admired his chutzpah.

I now understood why Seth had that scream within his mind. I was nearly there myself. The horrible memories wouldn't stop and the churning emotions of the people in the main part of the camp pressed in on him, even at this distance. A shuddering exhaustion paradoxically seemed to leave him too tired to sleep.

It hadn't felt safe to stay at Ganzfield. Seth had believed the invaders might return and try to shoot the remaining Ganzfield people from the air. They hadn't had time to tend to the dead.

We took care of them.

Good. We don't need our existence becoming public knowledge.

The survivors had gotten some supplies together. After a short discussion, they'd come here. With his greater telepathic sensitivity, the long drive down to this camp had been even worse for Seth than it'd been for me. His head had nearly exploded with the second-hand turmoil from the other passengers in the overcrowded van.

All I wanted to do was curl up someplace and not move—not think—until this all went away. However, with Dr. Williamson gone, that wasn't an option. *What do we need to do now?*

Warn other G-positives. Find Dr. Williamson. Get him out of wherever he's being held. Seth's thoughts flowed sluggishly, as though he was drunk from lack of sleep.

Okay.

The people up at the lodge have been contacting the G-positives in other places. The other people who'd trained at Ganzfield in past years were relatives and friends. If the Sons of Adam had declared open war, none of them would be safe in their colleges, homes, or jobs. The camp didn't have an internet connection and the single phone line in the lodge provided painfully slow e-mail access. However, over the course of the day, most of the recent Ganzfield alumni and their family members had been contacted. Some were coming here; a few were going into hiding; many were staying put and weighing their options.

Seth, it looks like Dr. Williamson's safe for now. He may be safer than the rest of us. Let's work on it in the morning, okay? Try to sleep.

Trevor and I silently walked back toward the lodge. I had only one phone call to make: my mom. She was a G-positive, too, which meant she could be in danger. I dug though my purse for my cell phone. As usual, it was dead. Why did I still carry the stupid thing? It couldn't hold a charge for even twenty-four hours and I never got any bars around Ganzfield, anyway. I'd tossed it in my purse out of habit when we'd headed out to the hospital.

I rummaged in my bag for the cord and plugged in at the closest unoccupied cabin. After charging for a few minutes or two, the startup screen lit up. To my surprise, I got a single bar.

"Mom."

"Honey! How are you?"

"I'm safe. But Mom, there's...there's been some—"

"What's wrong?"

"Some people are...targeting G-positives." I didn't want to tell her. I didn't want her worrying more than she already would and saying aloud what'd happened would just make it more real.

"Where are you? Are you all right?" Her voice had taken on an anxious edge.

"We're safe. We're not at Ganzfield anymore. Mom, keep alert. The people who...they're going after people like us. G-positives. You might be—" The thought of someone trying to hurt my mom closed my throat for a few seconds. "Mom, if you feel like someone's watching you or something like that...trust that feeling, okay?" A flash of unenhanced insight might be her only warning.

"What's happened, honey?"

"I—I can't go into it now, Mom."

"You know you can always come home."

"I know, Mom. I might do that." I had no intention of doing that. "Mom, I gotta go. I love you. Be careful, all right?"

"Maddie? What's going on?"

My voice broke. "I can't talk about it right now. I'll call soon, okay? G'bye. I love you."

"I love you, t—"

I closed the phone. Trevor silently shook his head when I offered it to him. *I…my family…they don't know about our abilities and…no, they wouldn't believe me.*

The lodge must have been the dining hall and rec room when this was an active summer camp. Long wooden tables and benches lined the walls. The huge fieldstone fireplace was tall enough to stand in and the blazing fire warmed the whole room. Fading amateur murals of nature scenes covered the walls. A life-sized painting of a moose gazed serenely out from the tall grass. It caught my attention for no particular reason.

Several people waited to use the single landline. Their anxiety for their loved ones crackled grey around them. I plugged my cell into an open outlet and silently handed the charger-tethered phone off to the first in line. Right now, I didn't care if I ever saw it again.

I sat down and stared into the fire. Trevor spoke quietly to one of the older McFees—another of Drew's uncles, or his dad's cousins, or something. After a quick mental *I'll be right back,* they left together. I ran my fingers through my hair and tried to keep the thoughts that hummed around me from flooding my mind.

Maddie? Trevor called to me from the doorway. He had our overnight gear from the van along with a small tent, two blue tarps, and some firewood. My legs felt like lead as we followed Drew's Uncle Gerry—technically his first cousin, once removed—on a wooded path to a small clearing. I sent a shower of silent gratitude to Trevor for arranging this. He'd understood that I needed to be out of other people's range, tonight of all nights. I didn't think I could handle a shared nightmare of the day's experiences.

Logs framed a stone firepit. We were now on the far side of the camp from Seth, and far enough away from the others that their mental voices were no longer in my head. Uncle Gerry brushed the snow out of the firepit, set up the wood, and then started the fire with a touch of his hand. I sat and watched the flames move along the dry wood. *Hypnotic.* I felt Uncle Gerry's mind grow fainter, leaving only Trevor within my hearing.

When I looked up, Trevor had finished setting up the small tent close to the fire. I felt guilty for not helping him, but the strain of dealing with everyone else's emotional turmoil—as well as my own—had overwhelmed me. Trevor slumped down next to me on the log and joined me in gazing into the fire. I leaned my head against his shoulder, wordless and exhausted. He wrapped his arm around me.

I felt like I'd aged several decades in a single day.

Fear sliced through my gut, colder than the night air. We stood crowded together. Silver-suited strangers pointed guns at us; their hatred burned me. They raised their guns to kill us all. I felt lethal energy surge through me to blast their minds, but the metallic suits blocked my line-of-sight. I couldn't let it out!

Powerless.

Panic clawed at my throat. "Trevor!" My eyes found him across the group. He ripped weapons from enemy hands and threw metallic figures in the air. *Too many!* They targeted him and the crack of gunshots split the cold air. Time oozed slowly forward as I saw him stop several shots, but the barrage continued. More invaders started shooting; their bullets ripped into him. Trevor's mind flashed the vivid purple shock of pain as he crumpled to the ground. *No, no, no!* His thoughts faded and were gone. I couldn't get to him, couldn't help him, and I was screaming, screaming—

I jolted awake with a cry in my throat. Trevor held me close and I felt his mind trying to reach mine, pulling me out of the dream's horror. My heart pounded wildly and I drew sobbing breaths as I clutched at Trevor. He was here. Warm. Unharmed.

It was just a dream. I didn't know if it had come from his mind or mine. *Just a dream.*

There was barely room for the two of us in the tiny tent. I didn't remember coming in before going to sleep, although I was in my sleeping bag with another pulled over me for warmth. I put my hand on Trevor's cheek.

Really here.

Firelight filtered through the tent fabric, outlining his features in flickering blue. I pulled his face down to mine and kissed him with fiery intensity—affirming that he was alive...that I was alive.

At that moment, I didn't care what we'd promised Dr. Williamson. I didn't care that it was freezing out. I didn't care about the consequences. I opened my mind to his—no holding back.

I want you. I want you in every way.

His mind echoed my passionate thoughts. We slid aside the sleeping bag and pulled at each other's clothing. Invisible arms supported him, keeping the bulk of his weight off of me. I thrilled at the sensation of his hands—his actual hands—on my bare skin. My insides went liquid. I trailed down and kissed his neck, his chest, and Trevor groaned.

Power flashed between us and we felt the world dissolve. Our energies merged instantly. We spun together, swirling into one another again and again to a passionate climactic intensity. Finally, we collapsed back in our bodies, holding each other close and trembling as we always did after we soulmated.

I wasn't sure, but I was beginning to think that making love—physically, at least—might not even be possible between us. *I think soulmating might be part of a divine plan to keep us from actually having sex.*

Trevor chuckled huskily into my ear. *You know what they say, "if at first you don't succeed…"*

I laughed and nuzzled in, kissing him gently. I felt healed—surprisingly whole. *Trevor, you're the reason I can face the bad things in the world. You make life good again, even when things seemed hopeless. I love you so much.*

His mind glowed with spring-green joy as he stroked my hair. *I feel the same way about you.* It was the first fully positive emotion we'd experienced in what felt like a long time, even though it had only been a single day.

And don't think I didn't notice that you're rethinking the whole sex thing, I added.

I can't help it. You're irresistible. However, the guilt had started pinging within his mind, eating away at his joy and contentment. He felt as though we'd gone too far. That, if we hadn't started to soulmate when we did, he wouldn't have been able to stop himself. *I didn't wanted to stop myself.* He hadn't cared about his promise to Dr. Williamson. He hadn't cared that we weren't being safe.

Well, if we keep doing things like tonight, we should at least have some protection on-hand. I didn't hold the promise to Dr. Williamson the same way Trevor did. I felt that only the two of us should decide how far we wanted to take things and Dr. Williamson had no right to impose restrictions on us. *I don't want you to ever regret being with me.*

I don't, but... His thoughts tread familiar paths of unhappy childhood memories and his desire to be worthy of his family. He'd made a promise to Dr. Williamson and he intended to keep his word. It bothered him now that he'd nearly broken it. He felt the need to prove to himself that he was a good person, to live up to his own standards. Trevor was...honorable.

I know.

I kissed him tenderly, trying to give him enough love to take the sting out of those thoughts. I might test the limits he put on himself, but I usually didn't push. Now I was feeling some of that remorse, as well. *So, are we out from under that promise when I turn eighteen?*

He pondered it a moment. *Possibly. But to be absolutely sure, I think I need to marry you.*

That would be the honorable thing to do, it's true. I smiled as a delicious tenderness filled me. Wow. Trevor made me think in poetry and love songs and I'd never been one for that sort of thing. *Does it have to be legal?* I flashed the concept of a lucid dream wedding to him, to see what he thought.

You really want to have sex, don't you? The idea of being so desired flared tingling, red energy around him.

I can't help it, I replied, echoing his earlier words, *you're irresistible.* He gathered me into an embrace of pure, overwhelming love and held me until I fell asleep again.

When I woke again in the grey dawn, Trevor was back on his tarp out in the cold—a safe distance away from me and from the remnants of the fire. He'd wrapped himself in two sleeping bags, although one had a huge rip down an entire side. Loose batting spilled from the torn nylon shell, leaving little puffs on the ground. Apparently, I wasn't the only one who'd had a bad dream in the night.

I offered up a silent prayer of gratitude to whatever Higher Power had put Trevor in my life. I felt emotionally intact again. *Whole.* Because of him, I'd be able to cope, to make it through the day. I needed to…we had a *lot* of problems to solve.

The morning air felt warmer and a little damp. It was above freezing—it might even make it up into the forties today. I followed the trail back to the camp, carrying a small pile of clean clothing and my toiletries. I needed coffee and a shower, preferably both as hot as possible.

Drew's mom, Viv, oversaw the kitchen in the winterized caretaker's cabin that sat next to the lodge. She pointed me in the direction of the coffee then put me to work cleaning dusty pans and chipped dishes while I waited my turn for the single working shower. Water to the outbuildings, including the shower house, was shut off for the winter so the pipes wouldn't freeze. This little cabin was the only building with heat and water. Fortunately, all the other buildings had fireplaces and were made from non-combustible materials. That must've been what appealed to spark firefighters to buy the old camp in the first place.

Viv McFee looked close to six feet tall, large-boned and a little plump. Strands of white shot through her blonde hair, which she wore tucked back in a braid. Her bright blue eyes were edged with what some people call laugh-lines, but I saw enough of her thoughts to know that most of them hadn't come from laughing. Her mind gave off a sense of endurance. More than once, I heard her think something like *we'll get through this. We've been through tough things before.* I'd met her briefly at Christmas, but apparently I hadn't made much of an impression. She didn't remember my name, but I didn't take it personally. I was terrible at remembering names myself.

I finally broke the kitchen's silence. "Who does this camp belong to?"

"Quentin and Gerry bought it a few years back. They wanted a summer place we could all come, even the active sparks." I saw their faces in her mind as she talked. Gerry had shown Trevor and me to our campsite last night.

"I'm so confused about how everyone is related. How are there so many G-positives in one family?"

"You don't know the story?" Viv gave me an appraising look. *Should I give her the public version or the real version?*

"Real version, please." I hoped I wouldn't offend her by picking the unasked question from her mind.

She cracked a wide smile. "That's right. You're the little telepath dating Drew's friend, Trevor. I remember you now."

I decided not to take offense at the "little" thing. Compared to Viv and most of the McFees, it was accurate enough. Besides, I was intrigued. What was in the "real" version that made a "public" version necessary?

"It all goes back to Gram. That's Nan Cochran McFee—my husband's great-grandmother. Andrew brought me up to meet her shortly after we started dating. She was a hundred years old that year. She died at a hundred and three, I think, back in the early 1990s."

I saw her memories of the old woman, whose body looked so hunched and frail but whose mind had struck Viv as being so strong. "When Nan was fifteen, she started having dreams of her future husband. Over and over she saw the same man in her dreams. She knew he was in America, and keep in mind, she was still back in Ireland at this point. Her family lore had always held that her mother's people had a bit of the 'second-sight,' so she took her dreams seriously. After months of dreaming of this same man, she finally decided she simply had to know if he was real. This was 1904, mind you, and decent teenaged girls simply didn't take off alone to cross the Atlantic. But she did. She ran away, booked passage in steerage on a westbound ship, and came to Boston.

"She kept dreaming of the man during the crossing and, the closer she got to Boston, the stronger her dreams became. She got off the boat, cleared immigration, and started walking. Then, as she went, she began to recognize more and more of the area around her. Finally, she came to the fire station in Roxbury. She'd seen it in her dreams many times so she knew she'd arrived. Nan walked right in, found the man she'd been dreaming about, and held out her hand."

Viv paused, scrubbing at a particularly resistant black stain on one of the pans. Her mind had switched to eradicating the mark, which left me hanging.

"So what happened?"

"What? When?" asked Viv, distracted.

"When Nan walked into the fire station! I mean...what did she say?" I felt amazed at the things this girl from another century had done. She must've been an RV, but how could she've located someone she'd never met like that? Especially without dodecamine?

"Oh, right. Well, Nan walked up to the man she'd seen in her dreams, held out her hand to him, and said, 'You're the one. You're the one I'm going to marry. What's your name?'" Viv laughed gently at this in a can-you-imagine kind of way.

"Well, Old Sean McFee was apparently rather surprised by this little piece of information, coming from this strange girl just off the boat. But something about her struck him as more interesting than crazy and he went for a walk around the neighborhood with her. She told him some of the things she'd seen him doing in her dreams, like knocking down a beehive by throwing an apple he'd bought from a green-painted apple cart. She pointed out the tree where the beehive had been and even picked out the right apple vendor when he happened by. By the end of the walk, Old Sean was convinced there was something special about this girl. After two weeks, they were engaged. They got married a month later, on her sixteenth birthday. He was twenty-one at the time."

Viv noticed that the drying cloth she was using was now too wet; she began to hunt for another. Once she found a new towel, her thoughts returned to the story of her husband's great-grandparents.

"Nan and Old Sean had five sons: Sean Jr., Seamus, Dylan, Ian, and Thomas. The boys grew up and Nan started having dreams of young ladies. She knew the dreams were like the ones that'd led her to Old Sean, so she told her boys what to look for. The first was the girl with the red hair who sang in the church choir in Walpole. Next came the one who worked as a maid in the big house with the columns in Belmont. She sent each son off to find the girl she'd dreamed for him. Ian had to go all the way to Kansas City. But each son followed the directions his mother had given him, and each time the girl she'd described was just where his mother had said she'd be.

"The young men brought these girls home to meet their mother. Once Nan had seen that each girl was the one from her dream, she gave her son the go-ahead to court her properly. Dylan brought home a young lady who matched the description his mother had given him—the daughter of a police officer in Sharon—but he'd gotten the wrong girl, according to his mother, so she sent him back to find the right one."

"The sons didn't mind dating the girls their mother had picked out for them?" The idea rankled against my modern sensibilities on several levels.

"Turns out, Nan knew what she was doing. The boys may've been skeptical at first, but once they met these girls, they liked them enough to get to know them better. They all fell in love, and the girls fell in love right back. So, they each got married and had families. And Nan's sons and grandsons all became firefighters— like Old Sean—in their turns. And many of them seemed to have his eerie understanding of how the fire was going to move and how to keep themselves and their teams safe."

"So the daughters-in-law were all G-positives?"

"That, or carriers. Not all of the grandsons had the gift with fire that Old Sean and his sons did. But enough of them did that now we figure Nan was a remote viewer who was able to locate G-positives, even though she didn't know what she was doing or how she was doing it.

"We believe she wanted her sons to find nice girls and settle down, and her unconscious mind did all the work. Between finding G-positives remotely and being a good enough judge of character, she unconsciously tracked solid matches for her sons. Then she did the same for her sixteen grandchildren when they were old enough."

Wow. I remembered reading something about how physical attraction was based on an unconscious recognition that the other person was genetically compatible. It looked as though Gram McFee had been breeding her own family of G-positives for generations. Perhaps it hadn't even started with her. The family lore of "second-sight" might be part of a long chain of remote viewers who'd unknowing selected people with the same genetic trait.

"By this point, her ability to match-make through her dreams had been accepted by the family. It was almost expected that, when a grandson or granddaughter was ready to settle down, he or she would talk to Gram. Gram would dream on it for a few weeks then say where to find the right person."

"So, when your husband brought you to meet her—"

Viv smiled at the reminiscence. "Her first words were, 'Ah, Andrew. You found her after all.'" I heard the Irish lilt in the old lady's voice in Viv's memory. The wispy tone still conveyed her joy, as well as a little touch of smug pride. Her rheumy blue eyes had sparkled with an I-told-you-so mixed in with her happiness.

"So, you're G-positive?" What was Viv's ability? I didn't know. Did she just not use dodecamine?

"I'm a carrier, but both of my boys are sparks. My Andrew was, too. He passed away from a stroke three years ago last January."

An aching loneliness filled her at the thought of her late husband. However, she refused to let it stay and take hold. Instead, she pushed the feeling aside gruffly and wondered what she'd been talking about before she'd been side-tracked.

"Meeting Nan for the first time," I prompted.

"Oh, right." She didn't notice I'd answered a question she

hadn't asked. "So, this whole big pack of sparks you see today was the work of an Irish lady and her second-sighted dreams. There are a few other types mixed in. We now have a couple of RVs and a healer; it looks like they got their mothers' gifts. But the fire-love runs pretty strongly through the McFee family."

Ellen McFee came out of the bathroom, absently indicating as she passed that it was my turn for the shower. Shadows darkened the pale skin under her eyes and a flashback of Melanie taking a bullet in the shoulder haunted her thoughts.

The overnight cold had thickened my shampoo and toothpaste into nearly unusable sludge. I tried to clean up as rapidly as possible; others were waiting to use the tiny bathroom. Once out, I grabbed a plate of scrambled eggs in the lodge and ate ravenously, realizing I hadn't had a meal since our McBreakfast twenty-four hours ago. Now I was rested and fueled, and there was a lot that I needed to do.

I filled another mug of coffee and carried it back to the clearing for Trevor. He was just waking as I returned, and he used the cup to warm his hands while he sipped. He'd slept the past night shelterless in a New England winter and he felt as cold as that sounded.

I rummaged through my bag for my laptop and power cable, and then Trevor and I went to the lodge. While he took his turn with the shower, I started making a list.

Dr. W—get him out

Warn others—list of names to contact?

I stopped. Something about a list. Hannah had a list—a list of the dead from Ganzfield. Was anyone missing from it? I knew that Zack was the only Ganzfield charm who hadn't been among the dead. Rachel was the only RV. Cold shock slammed through my chest. *The healers—Matilda and Morris Taylor.* I hadn't seen them lying in the snow yesterday. I tried to recall...Hannah hadn't registered them, either. I needed to check. Where was Hannah? Not here. She never ate breakfast. I tried to find her mind and couldn't. She was either out of range or still sleeping, and I didn't know which cabin she'd used last night.

Where was Rachel? I needed an RV. A quick mental search and—*whoa!* I abruptly winced and shied away. *Ugh.* I'd just mentally walked into her room without knocking. She and Sean were doing some "life affirming" of their own in one of the nearby cabins.

A blush still stained my cheeks when Trevor returned from his shower and joined me at one of the tables in the lodge. *What is it?* he smiled teasingly. *Have you been watching me in the shower again?*

I blushed further and flashed back to last night and the flickering blue light whispering across his silhouette as we'd touched. He flushed with remembered pleasure. Again, I hadn't been aware I was sending him my thoughts. *I think you're becoming telepathic.*

He tipped his head to the side as he considered that. *Only where you're concerned.*

Ahh, the hidden dangers of soulmating. If only they'd warned us in health class.

He laughed at that, but his joy abruptly faded as Zack flopped down across from us. His gaze fixed on me with the focus of a dog on a tennis ball. "So, what now?"

"Rescue mission." I felt my light mood leach away. Too bad charms were so useful; we couldn't afford to leave Zack behind. If things had been different, we might've been friends. But he was dangerous to me, and his presence made the muscle in Trevor's jaw twitch.

I guess that meant the "friends" thing was out.

I wasn't sure whether we'd be rescuing Dr. Williamson or the healers—wherever they were—but we were going to go do something, just as soon as we figured out a plan. We'd almost certainly need a charm and Zack was the only one we had.

Drew threw himself down next to Trevor with an enormous plate of food. "Rescue mission! About time. I'm in. When do we leave?" He started to eat with gusto.

"We need to find Rachel and Hannah. I have to talk to Seth, too. I'll do that now." I stood up.

"Do you want me to come with you?" asked Trevor.

"I'll just be a few minutes. You can finish eating." I felt his hunger; he really was being altruistic when he had offered to come. *Besides, I need to try something,* I added privately, giving his hand a squeeze.

As I headed toward Seth's campsite, I visualized my telepathic shield. Rather than the crude-but-effective brick wall, the bright mirror, or some of the other things that I'd practiced with Dr. Williamson, I took a deep breath then imagined covering my mind with an intricate, delicate, nearly-invisible web—strong, supple, and undetectable. I could feel it. Knowing how it'd worked in Zack's mind made me more confident that I could do it, too.

Now came the test.

I started walking again, slowly and quietly, toward Seth. I was about a dozen feet from the tent before he felt me. *Someone's out there!* Fear flashed cold within him. People didn't sneak up on him every day. Actually, people didn't sneak up on him *ever*.

Regret tinged my thoughts steel-grey. *Ah, hell.* Seth had been through enough. "Seth, it's me." I was afraid to try a mental contact. I didn't think I could broadcast thoughts and keep the shield in place, and my mind was so loud to Seth that I'd cause him a great deal of pain if my shield slipped this close to him.

"Me? Me who?"

"Maddie." I felt his confusion. Didn't he know my name? "The too-loud brat."

How are you doing that?

"I'm trying out a new shield. How's it working?"

You're about to blast me, aren't you?

"Not on purpose."

Get a little farther away, then. Just in case.

I moved back along the path toward the camp, and then dropped the spiderweb shield.

Ow!

Sorry! I moved back an additional fifty paces down the trail. I could no longer see his tent, although I still felt his mind clearly. *Better?*

Marginally.

Quick question. Did you see what happened to Matilda and Morris yesterday?

I told you—they took them.

You didn't tell me that! I'd have remembered!

I thought I did.

Isaiah has them, then.

Yeah, I guess he does.

What does he want with healers? Is he sick? A snort of mirthless laughter humphed out of me—we should be so lucky.

No clue.

We're going after them.

We?

Me, Trevor, Drew, Rachel, Hannah—and Zack, I guess.

Ah.

And Dr. Williamson?

We're going after him, too. Any ideas?

Yeah. Nick Coleman.

Who's Nick Coleman?

Williamson's lawyer.

G-positive?

Charm. One of the first through the Ganzfield program. He's in New York City. I don't have contact info, but he should be easy to find. If Williamson's being held officially, he'll be able to do something about it. Rescuing people from the Sons of Adam is one thing, but busting someone out of a federal jail is probably out of your league. And it's unnecessary, if you know a good charm lawyer.

We'll find him. It was a relief to remember that there were other charms in the world besides Zack—charms who didn't pose a threat to me. *New York City's only a few hours from here. We'll get the lawyer on the case, and then go after Matilda and Morris.*

Okay. Hey, take care of yourself, all right? You may be too loud, but you're the only one I can talk to like this now. Seth's loneliness and pain permeated those simple words.

I bit my lip as I choked up.

And Maddie? That new shield worked really well. I didn't hear you coming at all.

Good enough to go up against Isaiah?

If you were stupid enough to try, I guess it'd be good enough. If you have any luck or brains, you'll get them out without getting anywhere close to Isaiah.

But that wouldn't solve the bigger problem. *Take care of yourself, Seth. You're in charge while I'm gone.* As though I had any authority whatsoever.

Brat. His thought held a touch of fondness.

* * *

I mentally located Rachel and Sean in one of the cabins and knocked on the door. "Rachel, can you come find us in the lodge?"

Her unspoken response was full of reluctance and a few bad words. There were things she would *much* rather do, and Sean was determined to persuade her to stay and do them rather than come and talk to me.

"It's important." I ducked away before she could respond and before I could hear any more of Sean's "persuasiveness." Knowing so much about their intimacies made my skin itch. It made me feel a bit seedy, like I was a peeping-tom at the windows to their emotions.

I saw Hannah in the lodge, checking on her patients. All five looked whole and healthy this morning. Melanie rotated her shoulder for Hannah's inspection as I passed. She didn't have any more pain from her wounds; none of them did. My relief for them was selfishly tinged; I no longer had to endure their pain with them. Sea-green satisfaction emanated from Hannah—she loved what she could do.

Hey, my cell phone's still here! I hadn't really expected to get it back. I pocketed the phone and charger then gave Trevor a light kiss as I sat down.

Everything all right?

I nodded. *I think we'll be leaving this morning.*

Rachel and Sean entered the lodge, grabbing some food before they joined our table. They both looked flushed and their eyes were overly bright, as though they were high. Hey, there was a thought—what would the mind of someone drunk or high feel like? Personally, the idea of messing with my own brain that way freaked me out. Why risk addiction? Why risk being out of control? However, if someone else was already doing it, I didn't see the harm in telepathically checking out the sensation.

Once the entire group had gathered around the table, I told them what Seth and I had discussed. "I think we can get this charm lawyer on the case for Dr. Williamson. If he's being held by the police or the FBI or something, he needs legal help more than he needs what we can do."

"Charm lawyer?" Drew asked with an air of awed disgust, which was echoed by many other minds around the table. He glanced at Zack. "No offense."

"None taken." Zack was considering the possibilities of his own career in law. I had to admit, it was a natural fit for someone with exceptional persuasiveness. And hey, I'd heard that thought from him. I hoped that, as I learned how that spiderweb shield of his worked, I'd be able to work around it and read him better. It wasn't nearly as strong as the more noticeable shields I'd practiced—more like camouflage than armor.

"Rachel, where are Matilda and Morris now?" I asked. The golden threads shot out like a starburst from her mind. I reminded myself that most people, even most G-positives, didn't get to see this part of it—the emotions and energies the others used in these amazing displays of light and color. It really was beautiful, though. What a pity more people couldn't see it. I sent an image of it to Trevor.

You see this all the time? he asked, surprised.

You don't see your extra hands this way?

No. How do you see them?

I showed him the limbs of shimmering, golden light that seemed to flow from his torso—the energy that flowed through and strengthened the rest of his body and down his legs. I smiled as I recalled how those arms of light widened as he shielded me and how I felt surrounded by sunlight made solid. Not to mention how the energy shaded to red and ran over my skin when he kissed me.

Scarlet electricity flared between us. We reluctantly pulled back from the feeling when it took hold. *Show me more later,* he said, and I shivered in anticipation.

Work first. I took a deep breath and focused back on the world outside our heads.

Rachel seemed to travel along her golden beam, going south. "Other side of New York City. Looks like New Jersey, I think, or maybe Pennsylvania." We knew she could get us to the right spot as we got closer. In her thoughts, I could see Matilda and Morris tied to chairs in a dark room. They looked dirty and frightened, but alive and whole. If Isaiah had wanted them dead, they'd already be corpses. If he'd wanted to experiment on them—like with Trevor—they'd most likely be sedated and on operating tables. The memory made me shudder.

I told myself they were okay for the moment. *Right?* I had to make the decision—we needed to fix on a course of action. Something twisted deep within my heart. What if I was making the *wrong* decision? Should we be going after Matilda and Morris right now? Was I making a mistake? Were they in immediate danger?

Hannah was appalled that she hadn't figured out the other healers were missing sooner. "When I didn't see them among the dead, I was relieved. And I was so busy as soon as we arrived last night, I didn't think—" her voice broke.

"It's okay, Hannah." Trevor hated to see people hurting.

I tried to distract her. "How's the dodecamine supply?"

"The sparks salvaged eight vials from the infirmary. Four ccs each. Plenty of syringes, too."

"Can you find out what they can spare us?" I asked. It'd been six days since my last injection. "I'm due for a boost tomorrow."

"How much do you need?"

"Point-eight ccs a week."

If Hannah had been drinking anything, she'd have done a spit-take. Her eyebrows shot up. She'd never heard of a G-positive needing such a high dose. "*What?* That adds up to like…three times normal dosage."

"I know. Matilda thought it was better to give me smaller, more frequent injections."

Hannah considered that. Her thoughts filled with the possible side-effects that some rapid-burners experienced.

Yeah, I know. Stroke and brain damage, I told her silently, eager to move on to another topic. "Anyone else getting low? We might be gone a while."

"I am," said Drew. "I'll hit six weeks on Friday."

"I'm good for now," said Trevor. The others were okay for at least the next week or two.

"Where's it come from anyway?" asked Zack.

"A pharmaceutical company in New Jersey," replied Hannah. "It's written on the label."

Apparently, New Jersey was the new nexus of the universe. Everything we needed to find was probably right off the Turnpike. "I guess we're going to Jersey, then," I said.

Sean was set on joining us. He'd gone through an entire day thinking Rachel had been killed; now he was determined to stay close to her. How much could he add to the team, though? After all, Drew was one of the strongest sparks. I did a quick mental check with Trevor, Drew, and Hannah. *You guys okay with Sean coming with us?* Hannah didn't mind and the guys were both enthusiastic. Rachel was considering staying behind if Sean wasn't included. I didn't check Zack's mind; I didn't consider him truly part of the group. Besides, I couldn't read anything from him at the moment, anyway.

"You coming, Sean?" I asked, as though I didn't already know the answer.

Hannah got two vials of dodecamine and a bunch of syringes before we left. Drew and I would finish off the first one before the week was out. We now had a deadline. If we didn't replenish our supplies quickly, we'd start losing our abilities.

And then we'd be powerless against Isaiah when he came for us.

CHAPTER 7

It took over three hours to reach New York City. A quick internet search at a Connecticut rest stop had located the law offices of Nicholas Coleman on Seventh Avenue in midtown. We arrived just after noon on a damp, grey, New York day and left the van in a garage two blocks from the address. The parking fee used up most of the remaining cash Dr. Williamson had given us.

The City.

Thoughts from thousands of people simultaneously bombarded me. My mind was a stadium when everyone cheers, on and on in a never-ending barrage. I couldn't block it out. I kept talking too loudly, like someone wearing earphones.

Buzzing.

I wanted to swat away the confusion, as though swarms of insects filled my head. I'd had no idea it'd be so much more intense, being around so many people, hearing the rumble of all of their thoughts. The world pulled at me dizzily, like a carnival ride, making everything too intense.

Spinning.

I shook my head, as though the motion might clear the ache out of it. Okay, I *really* wasn't going to be able to spend a lot of time in cities from now on. I'd overload if I had to put up with this for long.

Ah, New York. Fast-moving people crowded the sidewalks. I heard the mental use of the F-word as a noun, verb, adjective, and adverb in the time it took us to walk the two blocks to Coleman's office. I also felt the swirling, chaotic intensity in the minds of not one, but two, drug addicts. I found the experience nauseating and confusing, without the euphoria I thought might be part of it.

Just like visiting New York as a telepath.

At Zack's suggestion, the guard at the security desk issued us passes instantly, without even checking our IDs. The elevators bustled with people going to or coming from lunch, so it took a while for us to get up to Coleman's office on the thirty-third floor. I squeezed my eyes shut and tried to hone in on the mind of a single individual, the way I'd sometimes tried to focus on the horizon when I'd felt carsick as a child. But I kept flipping from one person to another, feeling the frenzied thoughts of overly-busy people at every turn. I couldn't stand it.

Trevor took my hand. *Are you okay?*

So many minds. It's overwhelming—making me dizzy.

He winced. Either I was too loud in his head or he could feel the overwhelming sensation secondhand.

Crap. I decided not to connect to his mind again while we were in the City, if I could avoid it.

Next to me on the crowded elevator, my arm pressed against that of a sleek-looking man in an expensive suit. The contact made his thoughts especially clear and loud, and he hummed with excitement. *How can I ask that lawyer about investing this way? Am I incriminating myself if I just ask the question? Would that be considered conspiracy to obstruct the SEC?*

My mental antennae pricked but I kept from turning my head toward him. This was the sort of thing Dr. Williamson had been training me to do, although he'd never mentioned how intensely the city must affect him when he did it.

Is it really insider trading if I'm acting on unofficial approval? I can't believe we got such a huge government contract—we just took Locus Two public two years ago! Is there a way I can buy more stock before the public announcement without reporting it to the SEC? Can I buy it in Cassandra's name? She's only four.

Locus Two? I'd have to get online access soon to do some research on it. Hey, my mom was only an hour from here and she had my college fund, which I no longer needed for tuition. If this Locus Two thing checked out, I'd have a chance to start putting this ability to practical use.

Whoa—how crazy would that idea have seemed only a year ago? I shook my head as a little breath of laughter escaped me.

My life is surreal.

Locus Two guy got off the elevator on the twenty-ninth floor. We made it up to the thirty-third. I put on my game face as the doors slid open. *Pretend to be normal.* I concentrated on using a regular speaking voice with the receptionist.

"Please inform Nick Coleman that Maddie Dunn, Jon Williamson's god-daughter, is here to see him." I'd come up with the idea of identifying myself like this in the van. If we were meeting a strange charm, I was going to be "point," since I'd be immune if he used his ability.

This had seemed like a good idea in Connecticut. But now, with the mental energy of what felt like half the City passing through my head, I could barely think.

The receptionist looked at us through narrowed eyes. We'd

tried to clean up as much as possible, but compared to the refined and polished denizens of the fancy law office, we still looked like scruffy teenagers who'd been sleeping in the woods. Disapproval seemed to leak from each of her perfect, red nails. "Do you have an appointment?" Her mouth had moved, but I couldn't make out the words. At least her mind had echoed them loudly enough to make them understandable to me.

I smiled with what I hoped looked like confidence. "Just tell him we're here. I'm sure he'll want to speak with us."

Her face and her mind both clearly stated that she didn't share this view. However, she picked up the phone and spoke with Coleman's assistant. From down the hall, I felt an assistant's prick in recognition of Dr. Williamson's name. *Jon Williamson? Important client.* The assistant popped her head in the door.

I heard Nick Coleman's thoughts as he processed the assistant's words. His mind was slightly clearer than most others against the telepathic background noise. I again had the thought that G-positives might provide a stronger telepathic read.

I risked a quick connection and felt him startle at the contact. *We need your help.*

The assistant escorted us back and Coleman locked the door behind us. He was in his early thirties, athletically built and powerfully dressed in a ludicrously expensive suit. He looked handsomely lethal with a predatory gaze in his dark eyes. He wasn't wild about having the Ganzfield world intruding on the one he had here. *Did they raise anyone's suspicions? Who am I going to have to charm later?*

"Jon Williamson sent you? What happened at Ganzfield? I got a call last night that people were killed."

I shook my head. "Dr. Williamson didn't send us. He's in trouble and we thought you could help. He's in a holding cell of some kind. We think it's official—police or FBI."

"He's south of here. I think near D.C.," added Rachel. She'd RVed him again and he was still in the same cell. Dr. Williamson looked atypically scruffy, like he needed a shave. "They're probably federal."

"RV?" he said to Rachel, although I could hear in his thoughts that he'd already guessed. I remembered hearing somewhere that good lawyers don't ask questions unless they already know the answer.

Rachel nodded.

"I'm a corporate attorney; I don't handle a lot of criminal cases, but I'll see what I can do for Jon." Good. He was on the case.

I wondered if he could do one more thing for me. "You're a corporate lawyer. Can you also help me set up an investment account?"

"You're the new minder, aren't you? Jon's protégée?"

I nodded. Again, he already knew I was, and he knew how I intended to use that account. This was one of the main things he handled for Dr. Williamson. "You're Maddie."

I nodded, glad I could make out his words over the stadium-roar.

"He's mentioned you. I'll get one of my associates to set it up and make it look like a trust fund." He grabbed paper and an expensively-heavy metal pen, handing them to me. "I'll need your full legal name, address, Social Security number, date of birth, phone, and e-mail contact info. Give me a sample signature, too. I'll get the notary here to verify the papers after I sign for you. I'll give you a line of credit on one of the Ganzfield accounts. Jon said he wanted to do that when you started out."

Wow. The dollar amount in his head…*Wow!* Yeah, that'd do

it. The college fund could stay where it was. Good. My mom would've been reluctant to let me use it. She still thought college was a possibility. I jotted down the info and handed the paper back to him.

"So, what happened at Ganzfield?" he asked again. I focused carefully, closing my eyes and bracing against the background noise, and then sent him a series of brief mental flashes of the helicopters, the shootings, and the bodies.

Coleman turned grey. His hands shook as he lowered himself into his chair. Was my mental signal still too strong?

"Who did this?" His voice was no more than a whisper.

"Isaiah Lerner."

"But Isaiah's dead." Coleman had been at Ganzfield the last time Isaiah had targeted us. My words had just brought one of his personal demons roaring back into existence for him. He dropped his hands behind the desk to hide their tremors from us.

"He faked it to keep the RVs from looking for him," I said. "He's now going by the name Jonas Pike."

"The new head of the Sons of Adam?" Coleman's eyes went wide.

I nodded. Nick Coleman was well-informed.

"Geez," Coleman said aloud, although his mental word choices were more explicit.

"My thoughts exactly," I said, drawing a shaky laugh from him.

Back in the van, we headed toward the Lincoln Tunnel. The pressure from the mental voices lessened significantly while we were within it. I could only hear the minds of those in the cars around us, and they only numbered in the hundreds, not the thousands. I drew a deep breath of relief then regretted it; the air stank of car exhaust and something like pretzels. Once we were in New Jersey, Rachel RVed Matilda and Morris. Her golden thread trailed somewhere west of us.

The world outside the van looked grey and uninviting—typical for this part of north Jersey. But it was also warmer than New England, and there was almost no snow this far south. Both were welcome observations to people who couldn't always find appropriate shelter from the elements.

"Take Route 78," I said to Sean.

Rachel gave me a questioning frown. I knew she didn't know the roads around here and was at a loss to give directions, but she didn't like that I was in her head so much when she used her ability.

"Sorry," I said to her.

"You always follow along when I do that, don't you?" Her voice held a note of accusation.

"Can't help it."

She flushed hotly. *Oh, God. Maddie probably knows all about Sean and me—and what we did last night.* She felt her privacy had been violated. There was nothing I could say to that—she was right. The best I could do was to keep her secrets.

The highway took us past Newark Airport and through densely-populated, mentally-loud areas for several miles. We grabbed a late lunch at a drive-thru, filled the gas tank again, and then got back on the road.

After another ten miles, the population density dropped off and I could feel the pressure on my mind ease, as well. Unfortunately, the loss of those other minds just made Rachel's mortified, pink-grey fuming more noticeable.

At least I could connect with Trevor now without hurting

him. I leaned my head against his shoulder. *Hi again.*

You're exhausted.

Too many minds. It feels like thousands of people have walked across my brain today.

You didn't tell me.

When I connected last time, I was too loud.

I don't care. When you're hurting, you come to me, okay? He put his arms around me, protective and loving.

I felt the tension easing from me as our thoughts touched. He planted a tender kiss in my hair, hugging me closer.

We overshot our exit. Rachel's mental thread trailed north behind us, so we turned around and took 287 for a short bit, and then a smaller road, Route 206, ending up in Peapack.

Ka-ching! These houses were mansions. I had a vague memory of someone telling me that Jackie Onassis used to keep her horses around here. That could very well be true; the estates in this exclusive community were huge, secluded, and fancy enough for it.

We drove through the streets, honing in on Rachel's gradually-shifting golden thread and finally focusing in on one of the properties—tall brick wall, plenty of security, and a camera that followed us as we passed the gate. Drew noted the address.

Rachel concentrated her mental vision on Matilda. She huddled in a fetal position on the floor of one of the outbuildings—alone and scared. Seeing her like that—my hands clenched into fists and I suddenly wanted to blast somebody.

Our team started our assessment. Drew mentally reached out, feeling the electrical grid that fed the surveillance cameras and gate locks. Geez—who lived here, the frickin' royal family? I searched for a mind count. Near the front gate, I felt two security guards as well as three Doberman dogs, whose thoughts were hungry and vividly scented. I tried to stretch my mental range up to the house, knowing it was probably out of reach.

SOMEONE'S OUT THERE!

The voice in my head was extremely strong and very, very angry.

Oh, my God! I felt him running toward the front gate—toward *us*—with every intention of delivering a killing mental blast to the telepath he felt outside.

Crap. Isaiah! I startled badly. "Drive! Go, GO, GO!" I tried desperately to shield my mind, frantically throwing up a brick wall of mental energy. His telepathic touch burned into my thoughts.

Sean accelerated. After two blocks or so, I started to blink and breathe again.

"Maddie? What is it? What happened?" Trevor didn't loosen the invisible arms surrounding me.

"Isaiah. He was there. He could hear me." I wrapped my arms around my head, clutching my fingers in my hair.

Oh, hell! His range was so large and his thoughts were incredibly strong. I felt like a little kid pretending to be a grown-up—I was completely outmatched. How had Dr. Williamson ever expected me to go up against that?

"What would happen if we called the police and told them that two people were being held hostage?" Trevor asked. "It's not like Isaiah's a charm. He wouldn't be able to talk the police out of looking around. We could call 9-1-1 anonymously and say our friends were being held inside."

"How would we know that?" I asked.

"Maybe they'd managed to get to a phone and called us but someone discovered them and took it away."

My hopes for the new plan sank. "It'd work if he couldn't

blast them with his mind. I think he might kill the police officers."

"So it's up to us," said Trevor.

At the moment, that didn't seem like a very good thing for Matilda and Morris.

"Um, where are we going now?" Sean drove in the general direction of the highway, back the way we had come.

"287 North," I replied. Several sets of eyes looked at me curiously. "We can stay at my mom's house tonight." I tried to calm down. I still felt rattled from the contact with Isaiah. I needed to think—someplace safe. *Ah, hell.* How could we get Matilda and Morris out if I couldn't even get near the front gate?

My cell phone rang a few minutes later. Hey, the weak little thing had finally held a charge long enough to be good for something.

"Ms. Dunn?" Coleman's assistant informed me that the new account was ready to go and gave me the web address and initial password for my account. I rolled up my sleeve and wrote them down on my arm. *I really should carry a notepad or something.* I then called my mom's office and left a message, giving her the heads-up on the invasion of houseguests.

We arrived at my mom's house in Chatham a short time later. It was small, lily-pad green and, as both sparks mentally noted as we pulled up, made of wood. The second story protruded on columns over an open porch below, giving the house an overbalanced appearance, as though it might fall on its face. The room over the porch had been mine only a few months ago, but I suddenly felt like an outsider—like I no longer belonged here. Bringing this group of Ganzfield people into this world felt strange and slightly uncomfortable.

"Got any plans for the sleeping arrangements, Maddie?" asked Drew, again mentally noting just how wooden the house was.

"Any suggestions?"

"Actually, yeah. Was that a high school we just passed?"

"Uh-huh." I'd lived only a block away from it. The walk to the school took just under three minutes; I'd timed it last year.

"How do you feel about breaking-and-entering?"

I smiled. "I'm pretty okay with it. Do it all the time." I followed his thinking; the school was constructed of concrete. There were many fire-safe places there, if we could get inside, and Trevor could have plenty of room in the gym.

"Can you take out some security cameras?' I knew that he could, of course.

Drew nodded. "Piece of cake."

"Zack, I think there's a guard."

"No problem," he said. Everyone was up to speed.

"Okay, then those without special sleeping issues can have the house. Hannah, why don't you take my room? Zack, you can have the guest room."

I didn't know how to handle Rachel; she was unsure if she was going to be in the house or with Sean. Since she was already aware of my mental monitoring, I decided to use my powers for her benefit.

If it helps, he really wants you with him.

Rachel startled, then glared at me for a second before the silent words had their impact. When they did, she blushed and covered her smile with her hand. At least she was no longer fuming at me.

Once I showed Hannah and Zack where they'd be sleeping, I put out some snacks and sodas in the kitchen. I then went to my room, pulled out my laptop, and went online. Using the information that Coleman's assistant had given me, I logged in, launched the investment screen, and looked up "Locus Two."

Locus Two Systems: LCST. Current price: just over $12 per share. After a few moments of deliberation, I decided to buy $50,000 worth. Maybe I should make it an even number—five thousand shares. $60,000. Wait, was that too much? I had a huge line of credit from the Ganzfield account, but I didn't want to make a too-costly mistake if I was wrong…or if Mr. Sleek, the elevator man, was wrong.

Actually, even that much was making my hands clammy. Was I really ready to do this? That was a *lot* of money. That was a *whole lot* of money.

No, it'd be okay. I could do this. What was the worst that could happen?

I tried to remember all the things Dr. Williamson had taught me. Options might be safer—contracts I could pay a small percentage of the stock price for, giving me the choice of buying the stock at a particular price at a later date. The idea of using options made it easier for me to breathe. *Much less risky.* I picked a strike price and chose a date a month away. I wanted five thousand shares, so I put in an order for five thousand contracts and set up the system to handle the steps of the transaction and close the position automatically before the options expired.

I set my order to fill when the market opened in the morning. Dr. Williamson had walked me through all of this during our practicals. Still, the idea of making this decision with real money made my stomach clench and my fingers itch to tap nervously on something. I forced myself to get over it—it wasn't life or death or anything. I hit the final key that submitted the order just as I felt my mom drive into the driveway. I quickly logged off from the confirmation screen and went down to greet her.

I hadn't seen my mom since Christmas. Her plump arms enveloped me in a huge hug and I felt some of my stress melt away.

My mom loves to feed people. With the six of us gathered around her dining room table, she was happily stuffing us and we were happily being stuffed. She remembered Drew, Hannah, and Rachel from December and, if her smile grew a little strained when she greeted Trevor, I could only hope he wouldn't notice.

Okay, he did notice and it hurt him. *Crap*. My shoulders tensed. Suddenly, this visit suddenly seemed like it couldn't be short enough.

I introduced her to Sean and Zack. I thought she'd met Sean during her visit to Ganzfield, but he'd been lumped in her mind as *one-of-those-red-haired-guys-who-set-things-on-fire*, so she needed a reminder on his name.

Mom gave me some grief over springing houseguests on her unannounced. However, between her hostess-energy buzz and her relief that we weren't out in the world in peril somewhere, her words lost their edge.

I took a steadying breath. Hearing my mom's thoughts made me twitchy. I worried that I might hear unpleasant things, some censored disapproval that she didn't voice for fear of hurting me. I wanted her to be proud of me; criticism from her hurt more than when it came from other people. The fact that she disapproved of my relationship with Trevor rankled, but I had absolutely no intention of doing things the way she wanted when it came to him.

If she'd only try to get to know him.

I was sure she'd eventually change her mind. Trevor was simply the best person on the planet, and he made me so happy that I sometimes forgot to breathe. One or both of those facts should make a difference to her in the long run. At least, that's what I kept telling myself whenever I felt her negative thoughts about him.

We helped my mom clear the table then everyone but Hannah prepared to leave. My mom frowned. "Where are you going?"

"Sleeping in the high school," I replied. "You know about this. We talked about it at Christmas, remember? Fires, knocking down walls, throwing nightmares."

"You can't just break into the high school."

"Don't worry, Mom. We'll get the security guard's permission." I tried to soothe her.

"It's all right, Dr. Dunn." Zack's voice hummed with charm resonance.

"Oh, okay, then." She returned to drying the cooking pans.

I bit my lip. Zack had just charmed my mom. *Without even asking or anything.* True, it was benevolently intended and resolved the situation quickly, but still…my *mom*? I had a problem watching my mother being manipulated. Should I say anything? Should I tell him not to do it again? I felt myself scowling as we grabbed the sleeping gear from the van.

You okay? Trevor asked.

I didn't like Zack doing that.

Trevor nodded. *Got a better idea?*

It's either this or camping in the backyard. I really wanted to sleep somewhere warm tonight.

The walk to the high school took the same three minutes it had back when I'd lived here. Trevor opened the locked double doors without even breaking stride. A guard looked up in surprise from his desk in the security office.

"It's okay that we're here," said Zack, quickly. The guard relaxed. "My friends are going to sleep in the school tonight, all right?"

The guard nodded. "That's fine."

"In fact, why don't you go ahead and give them permission in writing right now?"

I was reluctantly impressed—that was a good idea. Someone else might show up after Zack left and this way we'd be covered.

"I'm going back now, okay?" he said to us, once we had the papers in hand.

I nodded. "Yeah. Thanks," It was awkward having him with us. Convenient, but awkward.

"Gym's at the end of the hall," I said, as we walked down the echoing corridors. It still had that high school smell. Posters for events I'd never attend lined the walls amid rows of green metal lockers. "Pool's through a passage in the back."

"Your high school has a pool?" said Sean, enviously.

"It's not my high school anymore." Being back felt wrong. I didn't belong here. I was an intruder into my old life.

"Dibs on the pool!" Sean grinned wickedly as the idea of skinny-dipping with Rachel filled his mind.

I let out a sigh of exasperation.

"The locker rooms have showers," I added, for Drew's benefit. "They're big, tiled rooms. Should be pretty fire-proof."

Drew nodded.

Trevor unlocked the gym door at the end of the hall. We turned on the lights with an audible clack from each of the long line of switches by the door. Large banks of humming neon staggered on above us, glowing green-white.

I froze. *Oh, my God.* Just inside the door was a large display—a shrine to the three student-athletes the school had lost this past fall.

Del. Mike. Carl.

Their faces shone large from the blown-up photos. Professional pictures—probably their class portraits. Smaller pictures and notes surrounded the large ones. In a few of them, someone had painted halos with glitter glue around their heads. I felt my stomach heave and my hands clenched into fists. Birth and death dates scrolled under each picture. The dates of their deaths were all the same: the day before I'd gone to Ganzfield.

I'd gone to Ganzfield because I'd killed them.

I bit my lip and pulled my arms tightly around my waist. The notes and pictures…people missed them. People's lives had been altered, saddened because of their deaths…deaths I had caused. But they'd attacked me.

They'd tried to rape me.

I'd acted in self-defense, but almost no one knew that.

Next to me, Trevor stiffened in shock and recognition. He knew these faces from my nightmares. Rage flowed through his mind in blood-red flickers. Seeing them—people who'd tried to hurt me—honored and canonized in an adolescent shrine sickened him. He restrained his urge to rip the pictures off the wall.

Rachel noticed our reactions and gave the pictures a second look. A vague sense of déjà vu touched her, possibly because these boys had appeared in a dream I'd once unintentionally shared with her. She saw the dates of death and made the connection with my arrival at Ganzfield. Something like an accusation began to form in her mind as she looked sharply at me.

Rachel, it was like Michael in the basement.

She physically took a step back. I'd never spoken to her, verbally or mentally, about the night I'd found her there. Her eyes flitted back to the shrine, and then back to me. She recalled the night we'd rescued Trevor—the night she'd seen me kill two people just by thinking them dead. I met her gaze and nodded.

Her glance went to Trevor. *And he knows?*

I nodded again. *He's seen them in my nightmares.*

Rachel didn't envy my telepathic ability. *Sean doesn't know about…about what Michael did to me.* I was startled by her admission, by her trust in me. I didn't know we had that kind of friendship. Perhaps this was where it would start.

I turned my attention to Sean. He and Drew were shooting hoops halfway across the enormous space. Their shoes made squeaking noises on the hardwood floor.

Not yet. He's not ready.

Rachel digested that for a moment then nodded and went to join Sean and Drew.

Maddie. Trevor's eyes burned into the shrine. If he'd been a spark, the display would've been reduced to ashes by now.

I understood. *I can't stay in here either.*

I'd rather freeze.

Want to check out the auditorium first? It's pretty big.

Just how rich is this school?

Best facility in the state. Or so they always liked to tell us.

We'll be in the auditorium! I called into the minds of the others as the doors closed behind us.

Trevor took center stage; the space seemed large enough that he'd avoid damaging anything. I put my own air mattress down along the open spot in the back row, normally used for wheelchairs.

Once I had my gear in place, I went to Trevor. His mind still tumbled with furious intensity. Taking his hand, I pulled him down to sit with me.

I really hated seeing that.

I swallowed hard. *Me, too.*

Halos? Really?

You noticed that, too?

I just want to kill them for what they tried to do.

I know the feeling. My words felt like acid.

Trevor's arms were suddenly around me. *Oh, Maddie. I'm so sorry. I didn't mean to—*

It's okay. I get it. I laid my head against his chest. *I get you.*

I felt the anxiety leave my body, replaced with the peaceful sense I only got from Trevor. His hands stroked my hair, brushing away the tension with his strong fingers.

CHAPTER 8

The fire alarm woke us both. *Crap.* I sat up on my air mattress, and the chambers made little whishing noises beneath my shifting weight. I looked around the auditorium. What a weird place to wake up; I felt like people could've been sitting in the chairs, watching me sleep. *Applauding my performance.*

Fortunately, the alarm silenced after a few seconds.

My eyes met Trevor's. *Do we want to know?* he asked.

I sighed as I rolled out of my sleeping bag. We both knew that one of the sparks must've done something and fire trucks were probably on their way. It wasn't even 6 a.m. Ugh.

We need to get out of here.

We grabbed our gear and met up with the others, heading to the front entrance. Sean and Rachel dripped with pool water and pink-tinted embarrassment. I picked up another piece of new, unwanted information about the mating habits of the North American spark. Apparently, they didn't just set accidental fires in their sleep—"intense" activity could cause things around them to burst into flames, as well.

Talk about having the hots for someone. There were now several scorched bleachers next to the pool where Sean and Rachel had been skinny-dipping.

So, do I want to know? Trevor glanced at Sean and Rachel.

I shook my head. *Not at all.*

Three minutes later, we were in my mom's kitchen. The fire truck had passed us on our walk back to her house. I started the coffee and Rachel grabbed the first shower. The house only has one bathroom; it's at the top of the narrow staircase that leads out of the kitchen and wraps back on itself halfway up. The single bathroom never had been a problem for my mom and me to share, but the logistics with so many people complicated the situation.

Once the coffee was ready, I grabbed a cup and sat at the kitchen table, staring out the window into the long, open backyard and at the bare-branched trees that lined the back of the property. I tried to force my brain to start working. We needed a plan.

Drew parked himself across from me, setting down his own coffee cup with a ceramic clack. "We need a plan."

I cracked a smile. "Are you sure you're not all becoming telepathic? That's like the third time someone's said what I was thinking."

Rachel returned to the kitchen, toweling her still-wet hair. Sean headed up next. Did we have enough towels for everyone? Would there be any left when my turn finally came?

"We need to go in for Matilda and Morris when Isaiah's not there," said Trevor.

"I think you're right." Rachel turned to me. "Maddie, I want to try something. You can project mentally. Can you send me images of an object you're familiar with—maybe something in the house here? I've never been as good at locating things or people I've never seen before. But if you can—I don't know—project that memory to me, I might be able to use it to locate things." She was warmer toward me than she'd ever been. Something had changed during that minute in the gym.

"Cool." Drew grinned.

"You think my mental contact with Isaiah might be enough for you to track him?" *Hmm...* If we could track him, we could rescue the healers much more easily. We'd just wait until he left the estate. Dr. Williamson would find this idea very interesting. I wondered when we might get a chance to tell him about it.

"I think we should try." Rachel's face lit up. "You up for it?"

"Absolutely. I think it's a great idea." But what image should I send to her? I really wasn't attached to things. The last time I had felt an intense connection to an object had been—

I concentrated on the memory of a present from my grandmother that I'd cherished as a child. The doll had been designed to be an object that people looked at; it was never supposed to be a plaything. But I'd loved the cool smoothness of the porcelain face, the crisp lace on the delicate dress, and the shiny black paint of the tiny shoes. I'd played with it often—very carefully.

Where was it now? I hadn't seen it in years. I sent the images to Rachel, giving her as much of the detail as I could—the essence of it. The starburst of gold from her mind seemed to shoot down through her body and through the floor.

I pulled open the door to the basement. The place had the damp, musty smell of a rarely-used, dark space. I followed the energy-line in Rachel's mind to the shelves in the corner behind the clothes dryer. A clingy layer of escaped dryer lint covered the blue plastic tubs stacked in the back. The golden thread seemed to disappear into one of them. It shifted with the box as I set it on the dryer.

Forgotten childhood treasures caused a surge of memories—old picture books, stuffed animals, a soccer trophy—"Participant"—from second grade. I unwrapped the doll from a piece of flower-printed flannel. My finger gently brushed against the painted hair and I felt a sad smile slide across my face. I carefully closed the box, sealing my childhood once again in a plastic tub in the basement.

"You did it," I told Rachel, as I came back up to the kitchen. Of course, she'd already seen that, but the others didn't know. She nodded but continued to frown. Would we be able to make the leap to tracking Isaiah? If we got it wrong, we might end up dead. Still, it improved our chances of success.

Lost in thought, we returned to the mundane functions of our morning activities. Drew took the next shower; Trevor pulled out a skillet and started making scrambled eggs.

My jaw dropped. *You cook?* How had I not known this?

A few things, he replied, modestly.

You know this is the last straw. I leaned up to give him a quick kiss. *You are now, officially, the perfect man.*

He laughed. *You might want to wait and taste it first.*

Whatever I might've said next was swallowed as my mother's ice-water shock splashed through me. *Someone's cooking in MY kitchen?* My mother uses food to express love, caring, and generosity. I'd never heard her thoughts in a situation like this.

Oh, crap. She felt insulted, as though our actions were a rebuke to her for not feeding us properly, therefore accusing her of being cold and unloving.

And then she saw Trevor at the stove. *Is he trying to usurp Maddie's every affection?*

I don't know what it is that Trevor sees when he looks at people. When I look, I see the changes in their faces. I understand the general emotions behind them—if someone's happy, or sad, or angry, or afraid—that sort of thing. Maybe I'm emotionally stunted or something, but Trevor sees the same twitch of facial muscles and suddenly comprehends so much more about the person's emotions from it. It's really clear if we watch a movie or TV, because then I can't pick up any mental cues, while he experiences this palette of complex emotions from each character.

So, when my mom came into the kitchen, Trevor's voice brimmed with apology. "Dr. Dunn, I hope that it's all right that I started making breakfast. We got up early and didn't want to trouble you."

My mom's eyes flicked from Trevor to me then back. Hostility and propriety waged a turf-war within her. *He's important to Maddie. He's good to her. And he even feeds her.* She pulled her face into a tight-lipped smile. I was amused—and a little offended—by her thinking. Was I so incompetent that I'd starve to death without someone making sure I ate?

The house felt over-full as we tried to get everyone breakfast and a shower in a place that was set up to handle just two people. When I finally got a turn in the bathroom, the shower was tepid and only a couple of hand towels remained in the linen closet.

My mom had left for work by the time I'd dried off, dressed, and returned to the kitchen. We crowded around the table. Zack was finishing breakfast. Hannah actually felt slightly ill at being in such close proximity to food so soon after waking.

"Maddie's got a plan." Drew broke the silence. All eyes turned to me.

"Not completely. Rachel may have found a way to track Isaiah. I think we can handle the security at the Peapack house if he's not there."

"Why are you so scared of this guy?" asked Zack.

I had the sudden realization that he hadn't been at Ganzfield in December. He hadn't heard Dr. Williamson explain Isaiah's history when we'd first learned he was still alive.

"He's a telepath who can kill people with his mind, like Maddie can." Drew explained.

Zack examined me with a new level of intensity, as though trying to see some visible sign of this lethal ability in me. Again, I picked up nearly nothing from his thoughts, which was frustrating—and a little creepy, like he was just a shell of a real person. But we had more important things to worry about right now.

"The main problem is that Isaiah has a much larger telepathic range than I do." They all needed to know exactly what we were dealing with. In my opinion, they weren't nearly scared enough of Isaiah. "According to Dr. Williamson, the last time anyone from Ganzfield had contact with him, Isaiah could read thoughts from more than three hundred feet and kill at more than forty. That's about three times further than my range. I also need line-of-sight to blast someone. He doesn't. So, if we go in when he's there, he'll feel us coming—like he did yesterday—and we'll all be dead before I can get anywhere near him."

"You can't shield?" Zack asked. I glanced at him sharply. Something felt off—like his mind held a strange inflection. My eyes squinted in concentration. It was almost as though I could see the spiderweb in his mind, protecting the inner layer of thoughts behind the façade. Trevor's concern flowed mustard-yellow around me. The others tried to figure out why Zack and I were silently staring each other down across the kitchen table.

His mental shield really wasn't strong; it was just hard to get a connection in order to focus. I concentrated on a tiny part of his mind and pushed with a sudden, sharp stab. A single, clear thought flared in the dark from behind the shield.

I gasped. *Oh, no. Oh, no, no, no.*

Zack knew he was hiding thoughts from me. He'd been testing me for the past few days, thinking things to provoke a reaction, seeing if I heard them, seeing if I responded to them.

And I hadn't had a clue.

"How long have you known you could do that?" I asked him, forcing a cool calm into my voice that I definitely didn't feel.

How long has he known he could do what? Rachel thought.

Hannah's eyes widened in alarm.

"Couple of days," he said, with nonchalant smugness. He knew exactly what I was talking about. "Since the infirmary at Ganzfield."

"Too bad you can't charm telepaths," I bluffed. "You're probably good enough to get close to Isaiah."

"You don't think I can?" The words held an ominous tone.

Don't even try it, I said into his mind. I was halfway surprised he'd heard it. I didn't know how well projecting thoughts would work when he was shielding. Would he hear them even if I didn't really have a good feel for his mind when I sent them?

And if I do? he asked, silently. I guess receiving projected thoughts wasn't a problem—and he had no problem framing his own back to me. *What can you do about it?*

I gasped. *Ah, hell*—he could even share thoughts while simultaneously shielding. Zack's ability was definitely strong and he had great control over it.

Could you stop me if I told you to do this? Zack deliberately imagined me kissing him.

Red energy snarled within me, making me feel strong, too. My jaw clenched and I thought about one of the last threats I'd used against charms who'd tried to intimidate me. *Yes, I could.*

And if you EVER try to make me do anything like that, I'll mess with your brain and alter your sex drive. You'll never want to do that with a girl again. I stamped each word deliberately into his mind.

Zack laughed aloud, startling the others whose thoughts were growing more confused and more alarmed. *So what? You do that and I'll just hit on Trevor.* He raised an impudent eyebrow and grinned at me. *That'd teach ya.*

I couldn't help it—I cracked up. The tension broke. We'd sized each other up, like two predators, and created a wary truce.

"So, we need to wait until Isaiah leaves before we go in for Matilda and Morris," I said, returning to the topic at hand.

"Why?" asked Zack. "We can get in shielded."

"You and I can, but you can't hurt him. You probably can't charm him. I might be able to shield well enough to get close, but neither of us can do anything with locked doors or guns. I'm pretty sure there will be plenty of both."

"If you can shield yourself, I can make the others shield themselves." Zack smiled smugly.

"What?" Rachel's voice filled with wariness. "What would you do to us?"

"I'd charm you into forgetting your abilities, forgetting the plan, so this Isaiah person can't read your minds and know what you're up to. I'd give you a false cover memory that'd fool him."

"So we'd be in there with no idea of who we were or how to defend ourselves or use our abilities?" Sean's arm tightened protectively around Rachel's waist. "What's the point?"

"Trigger words." The superior smile spread across his face again. "Maddie and I can use trigger words to release your memories. It's like hypnosis. Did you ever see the movie 'Push'?"

"Why? Is it any good?" asked Drew.

Trevor rolled his eyes. "Not really the point right now."

"It's like wiping our memories." said Rachel, coldly. "No. You're not going to mess with our heads and risk our lives based on something you saw in a movie."

Borrowed nausea twisted in my gut, mixing with my own. No way I'd trust Zack to do this to Trevor and the others.

"Wouldn't he sense there were strangers there?" asked Hannah. "How would shielding give us an advantage?"

"Look, that's not going to be necessary. If Rachel can track Isaiah, we can go in as soon as he leaves the place." I wanted to put a stop to this idea once and for all.

"What if he doesn't leave?" Sean challenged.

"I know we have to get the healers out, but that doesn't solve the bigger problem. We have this powerful guy trying to kill us. He's kinda like the Lex Luthor for G-positives. We need to take out Isaiah permanently." Drew had a point.

"I think I'll have to kill him," I said, quietly. Six pairs of eyes bored into me. "I may be the only one who can."

Trevor's cold horror leeched into my soul. *I don't want Maddie to become an assassin. It's wrong for so many reasons. She'll put herself in danger. Dr. Williamson's been trying to train her for this, to use her ability this way. She could be killed!*

Isaiah ordered the murder of everyone at Ganzfield. I met his eyes, silently pleading for him to understand. *He almost had you killed. I don't think any of us are safe as long as he's alive.*

But YOU won't be safe if you're anywhere near him! Trevor knew enough about my training with Dr. Williamson to fill him with fear. He switched tactics. *And what if we're wrong? What if he's not the one responsible? It would be murder.*

The sick feeling in his gut spread to mine.

If I get the chance, I'll ask him before I kill him.

You're serious about doing this?

I don't think we have a choice. But hopefully I won't be up against him now—or anytime soon. I'm not ready. The blood seemed to congeal in my heart as I remembered the power I'd sensed in the brief contact with his mind. *I know I'm not ready. Not by a long shot.*

I went up to my room to call Nick Coleman. Not that it was much quieter for me; the mental voices from downstairs continued as the others considered the best way to get into the Peapack place.

"Jon's being held by Homeland Security," Coleman said. "The feds think he's a domestic terrorist—that he's been running some sort of militia training camp up at Ganzfield. They got a tip from an anonymous source."

"Can you get him out?"

"Working on it. They take their time sorting out this sort of thing. They don't want to risk releasing someone who later blows up a building. But I should know more by the end of the day. I'll give you a call, all right?"

"Quick question: do you know anything about Isaiah and a place out here in Peapack, New Jersey?"

There was a long pause on the other end of the line. "Funny you should mention it. A large group of the Sons of Adam people are headed out there on Saturday."

Two days from now. "Who's your source?"

Another pause. "I left standing orders with a local member of the Sons of Adam. I…had a *few words* with him more than a year ago. Now he calls me when they're planning something." I understood that those "few words" must've been given with charm resonance.

Plan B began to form in my mind. "Can you give us some of

the names of the people going out there?"

"Maddie, what are you going to do?" Concern tinted his voice.

I wished I didn't have to speak aloud, but telepathy didn't work over the phone. "He's holding two Ganzfield people out there. We want them back."

"As your attorney, I have to warn you not to do anything illegal." His caution made me wonder if his phone might be tapped. Did Homeland Security know about his connection to Dr. Williamson?

Also, since when did I have an attorney? My life had gotten so weird recently.

"I wouldn't dream of it," I replied, too sweetly. "I simply thought Zack might have a quick word with some of them."

Coleman gave a quick laugh of understanding. "Would Zack be a particularly charming individual?"

"Some people find him charming." I mimicked Coleman's indirect way of speaking. *What if the phones really were tapped?* "Personally, I don't see it."

He chuckled. "I guess you wouldn't. I'll see if I can get you those names and call you later." He hung up.

I went downstairs to the kitchen. "New info."

"About Williamson or Isaiah?" Drew was getting into this.

"Both."

"Shoot."

I filled them in on Dr. Williamson's situation and the gathering on Saturday at Peapack. "So, I'm thinking Zack charms one of the Sons of Adam people to bring us in on Saturday. Even if Isaiah's on-site, a lot of other people will be there, too. For telepaths, other people's thoughts blend together when there's a crowd. It's like people all talking at once. So long as we're not mentally screaming our intentions and we don't get too close to him, we could pop a few locks, charm a few guards, and get Matilda and Morris out. If he's busy with this gathering, it could be hours before he even notices they're gone."

Nice.

Better than having Zack mess with our heads.

So long as no one gets killed.

I grinned. It looked like we had a plan. I felt some of the anxiety lift from my chest. We knew what to do and when to do it. We would get the healers out; they would be okay and—

Oh, my God in Heaven.

I don't know if I broadcast my shock to anyone other than Trevor or not. Perhaps they simply reacted to the simultaneous gasps of horror that Rachel and I emitted. I felt like I might retch. While we'd been talking, Rachel had RVed Morris and Matilda.

Morris's right hand was in pieces. Someone had cut off his fingers.

Cut. Off. His. Fingers. Of all the sick—

His face was ashen grey and he grimaced in pain. I could see Matilda trying to reattach one of the severed digits. The other fingers sat obscenely in a drinking glass filled with bloody ice. Trevor gave a sharp intake of breath; apparently I was leaking the images to him.

"I think they've been torturing Morris." My voice trembled as I spoke. Dark-yellow guilt filled my mind with a too-warm pressure. If only I'd been strong enough to take on Isaiah! We could've gotten them out before their captors did something so monstrous. "They cut off some of his fingers. They're right next to him…" I swallowed hard, trying to get the taste of bile out of my throat, "…in a glass of ice."

"They're letting Matilda heal him." Controlled anger ran like liquid steel through Rachel's veins.

"Why?" asked Zack.

"Healers can't heal themselves," Hannah explained. "We can't focus the energy into our own bodies properly." Okay, good to know, but that wasn't Zack's point.

"No, I mean why're they letting Matilda help him?"

No one spoke for a moment. In Rachel's vision, I saw Morris wiggle the newly reattached finger, testing it. Matilda fished another out of the bloody ice, checking it against the remaining stumps—probably making sure she didn't attach it in the wrong place. A fresh tear slid down one of the wet tracks that lined her face.

"She loves her brother," Trevor said.

I saw what he meant. "They might've forced her to do some healing on Isaiah and used Morris as the bargaining chip."

"If she did it, they'd let her reattach his fingers." Hannah finally understood.

"If she didn't, they'd keep cutting pieces off," said Drew.

It made sense. It was completely evil, but effective. "Why are they still alive?"

Hannah looked at me as though I'd suggested they both ought to be killed. *Ah, hell.* She really didn't think I had much respect for the sanctity of life, did she? "No, I mean, why is Isaiah keeping them alive? What does he need them for?"

Confused faces looked at me. "If Isaiah forced Matilda to heal him—and we don't know that's the case—now that she's done it, what else would he want them to do?"

No one had an answer. In Rachel's vision, Matilda began to reattach another of Morris's fingers.

Now that we had a game plan, we had very little to do until

Coleman called with the names of some of the Sons of Adam people going to Peapack on Saturday. Rachel and Sean started to watch a DVD, but they both fell asleep on the couch, wrapped in each other's arms.

Drew caught my anxious look from where he sat in the recliner. "Don't worry. I'm on it." As long as he stayed awake and alert, he could catch and put out any fires Sean might start in his sleep before they burned my mom's house down.

I resolved to check the batteries in the smoke detectors, just in case.

I went into the kitchen and found Trevor sticking a new battery in the smoke detector. *Is everyone reading my mind these days?*

It seemed like a good idea, with Drew and Sean here, he thought to me, almost apologetically.

Hannah had her laptop out at the kitchen table, writing e-mails home. Why did she stay with us? Why hadn't she returned to her family and friends in California? She'd been unhappy at Ganzfield, and now no one was training her as a healer. Once the dodecamine ran out, she'd lose her ability. I didn't float these questions into her thoughts, though—I didn't want to give her any ideas. Maybe she wanted to help Matilda and Morris—or was it because of her faith? She didn't talk about it often, but much of her mental activity focused on being a good Christian. Was she being Christ-like in staying with us?

Hey, did that make us lepers and sinners?

With so many other minds around when she was in range, I really hadn't focused on listening to the specifics of her thoughts— she was quieter than most. I only knew she hadn't made any plans to leave yet, which was good. We might need her.

I felt as though Zack was far away, at the physical limits of my ability, even though he was just upstairs. I scowled—I still couldn't get a proper fix on him. If I'd met him before I'd started all of this Ganzfield stuff, I think we could've been friends. However, he was a charm now, and one that I couldn't read.

What's he thinking?

I needed to know. What if he was planning something that could put us in danger? What if he realized that his mental shield interfered with my immunity to his charm ability?

Crap—did he already know it?

I stood in the middle of the kitchen, sensing Zack in the room directly above me. I tried to focus the way I had earlier, when I'd been able to connect through his shield. Normally, I just felt people's thoughts effortlessly, the same way I saw with my eyes or heard with my ears. But trying to read Zack was like straining to listen for a faint sound through white noise. I tightened my focus and felt my face scrunch in concentration. My hands balled into fists and my breathing seemed too loud.

Zack's anger washed through me. *They've drafted me against my will into a—a war! There's a good chance we'll all be killed by this psychopath! And now they're not even going to consider going with the plan I gave them. I've got this amazing ability and they won't let me use it! And who does Maddie think she is—the High-and-Mighty Princess of Ganzfield? Why do we all have to obey HER? Why is she calling all the shots? I don't know how she can kill with her thoughts, but I bet my mental shielding would protect me.*

I scowled as a sudden, twitchy urge to test that theory of his sparked within me. I took a shuddering breath to calm myself. We still needed a charm and I wasn't going to kill him just for thinking rude things about me.

Oh, wait a minute. Maybe I should try.

Not to kill him, of course. I didn't know if Isaiah could shield, but I probably should learn how to break through mental shields.

I'd have to talk to Zack about letting me practice on him.

I opened my eyes into Trevor's. His face was calm, but his swirling-grey thoughts didn't come close to matching it. *I don't like her focusing so intently in another guy's head like that.* He felt threatened by Zack, jealous and uneasy.

I put my hands around his neck. *You know you don't need to feel that way, right?*

He sighed, relaxing slightly. *It's just…I can tell he's interested in you, and now you're focusing on him like that—*

If it helps, I think I need to try to blast his mind.

Blast his mind?

Break through his shield and try to hurt him.

Trevor grinned. *Actually, that does make me feel a little better.*

I kissed him playfully. *I didn't know you had a dark side.*

Only when something might come between us. He pulled me closer, and I pressed against him. Our bodies reacted, speeding up our hearts and sending scarlet-red energy surging though us. The next kiss was deeper, slower, more powerful. It set my mind spinning, glowing.

An embarrassed disapproval brushed against me from somewhere close. After a few moments, I realized we were making out right in front of Hannah. She desperately tried to ignore us and focus on her computer screen.

Oops.

I took Trevor's hand and led him upstairs to my room. It gave Hannah the wrong idea, but at least got us away from her scrutiny.

Zack's awareness followed us through the closed door of the guest room. Once in the privacy of my room, I wrapped my arms around Trevor and felt his invisible touch on my waist, lifting me up to kiss him. I melted as the intense love between us swelled and connected us with dazzling swirls of red, then gold, then silver. The world seemed to dissolve away from us. There was only Trevor, the beautiful essence of his inner self. The energy between us brightened into an overwhelming light.

We returned to reality and abruptly fell over sideways, thudding to the floor. *Ow!* Pain from my hip and Trevor's elbow lanced through us both, shattering the afterglow of soulmating. Trevor pulled himself up to sit on the floor and managed a shaky laugh as he rubbed the pain from his arm. *Okay, doing that standing up—not such a good idea. How's your hip?*

Ow. I repeated, pouting as I rubbed the spot. I was pretty sure I was going to have a bruise.

Want me to kiss it and make it better?

I met his dancing eyes, feeling a smile pull at the corners of my mouth. I was still trembling, and my heart thudded rapidly against my ribs. I rolled up to my knees and gave him another kiss. I felt his invisible touch against my skin, gently caressing the injured spot as though he could pull the pain away.

My stomach suddenly lurched and I pulled away from Trevor. *What's wrong with us?* Why weren't we rushing in to save Matilda and Morris immediately? We'd gone in to rescue Trevor before we'd had a plan; the sense of urgency I'd felt had been overwhelming. Yet here we were, sleeping, watching TV, writing e-mails, and getting intimate as pure energy…while Matilda and Morris were being *tortured.* I felt the pale-green sense of guilt intensify and well up from my core.

Trevor picked it up from me—we were still tightly connected. *It was different when it was you. I couldn't wait. I couldn't stay still for a second when you were in danger.*

Trevor slid over the floor to sit with his back against the side of my bed. He pulled me into his lap, wrapping his arms around me and resting his chin on the top of my head.

It's going be okay. I think it'll work if we go in on Saturday. But I think it'd be safer if we let Zack put that charm shield on me.

Trevor took me by surprise with that one. "What?"

Well, I'm going in with you, and I don't want to be the weak link that gets us caught.

No way. Not going to happen. I didn't want to give Zack that kind of power over Trevor's mind.

Trevor felt it in me. *I'm not letting you go without me. This way, I can be useful.*

And you don't want to leave me alone with Zack.

True. But I really don't want to leave you alone with Isaiah.

The plan is to avoid Isaiah.

Trevor raised a skeptical eyebrow. *Maddie, how well do you think I know you?*

Okay, if I were ready and the opportunity to take him out presented itself—

You'd go in and try to blast him. And you might get killed. I'm not willing to risk that. You're too important to me.

He sent Dr. Hanson to VIVISECT you. He ordered the massacre at Ganzfield. None of us are safe while he's alive. We needed to end this situation, to fix this problem. So, either I take him out with my ability, or we get our hands on some missiles or something. Would anyone actually notice if we blew up part of New Jersey?

Maddie, promise me you won't go after him.

I kissed his lips gently. *How about I promise not to do anything that puts any of us in extra danger?*

Exasperation started, mixing in with his concern.

I'll include myself in that "any of us," okay? I added.

Is that the best offer I'm going to get?

Probably.

Okay, then.

"I promise I will not do anything that puts any of us in extra danger." I held up my right hand to make it official. Trevor wasn't satisfied with that, but he knew I wasn't stupid, and that I'd never break my word to him. He hoped that was enough.

"So, this is your room." He looked around. I saw it as though it was new to me, as well, scanning it with the eye of an outsider. What did its contents—the pale wood furniture, the forest green carpet and curtains—say about me? Well, not girly, anyway—the pink-and-sparkly stuff had disappeared years ago. Two large bookcases lined the wall on either side of the double windows that faced the street. They overflowed with creased-spined paperbacks, mostly fiction.

I had a small, glass-fronted case of trinkets and treasures by the door. Some of the contents held sentimental value. The small jewelry box, with its pattern of inlaid wood of different colors, was the only present I could remember my father giving me. He'd died in a car crash when I was four. A few other items were there for their value to my ego—like the copper medals for the Academic Olympiads.

A magnet board above my bed held cartoons, clippings, photos, and other memorabilia that, in my previous existence, had struck me as interesting or funny. I gave Trevor a mental commentary as he examined the contents of the room. Most of it seemed so trivial now. I felt like a different person than the girl who'd lived here—or at least a much older version of her. I couldn't believe I'd only been gone since last October. It hadn't even been half a year, but it felt like a past life.

Trevor perused my books. His mind lit up with green flashes of delight when he came across ones he'd also enjoyed. I considered books that I'd read to be trophies; I kept them as reminders of the stories within their covers, of the bodies of imagination that I'd conquered. I wanted them where I could see them—where I could glance over and recall favorite characters having interesting adventures.

How long had it been since I'd read a book just for enjoyment? My more recent reading back at Ganzfield had consisted mostly of neurology textbooks. I slipped over and joined Trevor. *Jane Eyre* caught my eye.

Is it any good?

One of my favorites. It's a great love story. He's proud, with a terrible secret. She's strong, with a terrible past. And yet they still manage to end up together, even when everything in their world seems to fall apart.

Ah, a chick book. He grinned.

Yeah, but in a good way. There's also stuff that guys can enjoy.

Like what?

Well, there's a crazy lady…and a big fire, too.

He pulled the book from the shelf. "You can't read when I do, can you?"

I shook my head. I'd never told him directly. I didn't want him to feel guilty. *It's as though you're talking to me. I can't focus on the book. It's okay, though. I pretty much follow along with whatever you're reading.*

Trevor pulled *Jane Eyre* from the shelf. *I think I need to read this one, then.*

You know you don't have to.

I want to. You know me—I can't resist a crazy lady and a big fire.

Why does that sound like the perfect Saturday night for Drew?

Trevor laughed.

We used up the last of my mom's bread and deli meat making

our lunch sandwiches. I added both to the growing grocery list on the front of the fridge before sitting down to eat. *Oh, crap.* We really were imposing on my mom by staying here. Feeding this crew—many of whom had huge appetites from fueling their abilities—how much would that cost? Could I get Dr. Williamson to reimburse her after he got out?

Geez, I was so self-involved. Dr. Williamson was trapped in a cell somewhere. He wasn't going to be worried about my mom's grocery bill. He might not even know what'd happened at Ganzfield. Did he even know why he'd been detained? At least he probably could pull that information from the minds of the people holding him. But who would've told Homeland Security that Dr. Williamson was a *terrorist?* I thought Isaiah was the most likely suspect. But Isaiah thought Dr. Williamson was dead, at least if he believed the Sons of Adam people who'd attacked Ganzfield.

Perhaps it'd been *his* Plan B. If the Sons of Adam didn't get Dr. Williamson, then the feds were the next thing on Isaiah's list. It was risky to involve the official law enforcement, though. There was a very real threat of exposure for all of us. I wondered how Isaiah, if he was behind this, planned to remain under the radar. Was his Jonas Pike alias a part of that?

Did Isaiah know Dr. Williamson was alive? If so, did he suspect that the rest of us were still alive, as well? We'd all been on his list of targets—he clearly considered us special threats. Would he connect the telepath who'd killed the two men at Eden Imaging with the telepath he'd sensed outside his front gate yesterday? A cold, tight knot of sick fear formed in my gut and began to spread.

Sitting next to me at the kitchen table, Trevor startled in reaction to my turmoil. *What's wrong?*

Just how well connected are we? I really think you're becoming telepathic. Seriously, I haven't had to choose to send you a thought for a long time now.

Maybe we're on the friends-and-family plan.

I laughed. *When I become telekinetic, then we'll know for sure.*

He became thoughtful. *Have you tried it?*

I frowned as I considered it for a few seconds. Then I looked at the empty soda can in front of me, concentrated, and imagined it sliding across the table.

Not like that. Pick it up like you normally would. Just don't use your hands.

I relaxed, and then tried to do it the way he'd described it. I just reached for it with my hand, but left my hand where it was.

The soda can flew across the table, over the edge, and clattered across the floor.

Holy—I gasped then looked at Trevor accusingly. *Tell me you did that!*

His wide eyes met mine and he shook his head slightly.

Seriously? You're not messing with me?

"Hey Trev, what'd that soda can ever do to you?" Drew assumed, as any rational person would, that when unseen forces sent things flying, Trevor was the one responsible.

"I didn't like the look in its eye." Trevor covered with surprising calm. He didn't take his eyes from me. *You actually did it! I was just—I didn't think you'd really be—you actually did it!*

What was soulmating doing to us? Were we becoming some sort of Trevor-Maddie hybrid? Was connecting as energy reshaping our brains somehow? Was it dangerous? Or perhaps— perhaps our connection allowed us to share our abilities with each other? Was I piggy-backing on Trevor's ability without his awareness, the way he was reading my thoughts without being telepathic?

Hannah watched us with concern; she'd noticed we were upset. Even from across the table, her healing ability gave her a sense of our stress reactions. Oh—*that's* why Hannah was so uncomfortable around romantic couples. She picked up on our biological reactions, perhaps even on the hormonal level. Between reading that information from us and framing it within the morality of her strong faith, no wonder she found it disturbing.

But that wasn't important right now, so I stored that little piece of information away for later. I had enough—no, more than enough—to think about at the moment. *Priorities.* Matilda and Morris. Rescue mission. And I didn't see how my clumsy new telekinetic ability would be of any use on Saturday. *Focus*—I had other things to worry about. This new development would have to wait. I'd have to play to my strengths.

We can do more with this later, okay? I told Trevor. *This afternoon, I need to blast Zack's brain.*

Yeah. He nodded absently, his thoughts preoccupied.

"Hey, Zack. You can shield. I need to learn how to get around shields. Can I practice on you?"

Zack met my eyes, but his face and mind were both unreadable. Finally, he smiled. "You can try."

Trying to blast Zack was like trying to pick up a layer of wet paint. We were alone in the backyard, back by the trees that edged the property. Pearl-colored clouds made the light diffuse and shadowless. The people in the house were out of my range here, so Zack's were the only thoughts I should've been able to detect. I could now feel the shield—subtle as a heat mirage—within his mind. With effort, I could even get a pinhole connection and hear some of his thoughts from behind it. But then the web would close up again.

"Whatever you just did, it sorta tickled," he said.

"You're mocking me, aren't you?"

He smiled smugly.

I felt the strong urge to slap him with a telekinetic hand, but that seemed a tad childish. Also, when I tried, it didn't work.

Was I going about this the wrong way? There had to be another route to focus within the brain. Maybe I could strike a specific structure or region if I couldn't get the normal connection. Perhaps his ability was the key.

"Zack, try using your charm voice."

"What do you mean?"

"You know, that special resonance you put into it when you want someone to obey you." What did he think I meant?

"It sounds different from my regular voice to you?"

I startled. Didn't charms hear the change? "Yeah, it's really obvious to me when you guys are charming someone. It sounds almost like more than one of you is speaking."

Zack considered that skeptically. "I don't hear any difference."

"Well, can you pretend that tree there is a person and tell it to do something?"

He rolled his eyes, unenthused. "Whatever." His tone changed with his next words, though. "Yo, tree. Bow before me."

I could hear the command in his voice. What's more, it penetrated his shield. *Yes!* It was as though part of it had to weaken to allow the charm-voice out. The breach felt like the little whirlpool in a draining bathtub, and the change in energy channeled me toward the weakened point.

"Keep going," I urged him when he stopped.

"Dance, tree. Dance for me." His voice was bored and sarcastic.

"Whip those leaves around. Ooh, yeah. Shake it."

I pressed hard, filling the weakness with a pulse of energy. Dr. Williamson and I had discussed using this focused overload technique, but I'd never put it into practice. I followed my pulse in, sensing the structure, feeling for the right position. Given what I knew of neurology, which after months of reading was significant, it seemed like the weak area correlated with the language center of the brain called Broca's region.

"Wiggle that trunk. Um. Twee. Moof." Zack looked at me in horror. *WHAT THE HELL DID YOU DO TO ME?* Fear and distress flooded from him, cold and clammy-yellow, strong enough to overpower his weakened shield.

Success! I felt a grin spread across my face and a weight lift from my mind. Maybe I could hold my own against Isaiah, after all. "Don't worry. It's just temporary." I told him, pretty sure that it was. But what if it wasn't? That would be bad. *What the hell am I doing?* "It should only last a few minutes, like a seizure."

Okay, maybe that wasn't the most comforting analogy. At the moment, I couldn't really make myself care. Giddy little tendrils of success flowered within me. I'd found a way though Zack's shield! The only problem was my new method wouldn't work on Isaiah unless, perhaps, he was actively trying to fry someone's brain.

Actually, that sounded like a distinct possibility for my next encounter with him, although it would probably be *my* brain he was trying to fry. Would my own shield weaken when I attacked, the way charming had weakened Zack's?

"Okay, Zack. Once your speech returns, we need to try it again. I have to see if I can do it while shielding."

You've got to be kidding me. He shook his head in disgust and headed back to the house. His shielding was erratic—many other thoughts leaked through, as well. Disheartened, Zack felt rattled—like a prizefighter who'd expected to win a match easily, only to be knocked out in the second round.

Guilt pinged hotly within me. I hadn't just taken his voice, I'd wounded his pride. *Ah, hell.* "Zack, wait!"

He ignored me, shutting the back door with unnecessary force.

Was this what I was? Was this the kind of person I wanted to be? Of all of the things Dr. Williamson and I'd discussed, focused overload had seemed like one of the most benign. It was both temporary and painless. How much worse were the other things I'd trained to do? Was I turning into a monster?

And just how upset was Zack? Was I finally getting a real sense of his emotions? I'd gotten so used to reading feelings from people's minds but, because of his shield, I'd had no warning that I was upsetting Zack so much. *Crap.* Unthinking. Selfish. *The High-and-Mighty Princess of Ganzfield.* My gut filled with a flattened ache and I pressed my lips tightly together.

By the time I returned to the house, Zack had retreated to the guest room—clearly avoiding me. Good bet he wasn't going to let me practice on him again. I guess I couldn't blame him. But that meant I'd have to learn as much as I could from this one experience. I replayed it in my mind several times, memorizing the relevant details. Our lives might depend on it.

Trevor was with Sean and Drew, watching a movie in the living room. It seemed to be *Push,* the movie Zack had mentioned. The guys took delight in heckling it. They mimicked the little noise that accompanied telekinesis as Trevor "threw" a decorative pillow across the room repeatedly. Some screaming guys with lizard eyes cracked them up. I bet this was what it was like when a bunch of naval aviators watched that old Tom Cruise movie. I smiled as I listened in from the kitchen.

Hannah and Rachel both bent over laptops in the kitchen. Rachel had Google Earth up, zeroing in on the Peapack property.

"Printer's in the little office off the dining room," I answered her unasked question. Rachel nodded. In her mind, I saw the aerial view. The property held a huge house and at least a half dozen other, smaller buildings. There was even a lake, artificial in its perfect symmetry. The main house wrapped around part of its shore.

I thought you were going to be busy all afternoon, Trevor thought from the next room.

Zack didn't like it when I took away his ability to speak.

Trevor's head popped through the kitchen door. *You did what?*

I took away his ability to speak. Just temporarily, I think. I hope. Dr. Williamson and I had been working on different ways to do it for a while. We'd talked about causing a petit mal seizure in one area of the brain, which would overload it and shut that part down for a while.

And you did that to Zack?

Yup.

Through his shield?

I nodded.

A shadow crossed Trevor's mind. *Why were you practicing this?*

Just in case.

Just in case?

In case Isaiah gets a mental whiff of us on Saturday. I might need to use it against him. I don't know if he can shield. Dr. Williamson didn't think so, but he might've learned since then. I picked it up in a week; he's had years.

Trevor looked at me sadly. *Maddie, you promised.*

I know I did! I'm not going to go looking for him. Really! This really is just in case. You know what a planner I am.

He relaxed. *You do like to plan.*

Want to try knocking over some more cans? I have some time before Coleman calls back.

Trevor frowned. *So, what do you think's going on with that?*

I don't think I'm becoming telekinetic or you're becoming telepathic. I think we're borrowing the ability in the other's mind.

Seriously?

Well, I wasn't able to slap Zack out in the backyard. I think it might be because you weren't there.

So, how are we going to test this theory? Go upstairs and slap Zack around for a little while?

I felt a pang of muddy-yellow guilt—I was pretty sure I'd beaten Zack up enough for one day. Also, Trevor seemed to like this idea a little too much. *What happened to my sweet guy who saw the best in people?*

He heard that. *I can't help it—the guy just bugs me. I told you, I think he's attracted to you.*

I reached over and took his hand, gently guiding him closer to me. *And I told you that you have nothing to worry about.* Our eyes met and held, amplifying the mental connection, laying all his thoughts open to me. He was afraid I was going to get into an unwinnable altercation with Isaiah and I'd be killed. Or that Zack was going to make a pass at me. Or that Ganzfield would no longer exist, that our abilities would fade as the dodecamine ran out, and then Isaiah would come for us and kill us when we were helplessly normal again.

Okay, you've got things to worry about. But you don't need to worry about us.

My love flowed shimmering white through him—filling him, soothing him, reassuring him. The world started to dim around the edges and we suddenly pulled ourselves out of the beginnings of soulmating, stepping apart and looking away from each other's eyes. *Not here.* The other people in and around my mom's kitchen probably wouldn't appreciate it if we did something like that right in front of them.

I led him by the hand into the tiny office off the dining room. It was barely large enough for two people. My mom's desk took up half the space and there was only one chair. I sat on Trevor's lap while I tried moving the pens and stapler around the top of the desk. I had very poor control, knocking most things around rather than picking them up.

Physical contact seemed to be the key. When I wasn't touching Trevor, I couldn't make anything move, even though he was still in my telepathic range. And Trevor could pick up thoughts from the other people in the house, but only when he and I were touching. However, he heard my mind much more clearly—even when we were in different rooms—even when I wasn't conscious of sending him thoughts. I hadn't realized how much I'd been sharing with him. With anyone else, I'd feel exposed and vulnerable, but this was Trevor.

He smiled at that. *Trust me, I know what you mean.* I'd been in his head for months, after all.

Okay, we could work with this. We'd been a little freaked with the possibility that we'd been changing each other's brain structures. I curled against him in the privacy of the tiny office, drawing comfort from his presence. The peaceful sensation reminded me of Aruba and a sudden thought hit me.

We haven't shared dreams in a while.

Embarrassed heat seeped across Trevor's mind.

I laughed when I realized why he'd deliberately avoided lucid dreaming with me. *I wasn't even thinking about that! I was just remembering Aruba. But if you think that doing things in dreams together would break your word to Dr. Williamson, I'll promise not to dream-ravish your chaste and noble mind.*

My mind is definitely NOT chaste and noble, he replied, and the images—the detailed, intense fantasies he showed me—made my heart beat wildly. I closed my eyes, feeling the electric-red thrill on my skin. My panting breath matched Trevor's as he showed me how he wanted to touch me, to do more than touch me, in ways that caused the heat to spread through my body, flushing my face and making me deliciously dizzy. *If we started doing things like this together in our dreams, I'm not sure I could keep myself from doing them with you in reality. You know how much I want you.*

I kissed him, feeling the quiver in my hands as my fingers traced the contours of his face. *I say we use three different kinds of birth control and just go for it.*

Trevor laughed, hugging me close. *I keep my word.*

We aren't sharing the church anymore, I pointed out, undeterred. *I think we could get out of that promise on a technicality.*

You really want to do this, don't you?

You're not the only one who has fantasies, you know. I showed him a few images from my own mind. *You don't fall deeply in love with a guy who happens to have an extra set of hands without coming up with a few ideas as to how those hands might someday be put to use.*

Trevor gasped, eyes widening then closing. A deep groan escaped from within him. Oh yes, he liked those ideas. We kissed deeply, shifting to get closer to each other in a desk chair that was clearly not designed for such use, when my cell phone rang. I had to pull away and get my panting breath under control before I could answer.

"Maddie, Nick Coleman here. I think this line is more secure than the one in my office, but we'll treat it as though someone might be listening in, all right? Let me tell you what's happening with Jon."

Coleman had gotten the location where Dr. Williamson was detained, a secure facility in northern Virginia. The feds hadn't allowed him to contact anyone. "I'll catch the Acela train to D.C. tonight and try to get in to see him in the morning. If I can talk to the right people, there's a good chance I can get Jon released tomorrow. Anything you want me to tell him?"

"Let him know what happened at Ganzfield—he might not be aware of it—and that we're okay. We're at my mom's. Most of the others are with Seth at a McFee place in Connecticut." I didn't know what else to add.

What about Greg? Trevor's question filled my head.

"Oh! Dr. Williamson had a driver with him. Greg…" I could never remember Greg's last name. I think he once said it was Turkish.

Greg Guchlu.

"Guchlu," I finished.

"I'll look into it. Anything else?"

"Did you get the names of the local Sons of Adam people?"

"Right. I got two for you: George Dovich and Robert Miller." He gave us addresses. Miller was in Madison, only a couple of miles from us, while Dovich was out in Blairstown, less than an hour away.

"Thanks," I said, sincerely.

"No problem. I'll give Jon the bill."

I wondered how much a charm lawyer charged by the hour. The answer came back to me like the punchline of a joke: whatever he wants.

* * *

My conscience tweaked again when Zack didn't join us for dinner. I took a plate up once we'd finished. I needed to make peace, and my mom's lasagna might be the key to solving the Middle East conflict—if only she could make it simultaneously kosher and halal.

I knocked—no answer. I knocked again, a little louder. I could feel Zack behind the door. Was he sulking? Still?

"Fine. Come in then." Petulance tinged his voice.

At least his voice was back. Good.

"Brought you dinner… " I put the plate on the little table next to the bed. My mom had decorated this room in reds and golds. The ridiculous number of little pillows that she'd arranged on the bed currently spilled in a haphazard pile on the floor. Zack sat on the far side of the bed, facing away from me, looking out the dark window. He winced when I turned on the light.

"What do you want, Maddie? Here to gloat?"

"No! I'm here to see that you're okay and to bring you food. I also needed to say I'm sorry."

"I don't need your pity."

I was getting annoyed. "No, you seem to be giving yourself plenty."

I felt the hot flash of red anger in his mind. Had I damaged his shield somehow? Was that even possible? He turned to look at me. "Look. You beat me today. You won. I lost."

I rolled my eyes. "It's training, not a competition."

It's not about training.

I suddenly understood. He felt especially humiliated today because Trevor was right—Zack was attracted to me. He'd wanted to impress me and instead, I'd sucker-punched his male ego.

"Oh."

His eyes locked on mine and his shield snapped back into place.

I needed to leave. Zack's face looked calculating…predatory… smug—as though he'd suddenly thought of a way to win, after all. He stood up as I headed for the door.

"Stay a little while," he said, pleasantly, and I found I wanted to. "You're not going to attack me again. You're going to leave my shield alone." All of that seemed very reasonable to me. Zack walked around the end of the bed. Standing very close to me now, he reached around me and quietly closed the door. I had a sudden flashback of Del and his friends in the van. Something cold ran through my core. It was suddenly hard to breathe.

"You're going to kiss me now," he said, moving closer.

My lips parted. *This is wrong.* In a corner of my mind, part of me started yelling. *Fight it! Fight back!* That part could see that he was using his ability on me, even though I couldn't hear the resonance in his voice. His mental shield allowed him to do this to me. A rush of blood-red energy gave me strength. *No.* I was *not* going to be a victim. Not back in the van—and not now.

Zack leaned in. I pushed as hard as I could against his chest. I felt like a weak little girl—he was physically much stronger than me. But I wasn't just a physical person. Struggling against his charm-orders caused pain to shoot through my forehead like a metal spike, but I had to do it. I stabbed at his mind with my ability, jabbing him with an echoing *no!*

It was one of my worst efforts—his shield prevented me from connecting properly. But it was enough to get his attention. He stepped back in surprise, prepared for an additional mental attack. Instead, I ducked around him, yanked the door open, and flung myself down the stairs.

I collided with Trevor as he rushed up, reacting to the distress he'd felt from me. He caught me in his arms and steadied me, holding me close. Being in physical contact intensified the transmission and he saw everything flash through my memory. His arms gripped me more tightly as his anger built.

Wait here, he growled, barely thinking in words.

He was at the top of the stairs in a single leap. The guest room door flew open with a bang. Zack didn't even have time to turn around before Trevor had an invisible hand at his throat, squeezing his larynx. Zack made a sick, wet sound as Trevor moved lethally fast to stand inches from him. The pure, white-hot anger from Trevor's mind hit me like a furnace blast.

Trevor leaned in close to Zack, looking down into his eyes. In a near whisper, he said, "If you ever try *anything* like that with Maddie again, I will squeeze your heart to a tiny pulp inside your chest."

Zack's eyes widened even further. He understood that this was a literal, not poetic, turn of phrase.

"Do you understand?"

Zack tried to nod, a difficult and painful thing for someone held by the larynx. Trevor looked hard at Zack's face for a moment, letting it sink in. He released Zack suddenly, stepping away from him as he slid to the floor.

"Hannah can fix up your throat later." Trevor closed the door behind him.

He came down the stairs, taking my hand but avoiding my eyes, as he nearly pulled me out the back door and into the deep blue evening. We moved quickly though the backyard, away from the house.

Trevor ran his hands first over his face then through his hair. *Is Maddie okay? I can't believe I lost control like that. I've never been that angry before. What's wrong with me?* He paced back and forth in front of me, as though the jittery, excess energy could be dispelled through the movement of his feet.

Finally, I caught his hand in mine. He stopped moving and looked at our intertwined fingers. I reached up and touched the side of his face. My hand trembled against his cheek. I couldn't stop shaking. Zack's actions had resonated with my most frightening memories, which made them seem so much worse.

Trevor still evaded my gaze. I slid my hand behind his head, bringing him closer to me until our foreheads touched. I closed my eyes and gave him full connection to my mind, feeling his jumble of turbulent emotions mix with my own. We stood there, letting the strongest feelings flash between us, wash over us, and then slowly subside. Our breathing slowed as the worst of my memories drained off.

Awareness filled my thoughts. I felt safe because of him. He was my true hero. *I can't believe you took on a powerful charm to defend me. You were so brave.*

He drew in a sharp breath and shook his head. *I wasn't brave. I was angry.*

In my experience, that's a big part of bravery.

Trevor sighed. He wrapped his invisible arms around me, held me close, and then floated me up as his hands framed my face. We lost ourselves in our embrace for a blissful while. Eventually, the cold evening penetrated our overheated minds and bodies. He pulled back to look at my face. *Seriously? That caveman thing did something for you? You?*

I felt myself melting at the memory: Trevor as my knight in shining armor, the literal man of my dreams. I felt so protected, so cherished. *Loved.* Trevor truly loved me. I'd never have asked him to do it, but having Trevor take on Zack for me had unleashed something primal within me.

I'm just as surprised as you are.

CHAPTER 9

Trevor and I returned to the kitchen, hand in hand.

Rachel, we've got a problem with Zack.

She looked up from the computer and paused as she focused on framing a thought back to me. *What kind of problem?*

Zack just charmed me.

Rachel gasped. *But you're a minder! Aren't you immune?*

I shook my head. *Not to Zack. He's a…special case. He…he tried to make me kiss him. And I don't know how far he would've taken it.*

Rachel's scowl darkened her face. She had personal experience with how far charms could take such things. *What happened, Maddie? Are you all right?*

*I still had some resistance. When I realized what was happening, I tried to blast him, and then ran away. And then Trevor—*I just supplied the wordless image of Trevor squeezing Zack's throat.

Rachel gave Trevor a satisfied nod. "Good for you."

Trevor flushed, embarrassed. I wrapped my arms around his waist and leaned into his chest.

So now we have an out-of-control charm in the house. There's no way Trevor and I can work with him now. I can't trust him on the team.

"Can we do this without him?" Trevor kept his voice low.

I shook my head. *We have to have a charm tomorrow if we're going to convince one of the local Sons of Adam to vouch for us. And if we're going to get in the front door on Saturday without me having to….* I remembered how clearly Seth had felt it when I'd blasted Michael and Victor in the Blake House basement. It was like sending up a telepathic flare. *The thing is, if I don't have to blast anyone, we've got a much better chance of getting in and out without Isaiah knowing.*

"So we need another charm," said Rachel.

Who else was there? Charms were now in short supply. Most of the ones I'd known had been killed at Ganzfield. Coleman was on his way to Virginia to help Dr. Williamson. I groaned when I realized I only knew one other. If this wasn't so important…

Rachel, can you call Cecelia? See if she can come?

She turned back to her computer. "I was online with her a little while ago." Popping up a new screen, she sent an Instant Message.

Emergency here. Need a charm ASAP. Can you come to NJ?

Cecelia sent a quick response.

I've got classes tomorrow. How big of an emergency?

She had just started at UNH this semester, less than two months ago. I sucked in a quick breath as I realized that, if she hadn't, she'd be dead now.

Rachel read the message then looked at me.

The image of Morris's severed fingers flashed sickeningly through both our minds. Isaiah had done that when he still had a use for healers. What would he do to Matilda and Morris when he was finished with them? "It's pretty much life and death."

Life and death.

There was a short pause.

This one of Maddie's plans?

Yes.

Rachel pinked slightly as she glanced at me, knowing I'd seen Cecelia's question as she read it.

The pause this time was much longer.

I'll come anyway.

We arranged a combination of bus and train to bring her south. She'd arrive after 3 a.m. at the train station in Newark. I suppressed a chuckle; Newark after dark used to be a scary place, one that I avoided. With a group like ours, I was no longer afraid of it.

"What do we do about Zack?" Rachel asked.

I'd been wondering the same thing. I wanted him out, far away from here. But we couldn't just turn a dangerous charm loose on the world. He could do so much damage before his ability faded. People would give him their life's savings, or they'd let him use them sexually, or they'd even kill someone, simply at his suggestion.

All he has to do is ask.

If only we had another charm, someone who could charm him into behaving. Did we need to wait to send him away until Cecelia could do that? She'd done something similar before…

I kept flashing back to that last minute, feeling my chest constrict as I did. How far would Zack have charmed me if I hadn't been able to resist? Was he as bad as Michael, who'd used his ability like a date-rape drug? I knew I didn't want to have Zack near me—near any of us. The thought of having to see him again threatened to bring up my dinner.

But Zack hadn't actually succeeded. He hadn't made me do anything. And he had a rare ability that Dr. Williamson wanted to study and cultivate. *Ah, hell.* That meant he probably wasn't going to be expelled from Ganzfield.

I'm pretty sure Dr. Williamson won't kick him out after this, I told Trevor and Rachel. *But we're in my house now. I want him out. Tonight.* It wasn't as though I had a soundproof cell in the basement here.

"What should we do with him?" Rachel's concern seeped through her words.

"Where would he do the least damage?" Trevor spoke softly, aware that Zack was in the room directly above us.

Sean came into the kitchen and wrapped his arms around Rachel, giving her a quick kiss on the cheek before taking the chair next to her. His feelings toward Rachel were so tender, I again felt like an intruder in their private world.

He glanced at our expressions and his brow furrowed. "What's going on?"

We brought Sean up to speed.

"Where's he from?" asked Rachel.

"Oregon, I think." I thought I'd heard him mention it, but I couldn't remember when.

"Let's just send him home." *It's far enough away that he won't be our problem anymore. We have problems enough.*

Despite my misgivings, I could see her point.

I found my mom upstairs in her room, reading. She was trying to give us some space, as though I was just a normal teenager whose friends had come to visit for a few days.

"Mom, there's a problem with Zack. He needs to go home."

Concern flowed pearl-grey through her. "What's wrong?" *Is he sick? Is his family all right?*

"I don't want to go into the details right now, but he needs to go home—tonight, if possible. Can I borrow your credit card to get him a plane ticket online? We'll pay you back." I hoped Dr. Williamson would, at least.

"Of course. If he needs to go home, we can do that. The card's in my purse in the hall closet. You know where it is."

"Thanks, Mom. Oh, and do we have any earplugs in the house?"

She rummaged through her bedside table for a few seconds then handed a little, clear plastic box to me. "Why do you need earplugs? You kids aren't planning to use power tools or—" Understanding flashed through her mind, and her voice dropped to a whisper. "Is Zack dangerous?" Her eyes searched my face intensely.

"Just about any of us could be dangerous, Mom. But Zack tried…he tried to use his ability against me. He tried to make me do something I didn't want to do." She made the correct assumption and I nodded. "I can't let him stay in this house another night."

"Are you all right, honey?"

"I'm fine, Mom. I can resist charm commands, and Trevor—" I paused, flushing with a smile as another wave of primal adoration washed through me. *My caveman.* "Trevor made it clear to Zack that his behavior was…unacceptable."

My mom's opinion of Trevor went up a notch. "It's after nine already. What can you do tonight?"

"We're going to take Zack to the airport, just as soon as we get the ticket."

Back in the kitchen, I handed the box of earplugs to Trevor. Neither one of us wanted me to talk with Zack alone. How damaged was his larynx? Could he still charm people? How angry was he with us right now? And just how dangerous was he?

Trevor molded two of the silicone plugs over the earphones of my iPod, sealing them into his ears. Then he cranked up the volume, and a classic Green Day song played through his mind to me.

Testing one two three…"Can you hear me?" I said loudly.

He didn't respond.

Did you hear me? I asked into his mind.

No. I think this'll work. Let's get it over with.

At the top of the stairs, I knocked on the guest room door. There was no answer, but I could feel his presence within. I pushed the door open. Trevor stood behind me, his hand on my shoulder.

"Zack." He huddled in the dark on the edge of the bed, his face in his hands. At the sound of my voice, a stream of ugly mental profanity bombarded me. "You're leaving. Where you go is up to you. If you want to go back to Oregon, we'll get you a plane ticket, but you're not spending one more night in this house."

"Am I out of Ganzfield?" His injured voice was a low, hoarse whisper.

So much had to happen before that was even an issue. Would we be able to neutralize the threats from the Sons of Adam and Isaiah? When, if ever, would Dr. Williamson get out? Would having him in custody blow our secret existence out into the open? What would the government do with us if they knew about our abilities? Would Ganzfield even exist anymore?

A sad ache filled me. I just wanted to go back to Ganzfield, for the place to be as it was. It hadn't been perfect, but it'd been home.

"I don't know." That was the truth, although I had a pretty good idea. "That's up to Dr. Williamson—when he gets back."

If he gets back.

Zack turned to face me. I flinched back and braced as though he was about to attack. Trevor stepped closer. He'd been trying to follow the conversation through our mental connection, but the music had made it hard for him to concentrate. His eyes zeroed in on Zack's mouth, watching for him to speak. I felt the light touch of his invisible fingers against my ears, ready to shut out any sudden charm commands.

"So there's a chance I can go back." A pale sliver of hope brightened Zack's thoughts.

I nodded, frowning at the idea. *Hope*—Zack wanted to go back. If he believed he still had a decent shot of keeping his ability and returning to Ganzfield, would he behave himself? The chances were definitely better than if we sent him out as a rogue charm with nothing left to lose. Hey, maybe Cecelia wouldn't even have to charm him into obedience.

"Probably a pretty good chance." As soon as I said it, I knew it was almost certainly true. If it were possible that Zack could learn to silently project charm commands—which I suspected was Dr. Williamson's hope—he'd want him back. That meant we hadn't seen the last of Zack.

"I want to stay and do this thing on Saturday. You need me."

"No way. We can't trust you."

"It's my shield, isn't it?"

"You tried to charm me!"

"So? Isn't that what I'm supposed to do?"

"Not to me!" I said, too loudly. Trevor's hand on my shoulder tightened in concern. "Not to any of us!"

The attack in the van flashed through my mind again, filling my gut with a clammy lump—linked memories of people trying to force themselves on me. I felt a flare of killing energy stir within me and I swallowed hard against it. I had to keep myself under control.

Zack changed tactics. His shield dropped—melting away—and his mind seemed to suddenly pop into the room. I usually felt people's minds increase in volume gradually as we came closer to each other. His hit me like a blaring stereo-blast.

Trevor's mental fingers sealed my ears. *What did he do to you?* He accused Zack with steel in his stare.

I'm okay. He just dropped his shield. It startled me.

Trevor let up on my ears, but remained in alert-protection mode behind me. I turned back to Zack and focused. *Why did you do it?* I asked directly into his head.

So clear! He was as loud as another minder and his unspoken response poured out his motivations—the things that drove him. Zack really, really liked to win. He wasn't evil. He wasn't sadistic. My ability to get through his shield had deflated him. He'd thought he'd win some of his lost self-esteem back if he could use his ability to make me do something. He hadn't planned to take it beyond a kiss, which would have been enough to restore his ego. Now he realized that he'd crossed a line with me and, after sitting up here in the dark, thinking he might lose his ability because of it, regret seeped bitterly through him.

I took a long, steadying breath, feeling calmer again.

Wait. Could he use his charm ability mentally? Was he fooling me right now? My eyes narrowed as I focused deeply on him.

No, it was okay. His thoughts were clear and open now. He wasn't like Michael. He wasn't like Del. He didn't get a sadistic pleasure out of the fear and weakness of others. Zack was more like a kid cheating at a game so he could always win. *Impulsive.*

Immature. But perhaps he'd grown up a little bit today.

There was no way he could remain here, though. The tension between Trevor and Zack would drive me over the edge if I had to be around it much longer. But maybe, if and when Ganzfield reopened, we could tolerate having him there. I wasn't happy about it, but I suspected it would work out that way in the long run.

"Zack, go home. When Ganzfield reopens, I'm pretty certain Dr. Williamson will call you back...*if* you don't do anything stupid in the mean time."

Zack thought of arguing, but after a moment, he realized I wasn't upset anymore. He considered that victory enough.

That bugged me. Had I given in somehow? Ah, hell. Let him feel like he'd won something, if it would keep him from doing anything overly harmful while he was still a dodecamine-filled, G-positive charm on the loose.

Just to be sure, I added, "Dr. Williamson interrogates charms when they come back after being away from Ganzfield to make sure they haven't been doing...well...things like you tried tonight. Don't do it, okay?"

"What are you going to tell Williamson?" He winced as the hoarseness in his voice made him sound more pathetic than he'd intended.

"I won't tell him, I'll show him. He'll get the full, surround-sound experience in 3-D, complete with all the emotional highlights." A small tremor started in my jaw at the memory.

Will it be bad enough to convince Dr. Williamson to kick me out? Zack wondered.

"I can show you, too." I sent him the full memory—including the sickening fear, the anger, the helplessness I'd felt. I recognized that my emotional reaction may have been overly-influenced by the previous attack, but that didn't make the feelings any less real or terrifying.

Trevor's hand tightened on my shoulder as he caught the show, too. I slid my fingers over his.

Zack turned white. His unfocused eyes widened as he looked within at what he'd done. When I finished, he sat there, breathing hard and shaking. He looked up and his pale face flushed red. "Oh, my God." He'd had no idea of the impact of his actions— of how much he'd frightened and upset me. Evidently, empathy had never been a personal strength of his. "Maddie, I…I didn't know. I—"

"You see now why you can't stay?"

He nodded.

"Pack up. We'll take you to the airport."

It was a little after ten when we left in the van. Drew drove; Hannah took shotgun. Trevor and I sat in our usual spots in the front-most bench. He still had the earphones in, just in case.

Zack sat alone in the back.

A few minutes out, I felt his thoughts fade. I turned back to him. "Keep that shield down."

Unshielded, Zack was a different person from the one I'd had around for the past few days. Loud. Full of conflicting emotions and ambition…and now shame. "Sorry." His thoughts popped back vividly as he played back the memory I'd shown him… again.

Ugh.

I crossed my arms tightly and told myself to suck it up. I needed to keep my focus on his thoughts. We'd be there in a few minutes. A few, eternal minutes.

Zack's guilt gnawed at me, making me feel too warm and nauseous. But at least he felt guilt. That was a good thing, right? A positive development in his life, making him into a better person and whatnot.

I just wished he'd do his soul-searching out of my range.

He drifted away a second time and I faced him again, seeing him silhouetted against the shine of headlights on the back window. "Keep it down."

POP. What was I, a masochist?

Huh…Zack had to concentrate on keeping his mind open—to keep from shielding. Was the mental block his natural state? Or, at least, what dodecamine did to him?

How unique and special. We're all G-positive snowflakes.

We pulled up to the long, glass-fronted departure area of Newark Airport and Trevor rolled back the side door of the van. Zack pulled himself forward, lugging his duffel as though it'd doubled in weight. Hannah brusquely laid her hands on his throat, healing the damage Trevor had caused. She didn't meet his eyes.

I handed Zack his flight printout and his gaze met mine for a second. A prickle of panic flashed down my spine, but I didn't look away.

I'm really sorry, he thought, his shield still down.

I nodded. "I know." My anger was gone. I'd spent time over the past months looking for redemptive capacity in many of the charms of Ganzfield. I believed the sincerity of Zack's apology.

I also knew that, if he wasn't sincere, Trevor and I could make him feel sorry in one or two other ways.

Zack knew it, too.

He jumped back as invisible hands closed the van door, nearly slicing into him. Trevor's unsmiling stare conveyed a final message as the van pulled away. Zack stood alone at the curbside, silently watching us leave.

We could all breathe deeply again, even though the air still smelled like New Jersey. Drew sighed and Hannah leaned back in her seat. Trevor took out the earphones, pressing both hands hard against his temples.

"Hannah? Could you do something about Trevor's headache, please?"

Trevor looked up, surprised. *I don't want to bother her with it.*

If you won't do it for yourself, then do it for me. I gently stroked his hair back from his eyes.

Hannah placed her hands on either side of his face and concentrated. Healing energy crackled through him—doing who-knows-what to muscle tension and blood-flow—and the pain dissipated for both of us.

"Thanks," Trevor and I said, simultaneously. I leaned against his shoulder.

Hannah watched us in the flashes of light coming off the highway. "You two have some kind of extra connection, don't you?"

I tipped my head back to meet his eyes and we shared a little flicker of soulmating memory that made my heart skip. He smiled at me. "You could say that."

"Like just then, you both reacted the same way, physiologically. I've seen you do that several times. It's like you...I can't really say. Like you're extensions of each other."

I hesitated; I didn't know how much I wanted to share with her. My connection to Trevor was so personal, so intimate. It went beyond words.

"It's like we were meant for each other. We're each other's other-half." Trevor squeezed my hand.

Yeah. That'd do.

From the driver's seat, Drew made a gagging noise. "Ugh. Cut the mushy talk or I'll set something on fire just to change the subject."

We all laughed, but I wasn't entirely sure it was an empty threat. "Hannah, thanks for staying with us. I know you haven't been happy at Ganzfield or with the team and our training and all, and…" I wasn't sure how to put it. "But you're here. You stayed with us, and that means a lot." I took a deep breath. "I don't know what shape Matilda and Morris are going to be in on Saturday and I really hope none of the rest of us will need your help. But thanks. Thanks for staying. You're a real life-saver in every sense of the word."

Hannah smiled shyly, although her thoughts filled with a quiet fulfillment—a warm sense of being appreciated.

Drew rolled his eyes. *That's still pretty mushy.*

We arrived back at my mom's house shortly after eleven. The night was clear and still above freezing. After a New Hampshire winter, it seemed relatively balmy to us. I suddenly realized that it was almost the beginning of March.

Since the fire alarm incident at the high school this morning, we'd decided not to risk going back there tonight. That made even more sense now, since we were charm-less. We didn't have anyone who could persuade the guard.

We found Sean and Rachel curled up sleeping on the living room couch. Rachel loosely held the kitchen fire extinguisher in her sleep-slackened hands. I frowned at this…this *irresponsibility*. My mom was upstairs, and this place was made of wood and filled with other flammable things. A line from an old Talking

Heads song drifted through my mind: *Three hun-dred six-ty five de-grees...*

Trevor gave a mirthless snort of laughter and the song continued to play in his head.

Drew frowned down at his cousin and considered beginning his explanation of fire safety by kicking Sean in the shin.

Wait! Let them sleep for now. We need to go get Cecelia in, like, three hours. He can sit watch while you get some sleep after that—and you'll get to stay indoors, too.

Drew contemplated kicking Sean for another moment, and then he nodded, pulled the recliner in front of the TV, and started channel surfing.

Trevor grabbed the camping gear. I went upstairs for the little travel alarm from the guest bedroom. All trace of Zack had been stripped from the room, almost like he'd been exorcized. My mom had changed the sheets and arranged her little red-and-gold pillows in an artistic pile in front of the headboard.

As I went out the back door, I set the alarm for 3 a.m. with a silent groan. Trevor had set up my tent back by the trees. He tossed his own sleeping bag on an air mattress and pulled me gently down to join him. I wrapped myself in the warmth of his arms and his thoughts and we gazed at a couple of lonely stars together for a few minutes before I reluctantly moved to my tent to get some rest.

The alarm dragged us from sleep. *Blech.* I rubbed my hand over my face. Even the thought of 3 a.m. annoyed me—simultaneously too late *and* too early. Inside, in front of the TV, Drew didn't even seem tired. He waved absently at us as we passed through to grab Sean and Rachel. An on-screen explosion filled him with delight.

Trevor drove, even though I still hadn't had a chance to use my new driver's license. Whenever we went somewhere, I needed to scan people's thoughts for hostile intentions. Was it really necessary tonight? It wasn't as though the Sons of Adam knew we were here in New Jersey.

Probably.

In the back of the darkened van, it was apparent that, in the thrall of their feelings for each other, both Sean and Rachel had forgotten that I was a telepath and that I was *right here*. Their PG-13 activities quickly drifted into R territory. *Ah, hell.* I should've said something earlier. Now if I asked them to stop, I'd deeply embarrass us all. I squeezed my eyes closed and tried to catch thoughts from the rare passing car.

The drive felt longer than the seventeen minutes shown on the dashboard clock.

"We're here!" Trevor called out loudly, studiously not turning around as he put the van in park. In the light from the streetlamps filtering through the windshield, I saw the flush in his cheeks.

Rachel and Sean went into the station to look for Cecelia. As soon as the van door shut, Trevor and I both cracked up.

Whoa, he thought, bemused and embarrassed.

I covered my face with my hands for a moment, and then leaned back against the headrest and tilted to look at him. "I guess they didn't have to give Dr. Williamson the same promise you did."

Trevor laughed again. "Guess not."

"At least, with Cecilia here, they'll have a chaperone for the ride back."

Trevor studied my face with thoughtful eyes. "You see things like that all the time, don't you?"

I nodded. "Especially from them. Rachel's crush on Sean was

one of the first things I felt after my initial dose of dodecamine."
It seemed so long ago. Was it really just five months?

"You never told me that."

"Just one of the many secrets I was planning to take to my grave. Now that they're together, it's not a secret anymore."

"That Rachel had a crush on Sean? That wasn't a secret."

"Really?"

"The way she looked at him all last summer? Incredibly obvious."

"How do you do that?"

"Do what?"

"Understand what people are feeling when they raise an eyebrow or clench their teeth. Before I got to Ganzfield, I got flashes where I just knew what people were thinking or feeling, but you do something different."

"Really? I thought everyone could see it. It's just in people's faces."

"So, you think you'd know what I was feeling, even if we didn't have this connection?"

"Most of the time. I noticed you before that first night in the church, you know."

"I remember."

"What do you mean?"

"I noticed you, too. I saw you in class that first day and you thought something nice at me after the thing with Michael in the dining hall."

"Do you remember what I thought?"

I nodded. "That I was brave, even though I was probably really scared."

"Was I right?"

I grinned. "Okay, you *are* good at reading people."

Rachel and Sean's romantic attraction flowered hotly in the distance. Cecilia followed behind them, resonating with what I considered her customary setting: long-suffering annoyance.

Cecilia nodded coldly in greeting as she tossed her bag onto the first bench and slid in next to it. Rachel and Sean got in behind her, drunk on each other. Actually, the second-hand giddy, blissful stuff was nice to read off of them. I found myself smiling from the contact high. Rachel's thoughts glowed with adoration for Sean. All she needed now was a notebook cover where she could scrawl "Rachel Fontaine McFee" or "R.F. loves S.M.," then draw a heart around it. Sean's thoughts tended to be more explicit so I tried not to focus in too much. Right now, though, he considered some of the other things about Rachel that delighted him, like when she'd said something funny. My lips quirked at that. I'd never heard Rachel say anything particularly funny, but it was nice that Sean thought she did.

Yeah, this was okay. As long as they could keep out of range with their physical stuff, I'd be happy. I really didn't like seeing mental porn, especially of people I knew—people I had to talk to with a straight face the next day.

I flickered to Cecilia and lost my smile. Her last dodecamine injection had been seven weeks ago, and she could feel her ability beginning to fade. *Crap.* No wonder she'd come when we'd asked. She needed a booster, but a full dose for her would take about half of our remaining supply. I'd also need another shot in the next day or so. We'd have to restock quickly after we got Matilda and Morris out.

Would Coleman get Dr. Williamson released tomorrow? Hopefully. I felt sure that Dr. Williamson would be able to get us resupplied. This scared, lonely, what-do-we-do-now feeling I'd had for days would be over as soon as he was out. He'd take charge, and everything would be okay. I sighed as I relaxed and drifted toward sleep, lulled by the almost hypnotic effect of the headlights on the highway. I had a vague memory of Trevor's arms around me, carrying me from the van to my little tent in the backyard.

CHAPTER 10

"You have *got* to be insane."

We'd all slept late; my mom had left for work by the time we gathered in the kitchen for breakfast. Cecelia wasn't happy with the plan.

"Got a better idea?" I asked.

"A better idea than going directly into the home of the killer telepath? Gee! How about *not* going into the home of the killer telepath?" Cecelia's voice dripped sarcasm. She sat with her arms crossed, leaning away from the table as though to disassociate herself from the rest of us.

She frowned as she absentmindedly rubbed the injection site on her arm—Hannah had given her half of our remaining supply of dodecamine. The muscles in my jaw tightened. Cecelia had taken some of our scarce resource and now she wasn't making herself useful.

"I'm pretty sure they're not in the main house." Rachel pushed a printout of the aerial map into the middle of the table. "I've been comparing the map to my visions, and I think they're...here."

She pointed to one of the outbuildings on the western edge of the property. It sat away from the others, isolated.

"How are they doing?" Trevor looked up from the stove. The smell of frying eggs wafted through the kitchen.

Rachel's silence only answered the question for me. In her mind, I saw Morris. His face seemed tight and grey; both his legs stuck out at unnatural angles. I winced with a grimacing, hissing breath.

The sound caught Rachel's attention. "Yeah. They did that late last night. Both his legs look broken," she explained to the others.

I shook my head. "Then they're definitely not in the main building. Isaiah's got a big range, at least three hundred feet. A telepath wouldn't keep someone in that much pain anywhere near him."

Rachel checked the scale of her map. From the large house, the little outbuilding would be well beyond Isaiah's range. Her confidence that Matilda and Morris were there grew.

How the hell I was going to hold it together around Morris? If his legs were still broken tomorrow, his pain would overwhelm me if I got too close. Perhaps Matilda could knock him out. He'd need to be carried, anyway.

"Where's Isaiah?" asked Drew.

"Still on the property, as far as I can tell." Rachel didn't feel as confident in her ability to track Isaiah. Her flashes of him were much hazier and unfocused. "He sticks mostly to the main house. He's got the entire mansion to himself, as far as I can tell."

"So, he's having a little luncheon with the Sons of Adam tomorrow, and you think this will be the ideal time to party-crash?" asked Cecelia.

"Actually, yes. We're better off blending into the crowd." I said. "Normally he'd notice a bunch of strange minds in his range, even if he's not close enough to read them clearly. But I think he'll be overwhelmed by all of his guests. We should be able to get the healers out while his head is full of other people's thoughts."

"Won't he hear you coming? Don't you telepaths hear each other more loudly?" She accused me with a scowl.

"I can shield."

Trevor placed a plate of eggs in front of me. He set a second plate down as he took the chair next to me. I met his eyes and smiled. *Thank you.* With the first bite, I knew his title as "perfect man" was secure. *I'm still shocked you know how to cook.*

Trevor's mouth tightened. *It's nothing, really.* A flash of memory: a much younger Trevor, alone in a house as the afternoon light faded, pulling a chair over to the stove so he could make himself something to eat.

Something tightened in my chest and I squeezed his hand. *It's not nothing. It's amazing. You're amazing.*

He ducked his head, but I could still feel his smile.

"You can shield?" Cecelia asked me, dubiously. I snapped back into the conversation.

"Well enough to sneak up on Seth." Did that sound a little smug?

Her eyebrows shot up. *Really? Whoa.* "So why do we need the Sons of Adam? You said you wanted one of them to get us in tomorrow."

"Yeah. We need you to charm them today. Get one of them to drive us in and vouch for us tomorrow."

"Why? Why go in through the front door at all?"

"You have a better idea?" asked Drew.

My eyes widened, reluctantly impressed. "She does."

Cecelia shot me an angry look. "I hate when you get in my

head like that."

I gave her an acid smile. "Oh, but I get such *pleasure* out of hearing the *sweetness and light* that fill your thoughts." My eyes narrowed as I considered zapping her Broca's area. It would shut her up *and* piss her off—a two-fer.

No, no, no. Bad Maddie. I needed to stop that high-handed, "Princess of Ganzfield" stuff. Zack had been right about that. However annoying I found Cecelia, we were still on the same team. Besides, she actually *did* have a good idea.

"Why don't you share with the rest of the class?" I halfheartedly attempted to get some of the sarcasm out of my voice.

Cecelia huffed as she considered it, but eventually her pride overcame her annoyance. "Okay, instead of going in with the Sons of Adam guys, I charm the people next door into letting us hop in from their side of the fence…here." She pointed to the map at the property line closest to the little house that Rachel had indicated earlier. "Then we can go in without anyone seeing us."

"How tall is the wall? Will we be able to get over it?" asked Sean.

"That's not a problem." Trevor smiled. Sean hadn't been part of our training, but he immediately understood how Trevor could manage it easily enough.

"I'll know for certain where they are when we're closer," said Rachel.

I looked at the map's scale, guessing at the distances. "I think I'll be able to hear people in that building from behind the wall. I'll know if Matilda and Morris are there—as long as they're conscious—and I'll be able to tell if there are guards." I spread my fingers across the map, frowning. With Isaiah's large range and the fact that minders are louder to one another… "It's close enough to the main house, though, that I shouldn't talk into your heads. Isaiah would probably hear that."

"So your part is to shut up and listen." Cecelia returned the fake smile I'd bestowed on her earlier. "What an important job!"

Again, I resisted zapping her Broca's region.

Trevor caught the thought from me and choked on a mouthful of eggs.

"Both you and Rachel will be working from behind the wall, so who's going in?"

"Trevor," I turned to him as I spoke, "we'll probably need locked doors opened, and Morris will have to be carried out if they don't let Matilda fix up his legs today." He nodded. "Ask Matilda to knock him out before you move him or I'll overload when you bring him back. You should probably get her out first."

"I can take care of Morris," said Hannah.

I looked at her in surprise. Hannah had been reluctant to go in at Eden Imaging, but she was closer to Matilda and Morris than she'd been to Trevor. She wanted to go in—no, she felt she needed to go in.

I nodded. "Okay. Good idea."

I turned back to the rest. "Drew can suppress any guns that guards might have, and fry the electronic surveillance equipment."

"What about me?" asked Sean.

Sean hadn't trained with us. How would he react in a stressful situation like this? How strong was his ability? I didn't know how much we could ask of him—how much we could depend on him. "Keep the engine running," I said, finally. "Make sure the way out stays open...and keep Rachel safe."

Sean considered it for a few seconds, frowning. *I want to do more than that. I want a real job.* Then Rachel gave his hand a squeeze and he nodded.

Rachel looked at me with relief. *Thanks. I don't want him in danger.*

I nodded to her, despite the little flash of jealousy that went through me. I didn't want Trevor going in without me, but it seemed the best way for this plan to succeed.

Cecelia let out yet another sigh of annoyance. "You want me to go in, don't you?"

"You can charm the guards, so...*yes.*" I refrained from adding "duh!" although I couldn't completely suppress the eye roll. "Rachel and I check it out first, and then you four go in, grab Matilda and Morris, and get back out. Simple."

"I don't like it." Cecelia crossed her arms again.

Does she like anything? Her negativity wore on Trevor, as well.

Maybe she'd like to be temporarily mute, I thought back. This was going to be a long twenty-four hours.

But that would deprive the rest of us of all that sweetness and light!

I laughed silently. When had Trevor developed such a flair for sarcasm?

Since we didn't need to seek out the Sons of Adam guys to get us into the party tomorrow, we found ourselves with a surplus of time. Drew popped in another movie; Hannah and Cecelia went online. But Rachel and Sean disappeared upstairs and the thoughts rolling down from them forced me to leave the house.

"It's *my* house!" I stomped across to the far end of the backyard. Trevor watched me without comment. It was damp and cold out, which increased my resentment. "Have they *completely* forgotten that I can hear them?"

I just wonder if they're being safe.

"The thing is, I actually know the answer to that! I don't want this much information! This is a textbook example of too much information!"

Trevor let me pace myself out for a few more turns. "Hey, why don't you hold still for a minute?" I forced myself to stop moving, crossing my arms tightly as I scowled at the back of the house. He stepped in front of me, and gentle, invisible hands began massaging my shoulders. I let out a deep breath and closed my eyes, letting my arms drop—letting everything drop.

You're wonderful, you know. I don't deserve you. I leaned forward into his chest.

Well, you're stuck with me now. You've ruined me for all other women.

"Good." I wrapped my arms around his waist.

The sound of his laugh made me feel so much better.

Rachel and Sean came back downstairs and they joined Drew for another movie. Apparently, the sparks at Ganzfield used to have a big TV set up in one of the cinderblock buildings. But after four units were crisped in less than a year, Dr. Williamson had stopped replacing them. Now Drew and Sean were enjoying some of the movies they'd missed. I felt a quick shudder. Had Drew or Sean been responsible for the destruction of those televisions at Ganzfield? If so, I hoped that they'd learned better control by now.

Coleman called late in the afternoon with an update. "I was able to get in to see Jon. We didn't know if we were being monitored, but thanks to 'that language the two of you use,' he's up to speed on everything that's happened."

Was Coleman just being paranoid with this euphemistic code stuff or was there a real chance that government agents were recording this phone call? Maybe his precautions made sense. After all, the government already knew that Dr. Williamson had been a neurologist with Project Star Gate. Even some minor display of extrasensory ability could make them suspect his true gift.

I felt cold fingers run along my spine. What would the government do with G-positives if they knew about us? Involuntary conscription into special ops? Medical experimentation? Forced sterilization? Concentration camps?

I wasn't naïve enough to believe they'd just leave us alone.

"The judge was in closed sessions all day," said Coleman. "I can't get in to see him until Monday. I'm trying to set up a meeting with the special prosecutor. If I can have a few words with her ahead of time, everything should run smoothly when we all meet in chambers on Monday. I hope I can get Jon released then."

I understood that the "few words" would carry charm resonance. If Coleman could speak privately with the right people, everything would be all right. I slumped into a chair with a tired smile. "Thanks."

My mom came home late from work. Her car overflowed with groceries. She shooed us away from the stove and started chopping and stirring with a Disney song in her head that made me picture a singing teapot.

The mood at dinner was subdued. Our thoughts focused on tomorrow—and on Isaiah. My mom sensed our anxiety but she didn't say anything. *Are they all so tense because the new blonde girl is here?* Since Cecelia's presence was a perfectly plausible reason for everyone to be stressed, I didn't enlighten her. I knew if my mom understood what we planned to do, she'd try to stop us. That was what mothers did—a big chunk of their job description involved keeping their kids from doing dangerous things. Breaking into walled compounds filled with murderous fanatics and their sociopathic leader definitely fell into that category.

I helped her clear the table then gave her a hug in the kitchen. "Thanks, Mom."

"What was that for?" she asked, surprised. I'd never been much of a hugger with her.

"For dinner. For the past seventeen years. For everything. I love you, Mom." I wanted to make sure she knew that...*just in case*. I still got a frigid twinge when I recalled Isaiah's mental touch. Our plan should work, but if something went wrong...

Trevor and I headed out to the back yard as soon as my mom went up to her room. We crawled into my tiny tent together; the nylon fabric whished around us as we kissed and clung to each other with tender desperation.

We drew together as pure energy almost immediately. It pulled up from our cores and twined in a pulsing, sinuous flow as we merged together. The power grew from deep within each of us, pulling us again and again into a blissful singularity that expanded until it gently shattered into a twinkling wash that closed over us.

I love you. The silent words came from both of us. We were thinking together, perfectly synched. My head rested on Trevor's chest and his heart beat against my cheek as we slowly drifted back to the physical world. The sound of our mingled breathing filled the tiny space and a warm contentment filled our minds. I'd nearly drifted to sleep when Trevor kissed me softly and reluctantly left the tent.

CHAPTER 11

"That's the one. He lives here," I said quietly to Cecelia. The red brick mansion at the end of the long, sweeping driveway wouldn't have looked out of place in a movie about Tudor nobility. Isaiah's next-door neighbor kept a showplace.

I concentrated on keeping my spiderweb shield up. Mentally invisible. *Nothing to see here. Please move along.* I wasn't sending thoughts to anyone in the group, not even to Trevor. Right now, we were too close to Isaiah to risk it. I wiped my palms against the legs of my jeans again.

"Excuse me!" Cecilia waved at the paunchy, slightly balding, middle-aged man on the other side of the gate. Cecilia's inner world remained as jaded and negative as I'd come to expect, but to this guy, she conveyed the bubbly, innocuous energy of a high-school cheerleader.

From out of sight behind the thick hedges facing the road, the nervous anticipation of the others waiting in the van trickled into me. Could Isaiah feel it, too? Had his range gotten larger over the years? If he came for us, would I be able to give them enough warning to escape? My heart thudded against my ribs. Dammit, I needed to focus!

The thoughts of the approaching man—*oh, ick.* I forced myself not to visibly cringe. *What a letch. He's old enough to be her father!* The sun in Cecilia's blonde hair drew him like a fish to a shiny lure. I pasted on a smile and tried to look like a perky teenage girl. Why were we acting like bait again? Oh yeah, we needed to get the man face to face since Cecelia's charming wouldn't work properly though the intercom system.

"Can I help you, ladies?" He imagined ripping Cecilia's clothes off with his teeth then—*ugh.* I suppressed my shudder. People like him were the reason my mother told me not to talk to strangers.

"Please let us in." Charm resonance heavily laced her words.

"Sure." He would've anyway, even without Cecelia's ability. The gate rolled aside with a sound like a peddling bicycle.

"Our friends are coming in, too."

"Okay." In his imagination, our "friends" were the cast of a porn movie shot in a sorority house. I could feel my molars grind as I forced the smile to remain on my face. Sean slowly followed in the van as we walked up the driveway. The gate closed behind us.

"You're happy that we're here," Cecilia said to the letch. His name was Bob, but I didn't care.

"I sure am." His "happy thoughts" made my stomach heave. Why did Jersey seem to have more than its share of skanky men? I couldn't wait to get back to New Hampshire where the creepy men just wanted to kill us. *No—focus.* I couldn't let strong emotion upset my shielding.

"Now, you're going to go into the house and leave us outside. Once we're gone, you're going to forget we were ever here."

"Sure will." Bob leered at her.

"Is anyone else here?"

"Nope, just me." Bob's thoughts confirmed it. His wife and daughter had gone shopping in the City and the housekeeper had the day off.

"Any dogs?" I added. Cecilia gave off a slight shiver as she pictured two Dobermans coming for her at full speed.

"Just Mitzy."

"Tell him to keep Mitzy inside." I said to Cecilia. "Mitzy" was a German Shepard—a really big one.

"Keep Mitzy inside. Is there any security on the perimeter wall?"

"Just a couple of cameras on the gates."

"Go turn those off as soon as you get inside." Her bubbly tone was long gone. "Erase the ones that show us or the van."

"Will do," said Bob, cheerfully. He was happy we were here, after all.

Sean drove the van across the grass to the property line. I wondered if Bob would be pissed later when he saw the unexplained tire marks in his professionally manicured lawn. We approached the wall as though it was the boundary to a dangerous land. In many ways, it was. The bricks rose about eight feet high and followed the slight slope of the land. A repeating pattern stuck out along the top edge, like scalloped frosting on a bakery cake.

Rachel closed her eyes and located Matilda. The golden thread in her mind led through the wall, across the grounds, and into the building on the far side. It was probably just Isaiah's guest bungalow, but it was larger than my mom's house.

Matilda looked exhausted and drawn as she sat on the edge of a bare mattress in a ground floor room. Rope bound her hands together in front of her, as though forcing her to pray. I could make out just a hint of her thoughts at this distance—the guesthouse was at the edge of my mental range. *Despair*—Matilda was filled with grey hopelessness. Without seeing Rachel's vision, I wouldn't have recognized her mind.

Morris lay unmoving on a twin bed in a small upstairs room. His legs still looked broken and his skin shone with the sick sweat of fever. Rachel and I watched his chest rise and fall a few times. *At least he's still alive.* I couldn't feel anything, not even pain, coming from him. He must be unconscious.

Where was Isaiah? Would he sense me this close, even while I was shielding? No way to tell. I walked forward until I touched the wall, and then focused on finding the other minds in the guesthouse. My palms left damp marks on the bricks as I simultaneously strained to listen while keeping my shield in place, both reaching out and holding back. The effort made my eyes hurt.

Wasn't it strange that mental shielding only kept other telepaths from reading me? Why didn't it interfere with my ability to read others? I'd been thinking of my shield as a wall, but that wasn't right. Walls stopped things in both directions. Blocking like this didn't stop the thoughts of others, but it prevented mental attack.

Didn't it?

Oh, crap. I went cold. Would my mental shield give me any protection from Isaiah at all, or would a burst of killing energy from his mind pass into mine as easily as a thought? Was it only camouflage, helping me avoiding detection? Or would it prevent Isaiah from focusing properly, like jamming his radar, keeping him from being able to send a blast to the right place? *Ah, hell.* I really should've thought of this stuff earlier. Now was definitely not the time.

I closed my eyes to concentrate, to focus on the rescue of the healers. Matilda and Morris needed us. "Four guards," I said, finally. "Two are outside. I think there's one in front of each of their doors. Matilda's downstairs in a big bedroom. She's conscious. Her hands are tied. Morris is unconscious in a room upstairs. He's still injured."

"Let's do this." Drew kept his voice low.

I squeezed Trevor's hand as he joined me at the wall. Anxiety clumped in my gut. "Stay safe," I whispered to him.

He trailed a finger lightly across my cheek. "You, too." Trevor felt oddly cut off—having me this close but unable to hear my thoughts. I guess that meant I was shielding well.

I made one last mental pass over the surrounding area, and then I gave them a nod. "All clear." My voice sounded raspy in my ears.

With an invisible boost from Trevor, Drew rose into the air, crouched over top of the wall, and then lowered on the far side. I felt him locate the security camera that covered this portion of the wall and melt its innards.

I held my breath. If someone had seen him fly over the wall, we'd know pretty quickly. I tensed, listening to the thoughts of the guards in the house. No reaction. Maybe the security people hadn't noticed the camera go out. If we had any luck at all, the guards would be too busy monitoring the Sons of Adam gathering to worry about what might—as far as they knew—just be a loose wire.

I gave Trevor another quick, jerky nod, and he lifted Hannah and Cecelia the same way he'd lifted Drew. He met my eyes for a breathless second then vaulted himself over.

Precognition isn't a G-positive ability. That's a surprising lack, actually. All of the "psychic" talents were usually clumped together in popular fiction, the way vampires and werewolves seemed to populate the same stories. What if we'd known then, when the team was going over that wall, that we wouldn't all be coming back alive from this expedition to Isaiah's?

We definitely would've done a few things differently.

I pressed my forehead against the brick, listening with my mind and my heart to Trevor's progress across the grounds. The ornamental plantings didn't provide much cover—our people would be seen if someone looked this way. I listened for the thoughts of alarm that I expected to feel if the guards spotted them. My pulse pounded in my ears and sweat dampened my clenched fists. Being left behind felt more stressful than taking part in a mission. I hated being separated from Trevor, especially when he was doing something dangerous. I couldn't help him from here. I couldn't do anything but watch.

My connection to Trevor kept his thoughts bright in my mind, even as the others faded into the edges of my ability. They paused at the side of the building as Drew fried the security camera covering the front door then focused on suppressing the guns while Trevor grabbed the two guards outside the front door. His invisible hands clamped their mouths shut and held them immobile as Hannah laid hands on their foreheads, knocking them deeply unconscious.

"They've taken out the first two guards." I whispered, for Sean's benefit. Rachel followed along with her visions.

Cecilia, meanwhile, opened the front door, calling out, "Don't move! We're supposed to be here!"

The guard downstairs smiled at her. After all, she was

supposed to be there.

I felt Matilda's despair flicker and fall away, replaced with hope. *"I'm in here!"* Her voice sounded thin and fragile through Trevor's thoughts. He reached within the mechanism and released the lock.

Matilda's anguish came through more strongly to me once Trevor was in the same room with her. *"He's a charm!"* Her words rushed out of her. *"Isaiah can charm now! And he's an RV. He can find G-positives, like Charlie Fontaine could. He has people coming here—you have to stop him! He's going to tell them where to find G-positives and send them out as killing squads."*

Her words dumped a bucket of ice water over my head. Everything clicked into place. The research looking into the brains of G-positives—G-positives like Charlie Fontaine, Rachel's uncle—hadn't been just to discover how to kill us better. Had Isaiah forced Matilda to use her healing ability to alter his brain structure, adding more G-positive abilities? I hadn't known that was even possible.

Oh, my God. If he could locate G-positives, we'd be the first people he'd find. Hell, we were almost in his telepathic range already. Did he already know we were here? *Crap, crap, crap!* I started shaking. This was so much worse than we'd thought. And he now had a house full of people who'd be more than willing to kill us, even if he didn't have the added power of being able to charm them into it. The charm component just made the killers more lethal. They'd become like suicide bombers, content to die so long as their targets died, too.

We were in terrible danger.

The survivors of Ganzfield were in terrible danger.

Even my mom was in terrible danger.

We needed to do something—*right now!* And I could only

think of one thing. I was shielding. I could get in there and I could blast Isaiah's mind.

I promised Trevor I'd avoid "extra danger."

I knew what he'd want me to do and I knew what I had to do, and they were two very different things. I was in trouble either way. At least, if I went in, I'd give the others a chance to get away and I might have a chance of stopping Isaiah forever. Isaiah would hear anyone else coming—no one else on the team could shield. No one else could come.

I had to go. Right now. Alone.

"Rachel," I dug into my purse for my cell phone. I tossed it to her with trembling fingers. After a second, I tossed my purse to her, too. "Call Nick Coleman. Tell him Isaiah's not just a telepath anymore. He's a charm and an RV and right now he's preparing death squads to send after every G-positive he can find." She froze, wide-eyed, for a moment, and then recovered with a quick nod and started flipping through my contact list for Coleman's number.

"Sean, I need a boost over this wall." I stepped into the basket he made with his hands, threw my free leg over the wall, and then leaned down to him. "Tell Trevor this isn't 'extra danger.' We're all dead if I can't stop him. Tell him I love him. Get everyone out of here and keep driving until it's safe." Sean nodded, committing each item to memory. "Don't wait for me. Go as soon as they get back."

Both Sean and Rachel had a bad mental startle at that, but I didn't know if I could survive this and I needed to know they were safely away before Isaiah could send people after them. "Don't stop anywhere. I'll call my cell once I'm out—let you know where to come get me," I added, glancing at the phone in Rachel's hand. I didn't know where I'd get a second phone. Hell—I didn't even know if I could remember my own phone number right now. I just had to make sure that Trevor and the others were on the move, rather than just sitting here as easy targets.

Rachel dialed Coleman; the phone rang in her ear as I slid over the wall. Rough bricks scraped my palms as I dangled, and then dropped to the ground. I could see the main house in the distance; it could fully be called a mansion. Modern design—a lot of glass. I took off running toward it.

I felt Trevor untie Matilda's hands and Cecilia release her from the "Don't move" charm command she'd uttered when going in. I passed out of range as they headed upstairs to find Morris. And then I was alone—in enemy territory.

I worked on keeping my shield up as I approached Isaiah's glass mansion. *He who lives in glass houses… No. Focus! Keep the shield up!* I slowed to a walk as I reached the line of parked cars, forcing my breathing rate down and my face to assume a mask of normalcy.

What were the names of the two Sons of Adam members Coleman had told me? If anyone asked, I could say I was here with one of them. One was Something Miller. Could I pick up enough information from the minds of strangers to fake an acquaintance? Possibly. The mental babble grew as I drew closer to the crowd. I closed my eyes, concentrated once more on the silver spiderweb shield in my mind, and took a deep breath. Then I pushed open the wide front door.

Large windows brightened the mansion's foyer. Several of the people gathered inside still wore sunglasses against it. I glanced around. Strange: their thoughts seemed so…*normal*. Most were pleasantly social as they talked in small groups, holding drinks and eating finger food off of awkwardly balanced little plates. Work, family, friends—these people weren't rabid hatemongers at the moment. I'd only encountered Sons of Adam members when they were actively hunting us. I hadn't considered they might not feel intense fear and hate all the time.

A strong mental presence broadcast from deeper within the house. I continued forward under a gracefully arching double staircase. Glass-paneled doors, now thrown wide, opened into a great room that stretched the width of the house. Windows ran floor to ceiling along the far wall. The lake caught the sunlight behind them, reflecting painful little jewels of sunlight from the water's rippling surface.

More people milled in this room, more than seventy or eighty here in all. The majority were male, and most seemed to be in their twenties or thirties. I felt mental pricks as several of the men noticed me. I still hadn't gotten used to hearing the idle erotic fantasies of men who didn't suspect their thoughts would be heard, and they set my teeth on edge. *No. Don't think about that now. Keep the shield in place.*

A few people thought I looked familiar; they were trying to place me. *Crap.* I felt myself break out in a cold sweat. My picture had been circulated as a target. No one had made that connection yet, but it could happen at any moment.

I moved with slow deliberation toward Isaiah. *So loud!* I could feel his thoughts too clearly, rehearsing the next thing he planned to say in conversation. His words bullhorned into my head and I still wasn't in range. His mind was so strong—too strong. I tried to swallow past the lump in my throat. I skirted a food-laden table covered in white linen.

A uniformed caterer bumped me, muttering an insincere apology. I gasped at the touch and my wire-taut emotions spiked before I recognized that it wasn't an attack.

Isaiah looked up. He'd felt something strange in the room.

Crap. I focused on my shield, keeping my gaze on the buffet table, as he scanned the crowd.

He looked so…*ordinary.* I'd expected his outward appearance to be more fearsome—to reflect his ability in some noticeable way. His short, grey hair receded at the temples. He had the wiry, forcibly-trim look of a man who kept himself physically fit in spite of getting older. Angular face. Straight nose. Strong chin. Ice-blue eyes that seemed to take in all of the details of the scene before him. He wore a white oxford shirt and khakis. Preppy. There was a very good chance that I was about to be killed by a man wearing loafers. Which part of that sentence was most wrong? *No, no, no. Stop it. Focus!* I tried to slow my breathing and keep the panic from flooding my mind.

At the far end of the room, near the window, the group that had gathered around Isaiah used the grand piano as a place to rest their little plates. They all shared a burst of laughter that caught the envious attention of the other clusters of people around them. It was clear where the center of power was.

Fifty feet from him—still more than halfway across the great room. I'd never blasted someone's mind from this far. I didn't think I could. I moved around another group of people, drawing nearer to Isaiah.

The distant sound of gunshots didn't register over the crowd noise. The relay came to me through Isaiah's mind as two security people outside opened fire on someone.

My heart seemed to stop beating. *Oh, my God.* Who were they shooting at? Probably someone I knew. I couldn't tell. The double distortion through other people's thoughts turned the distant targets into sinister-looking monster-people. Isaiah was distracted, listening to the confusion outside. *Now! This was my chance.* I started to close the distance directly. I'd blast him as soon as I got close enough.

"Everyone freeze!" Isaiah's voice conveyed both authority and charm resonance. The people around me instantly became silent, living statues.

No! I'm not close enough yet! I desperately felt for the area of his mind that'd sent out the command—*there!* I sent a blast of energy into it, just like I'd done with Zack in the backyard. But this time, I pushed, hard, trying to fill it with killing force. I shook as I felt the searing in his mind, the blaze of energy that I'd sent into him. The language center of his brain flared brightly, and then burned itself into a dark cinder.

More! I tried to expand the damage, move it through the rest of his mind, but I wasn't close enough. Only the use of his new charming ability had made the tenuous connection possible from here. Now I lost the focus and the connection melted away.

Half a second later, I realized my mistake.

I hadn't frozen.

I was immune to his charming ability so I was still moving.

And now he knew who I was.

Ah, hell. He wouldn't even have to walk around the room, listening to each mind up close, as he'd originally intended. My heart hammered in my chest as our eyes met for a moment of mutual shock—we both recognized our determination to see the other dead.

Isaiah silently launched a powerful killing blast directly at my mind. It hit my mental shield like a spray of dark acid and I gasped. I could feel it weakening, corroding under his continued onslaught. I forced my shaking legs to run forward. I had to get close enough to blast him before he broke through my shield.

I was in trouble. It was taking all of my mental energy to maintain my foundering shield. I couldn't draw away enough focus to attack. *Crap, crap, crap!* If I struck out again with my ability, I'd just give him a clear conduit to focus into my mind. My breath came in panicky little pants. This was bad. I felt Isaiah start to break through in pinpoints. He now could hear some of my thoughts. He recognized a flash of Trevor, the telekinetic he'd wanted to capture—*to vivisect.* He'd wanted to give himself that telekinetic ability, as well. He still did.

A sob caught in my throat. *No!*

Isaiah wasn't shielding. He simply attacked so powerfully that I couldn't counter him, like a champion boxer who hits hard enough that his opponent never gets a chance to land a blow in return. He pierced my shield again, mirroring the same focus point I had when I'd burned his mind.

I don't know what this'll do, but I bet it's something bad.

I felt a dark spot blossom in my mind, like spilled ink soaking into a towel.

He attacked again, stabbing his mental energy like a dagger into my consciousness. Something else went loose in my brain and my left leg gave out. I could still feel it, but I couldn't control it. The wooden floor seemed to rush up to meet me. I landed hard, catching most of it in my left wrist. A cracking pain shot up my arm, but the overwhelming torrent in my head drowned out the sound of my scream.

I couldn't stop—I had to do this. I tried to crawl closer. With every passing second, my shield grew weaker. Around me, the living statue people watched with silent revulsion as I inched along the floor, dragging one leg and pulling myself forward with my arms.

Monster!

—might be able to throw fire like the ones who attacked us up north—

—I can't move! What did she do—

Kill her!

The edges of my vision started to blacken, forming a tunnel until all I could see was Isaiah. He was striding toward me now, grim-faced and determined, still attacking my shield.

Oh, my God. I was about to die.

Isaiah knew it, too. He smiled maliciously as he planned how he was going to spin this to the observing crowd. What charmed words would he use? It wouldn't take much. *You all saw her try to kill me. She's a perfect example of how dangerous these people are.*

He didn't speak. He didn't gloat. He just came closer. Oily black killing energy seeped into my mind, stronger with every step. The parquet floor pressed cold and hard against my cheek. I was no longer moving, and everything was fading, spinning away, and Isaiah seemed to be flying as I left the world and the blackness closed over me.

CHAPTER 12

Dead.

I floated in the blackness.

Weightless.

The silence cocooned around me. I was alone in the dark.

Oh, no.

Trevor.

I'd never hear his mind again. I felt so empty without him, as though my soul had been ripped in two. The best parts of me seemed to've torn loose, leaving me adrift with my loneliness, my insecurities, and my pain. *My soul.*

Wait.

I was still self-aware. *I think, therefore I am. Right?* I still existed, somehow.

I heard a drumbeat, slow and steady. It took me a long time to realize it was a heartbeat, and even longer to realize recognize the heartbeat as my own.

That's a surprise. Cool.

Light filtered red through my heavy eyelids. My whole body

felt leaden, as though gravity was pulling on me extra hard now, making up for all that earlier floating.

I opened my eyes, squinting against the morning light. The sky seemed overcast outside my window, but it was still too bright. I lay on my side in bed. I was in my own room. Everything seemed so normal. All I could hear were the sounds of a few cars in the distance and the gentle patter of light rain.

Silence.

There were no thoughts in my head except my own. Had everything I'd experienced just been a dream? Hell, could all of Ganzfield been a dream? I drew a ragged breath and someone moved behind me, startling me.

"Maddie?" Trevor's voice was hoarse. I tried to move, but my body didn't want to obey me. Turning my head felt difficult and strange. An IV line in the back of my hand pinched with an itchy tightness as I shifted.

"Maddie!" Trevor's hands stroked my face and hair with tender desperation. He touched me as though he needed to convince himself that I was real. I tried to give him a smile.

Trevor looked terrible. Stubble darkened his grey-tinged cheeks and the inky smudges under his eyes were billboards of insomnia. I knew how he must feel; it'd been the same for me when he'd been unconscious after we'd gotten him out of Eden Imaging.

Unconscious.

I must've been unconscious.

I couldn't hear his thoughts. That made me feel even more isolated and alone. *Trevor,* I thought into the silence. *Trevor?* I didn't hear his mind and he didn't react. My ability was gone. Had Isaiah burned it out? Those last minutes flooded back into my memory. How was I still alive? "Luff."

Trevor's brow furrowed in confusion.

So did mine. *What was that?* I tried to say Trevor's name again. "Luff," once again came out of my mouth.

I watched something pass over Trevor's features. It was as though the new and fragile hope was pulled out of him with cold fingers. His face crumpled with pain. One of his hands left my face as he cradled his own forehead like he was trying to keep it from exploding.

Brain damage. *Oh, my God in Heaven.* Broca's area. I'd burned out Isaiah's, and then he'd done the same to me. I remembered the inky sensation as part of my consciousness had been blotted out. What else had he done to my mind? The thought started my whole body quivering.

No.

I needed to figure this out—assess myself. My thoughts felt clear enough in my head. I knew the words and I knew what I wanted to say. It just wasn't coming out of my mouth right. What was that called? I knew the term.

Expressive aphasia.

I couldn't speak. I couldn't use telepathy. A sense of claustrophobia rose within me.

Trapped.

I was trapped inside my own body, alone, without a way to communicate. "Ock."

Crap! I couldn't even get a good four-letter word out. If there ever was an appropriate time to use profanity…

Wait.

I had one more thing to try. I struggled to sit up. I felt so weak! My left leg felt funny—watery—but at least I could move it again. *Thank you, Matilda and Hannah.* I'd take a moment to appreciate that later. I pulled open the little drawer in my nightstand and rummaged for a pen. What could I…there! I grabbed the pad of post-its that I'd used for bookmarks.

Please tell me you can read this.

My hand shook but the words looked legible enough to me. I gave them a second reading, just to be sure.

Brain damage.

What if what I'd written was nonsense, too? Would I be able to tell? Did Broca's aphasia affect writing? Did I actually have aphasia or was it something different, something the medical community didn't even have a name for?

Maddie Dunn's disease.

It wasn't like there was a lot in the medical journals on telepathic damage, after all.

I reached for one of Trevor's hands. I could tell he was in terrible emotional pain, which made my heart ache—but I couldn't feel it. The world seemed colorless and numb to me. And Trevor, even though he was right here next to me, seemed far away.

I held up the post-it. It took a moment for his eyes to focus. I watched as the written words registered and the dashed hope returned, rekindling the life within him. His eyes met mine, searching for me within. I reached out and cradled his cheek with my hand, feeling the sandpaper stubble against my fingers. He took a few deep breaths, rubbing his free hand across his face. A little color seemed to return, washing away some of the grey cast from his skin.

"I can read that," he said quietly, after what seemed like an eon.

Relief trickled through me. I closed my eyes for a long moment and let out the breath that I'd been holding. I pulled off the top post-it.

Can't speak right. Can't hear thoughts.
But I'm in here and I love you.

I held the pad up to him again.

His hands framed my face. "Oh, Maddie." Desperate relief flavored his kisses. I felt as though he was drinking me in.

"You're awake." Hannah's voice startled us both; I hadn't sensed her approach. "Good. How do you feel?"

I can't talk. Broca's aphasia, I think.

With her medical training, she'd probably know the term. I frowned as I checked my spelling of the word "aphasia" twice; it didn't look quite right.

"You can't speak at all?"

My response came out as, "Aaht."

Hannah nodded, as if I'd actually said something that made sense. Her eyes were sad.

Resigned.

How long had she known about this?

"Matilda and I fixed what we could. When Trevor brought you out, we thought you were dead."

I thought I was dead, too. What happened?

Hannah and Trevor exchanged a look. What weren't they telling me? This was annoying. I frowned as I looked from Hannah to Trevor.

"She can't hear my thoughts. I've been trying to reach her." Trevor's hand kept gently stroking my neck and shoulder, but a part of me was still beginning to panic. How damaged *was* my mind? What'd happened in Isaiah's mansion? How had I survived? How had I gotten back here? Was Isaiah still alive? Were we being hunted by charmed death squads? Could they be coming here right now? My heart thudded up against my ribcage, and I swallowed hard to keep it in place. The questions in my mind threatened to overwhelm me.

"Her dodecamine levels are very low now," Hannah told him. I scowled. They were talking *about* me rather than to me. "She's a rapid burner and, after all of the bleeding in her brain, Matilda thought she had a better chance of recovery if she was off the meds for a while."

Bleeding in my brain?

That was a stroke—and a stroke was *bad*. I rubbed my forehead with a shaky hand. Was I more damaged than I felt? How would I know? Was there a point at which I wouldn't know what I didn't know? I felt fluttery and weak—and scared and sick and lost and…how much of that was emotional and how much was physical? Had Isaiah destroyed my telepathic ability or was it the result of being off the meds for—

How long have I been out?

I held it up to Trevor.

"What day is it?" he asked Hannah. He looked so tired. I felt another strong impulse to soothe him. As bad as I felt, he looked worse.

"Monday."

I'd been unconscious for two whole days? No wonder Trevor looked so haggard.

"Nine days."

My jaw dropped.

Nine?

Nine days? Trevor had been in that torture of uncertainty for *nine* days? The single day I'd experienced watching over him had been unendurable. I put my hand up to his face, looking into his eyes and seeing the shadows of anguish behind them. *Crap.* I'd put him through hell.

I'm so sorry.

I wanted to touch his thoughts and soothe his mind—try to make it better. I felt so useless, so helpless like this. I needed to fix this. I needed to fix myself so I could help Trevor.

Any dodecamine left?

I showed the little pad to Hannah.

"We have half a vial. 2ccs."

That was enough. More than I usually got. Nine days. No wonder my levels were low. I needed weekly boosters, and it'd been well over two weeks. That was good news, actually.

Hopeful.

Perhaps Isaiah hadn't burnt out my ability, after all.

Give me a shot.

I was going through a lot of post-its.

"I'm not sure you could handle it yet."

I frowned and tapped the pad with my finger.

C'mon Hannah! Don't leave me like this!

Hannah looked from the note and back to my face a few times. She gave a sigh of resignation. "Okay, but let me check you out first."

Trevor's hand slid down to hold mine as Hannah put hers on either side of my head. Her eyes closed in concentration. I felt nothing from her, just the warm, dry touch of her fingers on my temples. She wasn't actively fixing anything…at least, I didn't feel the pins-and-needles that usually accompanied her healing energy. Was that good? Did it mean I was better? Or was it bad? Was there nothing she could do to repair the damage she found? And why was this assessment taking so damn long?

"I think you should be okay. You want it now?"

I nodded emphatically.

Hell, yes!

This silence—this isolation—was torturous. I met Trevor's

eyes, trying to convey my hope that it wouldn't be long before we could hear each other properly again. He forced a smile and squeezed my hand, trying to reassure me right back.

Hannah returned a minute later. I'd never felt so happy at the idea of getting a shot. For just a moment, I felt like a junkie. How long would it take for the dodecamine to start working? I'd never been off it before and my initial dose had taken effect when I'd been asleep.

"I'll go call your mom, okay?" Hannah turned to Trevor. "You're here with her—of course you are." I heard her footfalls going down the stairs. Where was everyone else?

Trevor's fingers anxiously chafed my hand. "It's okay."

I met his eyes and suddenly felt like crying. What if it didn't work? I was counting on the meds. What if I was stuck like this permanently? I'd felt Isaiah's attack burn a part of my mind away. Did that mean that my speech was gone for good? Very possible. Matilda and Hannah would've repaired what they could.

Reality—I'd probably never speak properly again.

Oh, my God.

No! I couldn't live the rest of my life this way. I just *couldn't*. So weak, so useless..

So alone.

And what if dodecamine didn't work on me anymore? The flutters from my stomach expanded into my chest and I suddenly couldn't get enough air. The dodecamine had to work. It just had to.

"You know I get you, right?" Trevor cupped my chin in his hand.

I remembered a night, which didn't seem long ago for me, when I'd uttered similar words to him. I looked into his face.

"Like right now…you're feeling useless and angry and

scared." He slid into bed next to me and pulled me into his arms. His long frame seemed to fill the bed and his feet nearly hung off the end. Trevor was warm and strong and it felt so good to have him beside me. I slid closer to him, suddenly aware I was wearing what felt like an adult diaper under my old nightshirt.

Ick—who'd been changing me? At least the one I had on felt clean. I'd worry about the ramifications of such things later.

I tilted my face up his, searching his eyes for a flash of the soul within, the real Trevor, the part of him I loved the most. He seemed so maddeningly untouchable, like moonlight seeping through a window.

What good was I to him in this condition? I had nothing to offer him anymore. I wasn't special—I wasn't even normal. I felt damaged.

Defective.

A tear escaped my right eye, slipping down my cheek. Trevor's invisible finger brushed it from me, holding it up—a magically floating, flat little disk of water that caught the light between us. Trevor looked into it as though he could see the future reflected within its shimmer.

"I don't just love you, Maddie. I adore you. You are *everything* to me. Whatever happened, and whatever happens from now on, we'll make it work, okay?" His voice caught. "I'm the luckiest guy in the world. I get a second chance to be with you."

My heart felt like it was about to burst. I sniffed, unsuccessfully trying to stop crying. He kissed me tenderly, kissed my cheeks, my eyes. Kissed my tears away. Kissed the fear and the pain away. Finally, I was able to stop the shuddering sobs. I sniffled back into tenuous control of myself.

He pulled back to look at me—a devious twinkle lit his eyes. "It's okay if you never talk again, you know. You can just sit there and look pretty."

My eyes narrowed at the thought.

Trevor let out a quick laugh. "See? You hate that! I get you! I am attuned to your every mood."

I scowled. Was he *trying* to piss me off? Did he think that'd break me out of my little self-pity wallow?

"And now you're wondering if I'm trying to make you mad on purpose."

My lips twitched into a smile. I had to give him credit—Trevor knew how to read me. He still knew me, even without our mental connection. I felt my little funk begin to dissipate. It would be okay. Whatever happened, it would be okay. That's what Trevor was trying to show me. I felt my love for him fill me, or maybe it was his love for me. I looked into his eyes, grateful to whatever Higher Power had created this incredible man and put him in my life.

"I love you, too." Trevor lifted my chin to give me a tender kiss.

The first tendrils of connection to Trevor's mind sent a cool sense of relief through me. I could feel him there, breaking through the mental silence that had enveloped me. I let out the breath I hadn't realized I'd been holding. It felt as though my soul was unfurling. I suddenly felt…healthier.

Trevor?

I tried to concentrate—to project clearly. What if all I could send him was confused thoughts and random sounds? He didn't hear me, but a second world slowly came into focus around me. I could feel Trevor's presence—and his emotional turmoil. He was trying to put on a brave face to boost my spirits, but under his joy and relief, his thoughts thrashed with fear and anger and grief and a bone-numbing exhaustion.

I snuggled closer, stroking his face and hair, trying to pull the anguish from him as I waited for my ability to return more fully. *How long was this going to take?*

"It's only been twenty minutes," said Trevor, glancing at the clock by my bed.

The spike of joy hit us simultaneously. My *you heard that?* collided with his "Did you just ask how long this would take?"

You can hear me again? I'm not just sending gibberish into your head?

Trevor kissed me. *No gibberish.*

I'm so sorry I put you through this.

Trevor pulled away, a grey cloud of accusation filling his mind. *Why did you lie to me? You broke your word.*

Cold shock splashed through me. Trevor thought I'd taken off on my own little mission as soon as he and the others had gone in after the healers. He thought I'd planned it—and that I'd intended all along to break my word to him. He was feeling six different kinds of stupid for trusting me; for being too weak to leave for the past nine days; for sleeping in the yard like a dog, waiting for me to wake up.

I heard Matilda tell you that Isaiah was a charm and an RV and was about to send people out to kill us all. Didn't Sean tell you?

Sean's dead.

WHAT? I felt as though he'd slapped me. *Oh, my God. What happened?* Was it my fault? Had I been too late? Had Isaiah already sent killers after them? Were those the shots I'd heard through Isaiah's thoughts? Oh, poor Rachel. She'd been through so much; why did this have to happen, too? My empty stomach heaved sickly.

Something shifted in Trevor's mind as he realized I hadn't lied to him. A piece of his inner goodness—and his faith in me—seemed to re-inflate within him. How had he lived with all of these horrible thoughts and doubts for so many days?

You know I can't lie to you, right? I asked.

You can't?

Well, I could tell you something that wasn't true, but I think you'd hear the truth in my mind anyway. I suppose I could shield while I did it, but that would be a giveaway, too.

Really?

You accidentally pushed me in your sleep and broke my leg. I would've lied to you about that if I could've.

A hot sting of guilt shadowed his thoughts.

And we'd both be dead now if I hadn't needed the MRI, right? No more guilt! That accident probably saved both our lives! I only brought it up to make the I-can't-lie-to-you point!

Okay. So you decided to go after Isaiah alone after you heard what Matilda said. Why didn't you wait for me?

You can't shield. I was the only one who could get close—the only one he couldn't hear coming.

You were trying to save us. It was so much better than the torturous doubts that had been gnawing at him for so long. He'd wondered if Dr. Williamson had turned me into an assassin—had warped me to fill his own overpowering need to destroy Isaiah. Trevor had even considered the possibility that my love for him had all been an act—that I'd just been using him to get close enough to fulfill my mission. He'd been down some dark mental roads, alone with his own thoughts and insecurities for more than a week. I nearly started crying again. The pain Trevor had gone through was truly awful.

I reached up to stroke his face—to comfort him and take that pain away. I felt it retracting its talons from his soul. A knot of guilt lumped in my throat as the miserable realization hit me. *I've failed you.*

What?

If you didn't know—if I haven't shown you how much I love you— I was mangling this. How could I tell him? *I need to do better—so you'll always know how much I love you. I don't ever want you to doubt that again.*

Trevor kissed me and I felt his insecurities shrivel away. I wanted to make sure they never had a chance to take root again.

I couldn't let you go. I just couldn't.

What happened?

Trevor showed me his memories, the ones he'd been going over and over for the past nine days—his own personal footage reel from hell. He'd carried Morris back to the wall and lifted everyone over. When he'd jumped over himself, though, he'd discovered I was gone.

"She went after Isaiah," Sean had said.

Trevor's world had tilted with sickening dread. *Oh, my God. I have to stop her! Is it too late?* Trevor vaulted back over the wall and ran full out toward the mansion, using his ability to push himself faster. Two security people saw him moving with supernatural speed and opened fire. Trevor caught the bullets and kept running. *Find Maddie! Save her!* He hurtled through the open front door and wove through the silent crowd, looking around wildly for me.

The motionless people faded to inconsequence when he saw my crumpled body on the floor, shaking with effort just to stay conscious. He'd seen the man coming toward me, moving with the stalking gait of a predator closing in on its kill. Trevor had leapt at Isaiah, slamming his invisible arms desperately into him.

I remembered half-seeing Isaiah flying as I'd lost consciousness. I'd thought that it'd been part of the whole "the-world-stops-making-sense-as-I'm-dying" thing.

Now I knew that Trevor had run into a house full of Sons of Adam members and a killer telepath. He'd sent Isaiah hurtling though a plate glass window and out into the lake. He'd done this—this suicidally desperate thing—to rescue me. I felt his remembered terror and horror at seeing me motionless on the floor with blood leaking from my ears and nose.

Oh, no, no, no. Too late. Is she dead? She can't be dead. I was too slow. Too slow! I've lost her. She's gone. Please, God, no! She can't be gone.

Trevor had scooped me up and carried me out of the house, through the crowd of eerily frozen people. He'd reached the main road ahead of the van. Drew pulled to a stop with a squeal of tires. The door slid open and Trevor froze. Blood and grey matter dripped off the bench from Sean's head wound. Rachel clutched his limp hand, keening and rocking in her grief. Hannah and Matilda still tended him, but their faces showed they had no real hope. Sean was gone from the moment he'd popped his head over the wall to see who was shooting at Trevor. The bullet had gone in through his forehead, smashing a fist-sized chunk out of the back of his skull. Blood darkened his red hair nearly black around the wound. Trevor's guilt splashed sickly-green between us. *If he hadn't been checking on me, it wouldn't have happened.*

The wounded and dead overcrowded the van. Morris lay unconscious across the second seat. I'd taken up the third as Matilda and Hannah had worked over me in the swaying vehicle.

Trevor had watched as the healers worked, feeling overpowering, helpless grief. Every comment they'd exchanged about the damage to the different parts of my brain had burned into his thoughts like a brand.

A bad bleed in my right motor cortex—that explained the problem with my left leg. Other bleeds, localized seizures, and a dead zone—an area seared away in the expressive language center of my left hemisphere—Broca's area. They didn't know how to fix that; there was nothing left to heal. The cells in the entire region were completely dead…and brain cells don't regenerate.

They'd been able to halt the bleeding before it'd drowned my neurons. At one point my heart had stopped, and Trevor had felt like his own heart was being ripped from his chest as Matilda had used her ability to shock it back into rhythm. Their work continued back to my mom's house. Trevor had stayed at my side, feeling powerless and angry and so, so alone.

He'd witnessed my mother's horrified reaction as he'd carried my unconscious body into the house. She'd sat down heavily as she'd taken in the blood on everyone's clothing and the grief on their faces.

Matilda had talked her out of taking me to a hospital. "They can't do much for injuries like hers."

"And you can?" Tear streaks lined my mother's cheeks but her face blazed with maternal protectiveness.

Matilda looked at her with compassionate eyes. "I think we're her best chance."

Trevor's anguish had squeezed his heart. *If there was really much hope for Maddie, Matilda would've said something more positive—more comforting.*

I choked up again, covering my mouth with my hand. Dammit, I'd caused him so much pain.

I saw his next few days—barely eating, reluctantly leaving me only when he could no longer stay awake, knowing he could bring the roof down on me if he fell asleep at my bedside. Trevor and my mom had kept vigil on either side of me. At first, they'd endured an awkward silence. Eventually, my mom had started to talk, sharing her memories of me—stories from my childhood. Trevor had listened intently, as though each word gave him a tiny connection back to me. Talking about me was their way of keeping me alive.

My mom rushed home just before lunchtime, as soon as she got Hannah's voicemail message. She'd been in session with a client when Hannah had called. Her excitement and relief reached me before she'd even parked.

My mom's here.

Trevor discreetly moved back to the chair next to my bed. He'd made good progress in his relationship with my mother, but that progress would almost certainly be derailed if she came home and found him in bed with her underage daughter.

My mom seemed to fly up the stairs, but she stopped still as soon as she saw me. Drops of cold rain clung to her hair and shoulders; she hadn't bothered with an umbrella. Both hands flew up to cover her mouth, as though to hold in the overwhelming emotions.

Little good that does me. I started to cry from the intense waves of mother-love that rolled off her.

Hi, Mom.

She faltered for a moment, frowning. I usually didn't use telepathy with her. "Oh, honey. How do you feel?"

Not bad. I've got a form of aphasia, though. Good thing about the telepathy, huh? I smiled, trying to make the situation as light as possible.

My mom pulled me into a softly fierce hug. "My brave girl."

As a psychologist, she knew what aphasia was. She held me close, happy I was alive. But she simultaneously mourned the normal life she now felt was lost to me.

Mom, my so-called normal life ended last year. But a part of me felt the same sense of loss. Before today, I'd always known I had the same option as Dr. Williamson's niece. Ann had been a minder at Ganzfield until last fall, but she'd chosen to stop taking dodecamine and had gone back to being a "normal" person.

Now, if I went off the meds, I'd be disabled. I'd probably have to go through months of therapy or something just to learn basic communication skills. Would I have to use sign language? Actually, would that get as garbled as spoken language without a functional Broca's area? I didn't know. I just knew that "normal" was no longer an option.

My mom frowned. Guilt colored the energy in her mind dark-yellow, which surprised me. I'd been expecting her to be mad at me for doing something reckless and stupid. But no, she felt sick at heart because she'd gone back to work after two days. She'd wanted something to do—something that would distract her. Now she felt a need to prove that she loved me, even if she hadn't spent every moment by my bedside.

I knew a way to fill that need.

Trevor's thumb stroked against my knuckles, nervously soothing. *Should I give Maddie and her mom time together? I'm not even sure I can let go of her hand, let alone leave the room.*

My mom glanced at Trevor. *I know he wants to be here, but I really wish he'd back off a little. Maddie's my daughter—my only child—and I almost lost her.*

He picked this up from her glances at him and felt torn.

Please, stay. I want you with me, and she'll want to feed me.

To her I sent, *Mom, I'm starving. I haven't eaten in days. Is there anything—*

No need to finish that thought. My mom lit up at the idea—love through food was her thing. Her mind flashed through the ingredients she knew were in the house. I didn't want to trouble her, just give her something to do that would make her feel better. Leftover chicken parmagiana? That'd do.

Do you need some time alone with your mom?

Not right now.

I swung my legs over the side of the bed. What I needed right now was to use the bathroom. I suddenly felt Trevor's invisible hands around my waist.

No.

When you gotta go, you gotta go.

Your leg.

Okay, he had a point. I could tell it wasn't quite right. It only seemed weakly obedient compared to the other. I tested it, doing a couple of leg lifts. It felt rubbery and I wasn't sure it would support me.

Please don't make me use a diaper. That sounded more pathetic than I'd wanted to. *If you can get me to the bathroom, I'll be able to handle everything else, okay?*

He lifted me in his arms and carried me across the hall. From behind the closed door, he filled the hall with his anxiety. I awkwardly managed to do what I needed to, keeping my weight on my good leg and holding onto the edge of the sink. I washed my hands and brushed my teeth, reveling in the non-fuzzy-mouth feeling that resulted.

I wrapped my arms around Trevor's neck as he brought me back to bed. *You know I was joking when I said I'd need to come up with a new reason for you to carry me around, right?*

His hand lingered on my shoulder then moved to the side

of my face. *Oh, my God—I almost lost you!* The overwhelming thought hit him like a tidal wave. His eyes clenched shut against it.

I pulled him close. *I love you. I'm okay.* I repeated it over and over until the wave receded.

"Sorry," he said aloud. "I just—"

I know. I felt the part of his exhausted mind that cried out for sleep, but the thought of leaving repelled him. We needed to be with each other.

My mom returned with three plates on a tray. In the kitchen below, Hannah enjoyed a sandwich while she continued to work on her laptop. I felt a warm rush of gratitude when I realized that she was online, researching aphasia.

Food.

Food was good. I was quickly full, having eaten less than half of the portion my mother had provided, but Trevor polished off his entire dish of chicken parm as though he hadn't eaten in days. I switched plates with him when my mom wasn't looking; it would detract from the love-through-food effect if she saw me give away her offering.

Trevor's awareness of the world had shrunk to this single room once they'd brought me back. My mom had kept going. Had Cecelia charmed her? Taken away some of her worry and given her extra strength?

Probably. Cecelia tried to charm me.

What? I felt a protective anger well up.

Trevor's embarrassment ran hot-pink through his mind. *I pinched her larynx as soon as she said my name. Reflex. I realized later that she probably wasn't trying to do anything harmful.* Cecelia had avoided him after that, though.

My mom filled me in on all that'd happened in the past nine

days. "Dr. Williamson and Greg came here; I guess it was a week ago, now. That lawyer, Nick Coleman, got them to drop all of those ridiculous charges. He said the prosecutor's office had even issued a formal apology." She paused as she polished off another forkful of chicken. "Dr. Williamson and Cecelia went out to Isaiah Lerner's house. They released the people there; they'd been held in a charm command to freeze for *days*. Another day or two and they probably would've started to die of thirst. That nice Cecelia rechanneled their energies into helping inner-city kids." My mom smiled. "I really like her. Did you know she wants to be a therapist, too?"

I nodded, eyes wide. My mom now thought Cecelia was *nice*? And I'd always considered her such a good judge of character.

Trevor's lips twitched but he kept his eyes on his plate.

"You know, the therapeutic potential of a charm voice is really…well…it's practically limitless. I've offered her an internship in my practice, when she's ready."

Oh, man. On what planet would my mom bond with Cecelia? Just how long had I been in a coma again?

I really didn't understand Cecelia. She seemed so negative to me, yet she kept doing good things. Maybe it was just her reaction to me—she hadn't liked me from the moment we'd first met and, to be honest, I really didn't like her, either. I guess it didn't matter, in the long run. She was a fundamentally decent person, even if I personally found her to have a fingernails-on-a-chalkboard personality. Perhaps good personality traits didn't always go together.

My mom didn't seem to know the whole story, though. There was no way Dr. Williamson had gone to Peapack out of an altruistic need to help our would-be killers. Hell, some of them had probably been in the silver suits the night of the massacre. I was sure he'd gone looking for proof that Isaiah was really dead.

Crap. Isaiah's dead, right?

Trevor shook his head. "They didn't find a body." Ambivalence twisted within him. He'd wanted to kill the man hurting me, but he didn't want to be a killer.

Could Rachel—?

My mom's face fell in sympathy. "She's having a hard time right now. Grieving. She wouldn't even let Cecelia help her. With Sean gone, she doesn't want to feel better. I think she needs time to deal with her loss."

But this was important! I sat up suddenly. Trevor put a hand on my arm. Strong emotion shorted out Rachel's ability, and I hurt for her, but more people would feel that same grief and pain if Isaiah came after us again. I rubbed my forehead with both hands, trying to calm the anxiety welling up within me. *So no one knows where Isaiah is now?*

"Dr. Williamson told me that Rachel's vision didn't get more specific than 'somewhere in Europe, maybe Switzerland,'" my mom said.

Europe. Okay, that sounded far enough away for me to relax, at least for the moment. *So death squads aren't about to break down our doors?*

Trevor shook his head. "No death squads."

Good to know.

Actually, if I'd been successful in burning out Isaiah's Broca's area, he was never going to charm again. That was something—it might even have been worth losing my own voice.

Maybe.

I knew I'd keep thinking about what I'd done wrong that day—rehashing it over and over, haunted by the things I could've done differently. If only I'd stopped moving when he'd said to freeze! If he'd come through the crowd, mentally sniffing us one-by-one, I could've waited until he was close enough and—

I squeezed my eyes shut. The what-ifs definitely were going to torture me.

Where's Dr. Williamson now?

"He's gone back to re-open Ganzfield. He said he was going to stop someplace in Connecticut overnight then take the people who wanted to go up to New Hampshire with him the next morning."

Did everyone else go with him?

"Everyone except Trevor and Hannah."

Hannah had stayed. Was she ever planning to go back? I'd ask her later.

Are the others okay? Matilda? Morris? It hadn't been for nothing, right? Not if we saved them. A lump filled my throat—*Sean... Rachel.*

"Matilda is fine. Morris…he was walking normally when they left." *He seemed traumatized, like he had PTSD. What had those people done to him? What other dangerous things has Maddie been doing? How can I keep my little girl safe? Will she even listen to me anymore?*

Crap. My mom was building up steam for a crusade. I needed to distract her before she decided to lock me in the attic "for my own safety."

Mom, what time is it? Are your afternoon clients the same ones you cancelled on last week to stay home with me?

My mom frowned.

Trevor's eyes met mine. *Kinda manipulative, don't you think?*

She's getting upset. She needs to help people, but I don't want her focusing that help on me. I turned to her. *Mom, I'm fine. You can go back to work. I'll be here when you get home.*

"You'll be okay?"

I smiled and nodded reassuringly, glad my mom wasn't a telepath. I had an idea, but it would work better if she weren't in the house.

I pulled Trevor into bed with me as soon as my mom's car had backed out of the driveway. *Sleep,* I ordered him.

I can't. I might hurt you.

I shook my head. *Sleep. I'll wake you when you start to dream.* He was so tired and the weather was too cold and wet for him to be outside. If the sparks could sit watch over each other's firestarting, I could do this much. I wasn't tired, which didn't surprise me. Hadn't I been sleeping for the past nine days?

Trevor normally would've put up more of a fight, but the combination of exhaustion, bad weather, and simply wanting to stay close to me won out. He wrapped one of his long arms around my waist and was asleep in less than a minute.

I picked up the only book within reach—a book Trevor must've been reading during his long vigil at my bedside.

Jane Eyre.

Had he been reading it to me, trying to reach through my unconscious state to connect to me? I smiled. Yeah, that sounded like something he'd do.

Trevor's face was loose with sleep, the tension of the past days erased. I felt his breathing, even and slow, and a soft smile pulled at my lips. I'd often fantasized about us sleeping in each other's arms.

I'll take what I can get.

A scrap of paper marked a place near the end. I opened the book to it, read for a moment, and grinned. It was one of my favorite parts—after Mr. Rochester has been injured and blinded in the fire, when he feels unworthy of Jane, but he's still so in love with her. He tells her how he's yearned for her to return to him:

"I pleaded; and the alpha and omega of my heart's wishes broke involuntarily from my lips in the words— 'Jane! Jane! Jane!'"

"Did you speak these words aloud?"

"I did, Jane. If any listener had heard me, he would have thought me mad: I pronounced them with such frantic energy."

"And it was last Monday night, somewhere near midnight?"

"Yes; but the time is of no consequence: what followed is the strange point. You will think me superstitious,— some superstition I have in my blood, and always had: nevertheless, this is true—true at least it is that I heard what I now relate.

"As I exclaimed 'Jane! Jane! Jane!' a voice—I cannot tell whence the voice came, but I know whose voice it was—replied, 'I am coming: wait for me;' and a moment after, went whispering on the wind the words—'Where are you?'"

When I first read this book, I'd loved the supernatural component of their relationship—how Mr. Rochester had called for Jane and she'd felt his mental touch and had come back to him.

Maybe Charlotte Brontë had been an unenhanced G-positive.

Trevor slept for just over three hours before he started to dream. When I felt his mind stir into REM sleep, I called his name aloud. At least, I tried to.

"Luff!"

I rolled my eyes at my stupidity. How could I forget that I had this problem? Was I brain damaged, or what? It'd just started a few hours ago! I stroked Trevor's hair, pulling him reluctantly from sleep, leaning down to kiss him when I felt his conscious mind stir. His eyes opened, meeting mine.

I didn't do anything to hurt you, did I?

I shook my head. *Nope.*

Thanks. I really do like sleeping inside in a real bed! He stretched out with a smile. That haunted, grey look was gone and his contentment filled my soul with a spring-green wash of joy.

If you didn't need to dream, I'd watch over you like this every night. I think you'll have to settle for a daily nap. I'd enjoyed the quiet closeness of him. I'd never been able to read with Trevor so near. Usually his thoughts and the written words bumped up against each other in my head.

What happens if I don't dream?

After a while? Memory loss. Mental confusion. Eventually, you'd go into a dream state even when you're awake, like a hallucination. Thank you, neurology textbook.

He appeared to consider it. *But on the upside, I get to sleep with you?*

I laughed, rolling until I was lying across his chest. *So, what do you want to do for the rest of the afternoon?* His first thought involved us doing pretty much what we were already doing, but without clothes. Little tingles of red energy began to dance along my skin and I laughed again.

Your laugh still sounds the same, he thought to me, happily. I was glad he wasn't pretending that nothing was wrong. Or, at least, that he didn't notice anything wrong. He heard that, of course—our mental connection was as strong as ever. *I told you we'd deal with it together.*

There IS something you can help me with this afternoon. It's been a while since I had a shower—

Red electricity seemed to crackle over him and hunger for me filled his thoughts. Part of him was fully ready to go further; the rest of him was holding that part back with a heavy leash of obligation, promise, regret, and concern that he wouldn't be doing what was best for me. I loved both parts of him.

I rolled off of Trevor and put my feet on the floor. Again, his invisible hands prevented me from standing. His thoughts were turbulent and erotic. *Where do you think you're going?* He wasn't sure if he was preventing me from falling or about to pull me back to him and put all of those electric red thoughts into action.

I told you. Shower. I smiled with false innocence. *Unless you want to give me a sponge bath…*

Trevor groaned, lifting me as he stood. His self-control stretched to the breaking point. I laughed again, feeling the delightful, giddy red energy flush across my skin. *Don't worry— we'd be soulmating before you got to second base.*

His eyes met mine and the connection flared between us. *Tease.* Then his mind took a playful turn and he smiled widely. "So, you want a shower, do you?"

You WOULDN'T! I gasped as invisible hands swooped me up. We both laughed as he carried me into the bathroom. He stood me in the shower stall—still in my nightshirt—pulled the shower curtain closed, and turned on the *cold* water.

I shrieked as the icy spray assaulted my head and shoulders. It was too cold to breathe! Downstairs in the kitchen, Hannah reacted with alarm to my scream. *We're okay,* I told her, as she started up the stairs.

Do I want to know? she thought to herself.

No, you really don't.

I fumbled for the hot water knob. It took forever for the water temperature to get above "arctic." Trevor's invisible hands held my waist, keeping my weight off my leg, but also keeping me centered in the freezing spray. The water seemed to move around them, leaving the suggested outline of hands and arms in the cascading droplets. I remembered that he didn't feel hot or cold with them. My eyes narrowed as I sent a full sense of the cold water on my skin through our mental connection.

He gasped as though I'd thrown ice water in his face. In a sense, I had.

The water warmed and I found I could breathe again. I was still laughing. *You're lucky I'm not furious.*

Serves you right, you tease.

It's only teasing if you don't intend to follow through. Otherwise, I think it's called foreplay.

The invisible hands on my waist seemed to tremble slightly. I struggled to pull my soggy nightshirt over my head. The water made it ridiculously heavy. I hung it from the soap dish. The warm spray felt wonderful on my skin. I closed my eyes with a sigh and let it run over me. *Ahh — clean.* I washed and conditioned my hair then took the soap and started lathering my body.

From behind the shower curtain, Trevor groaned. *Oh.* I couldn't contain my smile. I normally popped up a mental shield when I showered at Ganzfield, since I never knew if one of the other minders would be in range. Oops—I guess I "forgot" this time. I started moving the soap more slowly, sensuously rubbing it against my skin, moving toward more strategic places—

One invisible hand briefly left my waist and turned off the hot water. The sudden cold spray hit like a wall, making me shriek again and dive for the knobs. After rinsing, I turned off the water. A solid hand stuck itself around the shower curtain, unceremoniously holding out a towel. I took it, dried myself off, and then wrapped it around my body and pulled the curtain open.

Trevor stood just outside, his eyes shut tight and breathing heavily, desperately trying to think about Fireball.

You can open your eyes. I'm decent.

Hardly. One eye opened narrowly, making sure I was covered. I tried to lean in closer, intent on kissing him, but his invisible hold kept me out of reach. *Clothes.*

I noticed that Hannah's mind was no longer within my range. Was she taking an afternoon nap or had we driven her from the house?

Back in my room, I grabbed some clothes from my dresser and closet—jeans and a brown jersey. *Unsexy enough?* I asked, holding them up for his approval.

He looked at me intensely and gave a little head-shake. *You could be wearing a sweatshirt or a granny gown or a trash bag and you'd still look sexy.*

My heart did a little flip.

Trevor shut his eyes. Red energy pulsed off his skin as he caught mental glimpses of what I saw in the mirror as I dressed. I slid my arms around his waist, feeling his tension—the strain of holding himself back.

Don't hold back with me. I leaned up to kiss him.

Trevor seemed to ignite. His kiss lifted me off my feet, pulling me to the bed. His arms drew me close to him and we met as pure energy in a thermonuclear blast of soulmating, leaving dark afterimages in its wake.

Our hearts beat together in the same, wild rhythm. Our breath mingled between us as we lay with our heads on the single pillow. We looked onto each other's eyes, but saw so much beyond them.

For one thing, I seemed to be glowing—literally. A golden light surrounded me. Was I glowing with Trevor's love? *Aww.* It took us a few seconds to realize why it looked familiar. *Sean looked like this when Rachel used to view him remotely.* We shared a deep aching for Rachel—for her loss. The next thought hit us simultaneously.

Is an RV...?

I think an RV's trying to find me and they're close enough for me to sense the trace in their thoughts.

Cold horror washed through me and my heart seemed to stop. *Oh, my God—*

Isaiah!

He came straight toward the house, a burning seed of hate moving through the cold rain. His fierce anger had a single focus: *extermination.* He wanted to kill us for destroying his voice, his plans, and his cover as Jonas Pike.

Before we could do more than sit up, he sent a lethal blast at Trevor's mind.

CHAPTER 13

In my first week at Ganzfield, Dr. Williamson had tried to read something too personal from my thoughts and I'd automatically shielded. When Isaiah launched his attack against Trevor's mind, I threw a wall up against it—and this one wasn't the subtle spiderweb. It was solid steel—the hull of a battleship— surrounding both our minds and shared consciousness. I squeezed my eyes tightly shut, focusing. Trevor's *life* depended on it. I tasted blood; I must've bitten my lip. My hands balled into fists as my whole body trembled. Oily-black killing energy battered against us, but the shield held—strong and powerful.

Trevor and I communicated faster than thought. We knew what the other was thinking because there was no other. In the wake of soulmating, we were a singularity.

Isaiah's out of our range. We can't fight back from here.

Trevor pulled me up in his arms.

The mental attack faltered and died. Isaiah flicked a golden RV thread against us again—a mental periscope. *Why isn't the boy dead?* Anger and frustration flared cold and grey against us.

That should've killed him. We felt him pull the gun from his jacket pocket. *There's always the old-fashioned way.*

Isaiah's fingers shook as he clicked off the safety. The gun felt heavy in his hands. *The telepath girl's got to die. Now! And without the healers, I can't adapt the telekinetic's ability. There's no reason to keep him alive.* Still-painful, puckered slashes pulled rawly at his scalp and arms as he moved. *Payback for throwing me through the window. God, they almost killed me. No, I can't let either of them live. They might try it again.*

"Maddie!" Trevor wrapped his invisible arms around us as bullets came through the front windows. Shattering glass and splintering wood bounced off the arms of golden light that spread wide around us.

I tucked my head down against his chest. *Focus! Keep the shield up!* Bullets hung inches from us, imbedded in midair. I winced as something slashed into the skin near my ankle, below the invisible shield. Trevor and I felt the pain together.

Trevor's golden energy mixed with the silver of my mental shield, blending together. *Electrum.* We were safe with each other, protecting each other. Isaiah couldn't harm either our minds or our bodies because we shared our souls.

The rain of bullets stopped. I opened one eye and felt for Isaiah's mind. Did he need to reload? Was he going to try something else?

No. Something was wrong with the gun. Isaiah clicked the trigger with impotent rage.

What the hell? We all felt the minds of several other people closing in, focused on Isaiah. In the distance, a siren began to wail. Trevor pulled me close and started to dash downstairs.

Oh, God! Pain slammed into us, a purple-black cloud that obscured our vision and knocked the air from our lungs. Burns bubbled on the skin of Isaiah's chest. Even secondhand, it felt like a liquid scream.

Isaiah ran away from the house, back through the rain. The pain faded with the distance. Trevor staggered downstairs, his equilibrium knocked out of balance by the burning agony we'd felt from Isaiah.

From the front porch, we saw six sparks emerge from various points along the street, converging on Isaiah. From the looks of them, four were McFees and the other two were Underwoods. They rushed toward Isaiah, yelling to each other.

"Faster! He's going for the car!"

"Keep focus on his chest!"

"I'm trying!"

"This damn rain! I can't get the fire to stick!"

"Dave, the gas tank!"

"I know! It's too far!"

"Dammit! He's getting away! Move, move, move!"

"Do it now!"

Somehow, they'd figured out how to combine the effects of their abilities to extend their range. But they were unpracticed, and the rain weakened their ability to light things. Isaiah gunned the engine and was gone.

The sparks gave up their pursuit. Several swore in dripping frustration. They regrouped around us on my mom's front porch.

One of the McFees pulled out a cell phone and made a quick call. "He got away." Disappointment colored his thoughts dirt-brown.

I heard Dr. Williamson's voice through his mind. *"I'll be there soon."*

Another of the sparks looked us over. He was probably in his early twenties, with the standard-issue McFee compliment of red hair and freckles, and was built as solidly as a tree. "You're Maddie and Trevor, right? I'm Dave McFee. You two okay?"

He was pretty sure we weren't okay.

Trevor still held me against his chest. Blood dripped off the end of a four-inch-long sliver of wood embedded just above my ankle. Dave couldn't see the golden shield that Trevor still had wrapped protectively around us, or the silver shield I still maintained over our minds.

The eight bullets floating like a frozen swarm of metal bees caught his attention, though. *Wow. Cool,* he thought, as he realized what they were.

Trevor and I were still too shocked to care. *We almost died.* Isaiah should've been able to kill us. The mental blast should've destroyed Trevor, and then the gun should've destroyed me.

We were still alive because we'd done something we didn't know was possible.

Hannah. Where was she? Had Isaiah done something to her?

"Where's Hannah?" Trevor asked for me.

"She's with the others, a few blocks away," said Dave. "We got her out when Claire said Isaiah was on his way."

They'd known Isaiah was coming? *Why—?*

The police car turned the corner, coming fast. "We don't have a charm with us. We've gotta fake normalcy for the cops, okay?" Dave's worried eyes gave us another once-over.

A half-laugh escaped me. Apparently, Trevor and I didn't look very normal at the moment.

Trevor scooped the bullets from his shield and tossed them back into my room through the splintered remains of the front windows. Any forensics experts would find their positions inexplicable. *What're we going to tell the police?* We needed a plausible reason for someone to've shot up my mom's house.

My mom—the *psychologist*. She dealt with people with mental problems every day. I dropped the shield from my mind and Trevor's, feeling exposed and vulnerable as I did so. However, we had only seconds and I needed to give everyone the same story.

A crazy guy drove up while we were all hanging out, watching a movie. He yelled at the front of the house then opened fire and ran away. Got it? You've never seen him before. You had no idea what was happening. Don't give details except what he was wearing and what the car looked like.

The police car drove up onto the lawn. Two officers jumped out, guns drawn.

I'm in trouble if they ask me any questions, I told Trevor. *I can't answer out loud.*

You're in shock, of course. Look dazed.

No problem. I really didn't need to act for this one.

Once the police officer had established we were unarmed, the sparks did a good job of coordinating their stories about the "deranged man" who'd yelled at the house, and then opened fire.

I mentally supplied the phrase, "Stupid shrink, you ruined my life!" to their stories.

The cops bought it.

My mom drove up. She threw her car into park on the street and ran up in near-panic. She'd had this nightmare before, the one in which she came home to find the house where she'd left her child was now a crime scene.

Mom! We're okay. I'm okay. She shook her head, unused to having my voice in her mind, and didn't even break stride.

I'll believe Maddie's really okay when I can put my arms around her. She kept coming, fast.

A cop stepped forward. "Ma'am, this is a crime scene."

"This is my house. My daughter's in there. You want to stop me, pull a gun on me."

The cop took a moment to assess the look on her face, and then stepped back. I would've smiled, but I knew she was coming for me next. My mom took in the scene from the living room doorway. I sat on the couch, and Trevor's arm protectively circled my shoulders as a paramedic treated the gash above my ankle.

Oh, thank God she's all right. My mom enveloped me in a hug.

Mom, it was Isaiah. She took a flanking position on my free side.

Why didn't that boy do more to keep her safe? Her eyes moved from the blood-soaked bandages on my leg to Trevor.

Mom, don't start. Trevor just saved my life. He stopped the bullets —

An overwhelming sense of *holy crap* hit me. I met Trevor's eyes as I started trembling. It was just as well I had to act like I was in shock.

Actually, who was acting?

Trevor said all the right things to the police. They didn't press me to answer questions with more than a nod or a headshake. I leaned against him and his heartbeat against my cheek soothed me.

The paramedic looked at me critically. "I want you to go to the hospital. You need stitches." *And psychiatric observation for shock and posttraumatic stress.*

I shook my head—not gonna happen. Hey, could my mom talk the paramedic out of that? *Mom, you've got to reassure them that you can handle any psychological problems I may have.*

She met my eyes. "Maybe you should…"

Mom, I'm fine. Really. Did I sound convincing? *And talking to a therapist's not really an option right now, you know?* Geez, and I'd thought my life had been bizarre *before* I'd encountered the killer telepath.

"She'll be okay with us. We'll take care of her," she told the paramedic.

You also can tell the cops that the description of the shooter sounds like a former patient of yours named Jonas Pike, okay?

My mom frowned. She didn't want to lie to the police.

If you tell them the truth, they'll probably commit us both. Dr. Williamson's on his way—he'll explain everything.

It took more than an hour for the police to finish asking us questions. Our shot-up house now had yellow crime scene tape around it. Neighbors returning from work gawked curiously at the shattered windows and the array of police cars on the lawn. My mom had told the cops that we'd stay with friends until they caught the deranged mental patient, Jonas Pike, who'd done this.

One of the officers knew the name. *Jonas Pike. Isn't he a higher-up in some crazy group that claims that people with evil superpowers are among us?*

I hid my smile. That'd actually synched up better than I'd hoped.

In the town car on the next block, Dr. Williamson waited with a shield around his mind. How did he get here so fast? Apparently, he hadn't gone back to Ganzfield after all. I wanted to pepper him with questions, but he stopped me. *Pay attention to the police right now. Make sure the others have the right answers to give them.*

I reluctantly returned my attention to the situation around me. Yikes—just in time. Upstairs, in my destroyed bedroom, the investigating officer scowled as she noticed that the bullets were in the strangest pattern she'd ever seen. *It looks like they were just dropped around the crime scene. What's going on here?* She took several digital pictures, and then started bagging the bullets.

I caught Dave's eye. *Dave, a cop's in the bedroom upstairs. Her camera needs to fry before she leaves, okay?*

Dave smiled and gave me a barely discernable nod. He headed to the top of the stairs to intercept the officer as she left. *Crap.* What if there were pictures of other crime scenes on that camera? Oh well.

The last of the cops pulled away. Dr. Williamson's car arrived less than a minute later, trailed by a black Ganzfield van. I didn't recognize the minds of most of the arrivals.

Hannah found me in the living room. Her thoughts were full of remorse.

What happened? I asked her. *Are you okay?*

"I'm so sorry, Maddie!" She was nearly crying. "I forgot to call right away! I left a message for your mom, and then I had an idea I needed to check out about Broca's area. I didn't call until after lunch!"

"Call?" asked Trevor.

"I was supposed to call Dr. Williamson if Maddie woke up." Hannah suddenly noticed the bandage on my leg. Without asking, she laid her hands on either side of the gauze. The pins and needles started and the laceration healed over cleanly. I decided to leave the bandage on for the rest of the day, in case the police came back.

Dr. Williamson entered the house. As always, his suit was perfect. Cool relief soaked into me. I could relax—Dr. Williamson was in charge now. Everything would be okay.

We all crowded into my mom's living room, pulling chairs from the dining room and the kitchen to find enough seats.

Do I have enough food in the house for all of these people? My mom's thought made me smile.

Dr. Williamson caught sight of our little group huddled on the couch. "Maddie, how are you doing?"

Woke up from a coma this morning, got shot at this afternoon. So, you know, the usual. You?

He smiled, but it didn't reach his eyes. His mental shield grew stronger, and my brow furrowed. It was as though I'd be able to see through the block in his thoughts if I just concentrated more. Something was upsetting him, something more than Isaiah still being on the loose. A hush fell expectantly over the living room as Dr. Williamson cleared his throat.

"It didn't work," he said. "What went wrong?"

What didn't work? I thought. Next to me, Trevor had the same thought. Were we still mentally synched, or just equally out of the loop?

"I called you too late," said Hannah, miserably.

"The rain shorted us out. We should have been able to fry him at that distance." Dave still felt frustrated about that.

"I didn't tell them to move into position in time," said the young woman next to Dave. "I didn't have a strong enough fix on him." Guilt flashed within her, muddy-yellow and acidic. Was this Claire? She was tall with pixie-cut, nearly-black hair and startlingly blue eyes. Dave put a hand on her back and she leaned against him.

"We've had this trap ready for nearly a week. Maddie was put in danger by your incompetence." Dr. Williamson let everyone feel how disappointed he was. I caught a flash of anger underneath that, although I was pretty sure he wasn't trying to broadcast it.

Trap? I asked.

"Why don't you speak aloud?" he asked, chastising me for my latest breach of telepathic etiquette.

Would if I could. I felt my anger rising. I projected into everyone's minds—I still could follow the spirit of the rule, at least. *Isaiah burned out my speech center a week ago last Saturday.*

The shock Dr. Williamson felt was genuine. "What?"

Didn't Hannah tell you when she called?

"I didn't have a chance," interrupted Hannah. "I just told him that you were awake and he asked if you'd been given dodecamine. He hung up as soon as I said yes."

"Once you were awake, Isaiah could track you," Dr. Williamson explained. "He modeled his RV abilities on scans of Charlie Fontaine. Charlie could find G-positive minds as long as they were conscious, even without dodecamine. The ones on dodecamine were like beacons to him; they practically shouted their presence."

So that was why Charlie Fontaine had left Ganzfield—the home of the Screaming Beacons.

Maybe that could be the name for our sports teams.

"I knew Isaiah. I knew he'd feel compelled to come after you. You're a big threat to him."

Next to me, indignation seemed to explode from Trevor. "You used Maddie as *bait*?" His arm tightened protectively around my shoulders.

On my other side, my mom's thoughts filled with dismay.

Dr. Williamson stared back into Trevor's anger. "We needed to get him out in the open and distract him enough that we could get our people close to him. He'd holed up on a farm out in Pennsylvania. We had no way of approaching without him sensing us."

Rachel, I thought.

"Rachel found him last Monday."

"Not in Switzerland," said my mom. *He lied to me.*

"Not in Switzerland. I'm sorry I couldn't tell you the truth, Nina. We couldn't risk Maddie overhearing your thoughts and Isaiah overhearing hers before we sprang the trap."

How did the sparks get so close? I asked.

"We didn't," Dave interrupted. "Since the attack on Ganzfield, we've been up at the place in Connecticut, working on combining our abilities to spark things over long distances." His frustration filled him again, making him wince. "If it hadn't've been for the rain, we would have had him."

You got him in the chest pretty well, I told him.

"We did?"

"It hurt pretty bad," Trevor added, wincing at the memory. "I think he'll recover, though."

"How do you know?" asked another spark. I think her name was Mary. "You're not a telepath."

Trevor and I both blushed as every eye in the room fell on us. "Maddie and I…share a special connection."

I squeezed my eyes shut as the mental barrage of R-rated "special connection" images hit me. My cheeks got even hotter.

"That's enough." Dr. Williamson nearly growled in annoyance. His mind remained opaque to me as he looked closer at us. "Did he get close enough to attack?"

Isaiah… An intense wave of nausea rolled through me with the memory. *Isaiah went after Trevor first.*

Dr. Williamson frowned. "How did—"

I tossed up the mental shield around Trevor and me. It no longer felt quite as strong, since the connection between the two of us wasn't as intense as it'd been just after soulmating, but it was enough to make Dr. Williamson take an actual step back. His mouth opened, although no words came out. He looked from Trevor to me. We were completely blank to him. He could sense the shield, but nothing of either of our thoughts.

"What did she just do?" asked one spark in the corner.

"She just showed me what a real 'special connection' is." Dr.

Williamson stared at us. There was something new in his voice. Was it respect? Was it concern? The core of his thoughts was still unreadable and I'd had enough of that.

I lowered the shield again so he could hear me. *Trevor could've been killed.* The thought made my stomach give another heave and tears pricked at my eyes. *You set us up as bait with no warning, no protection —*

"Isaiah wasn't supposed to get that close to you. It was a calculated risk."

Dark-red anger geysered up within me and I suddenly wanted to blast Williamson's mind. I felt...what?

Used.

I'd been used by this man I'd considered to be like a father to me. Betrayed. *Would you've used Elise as bait like that?*

Williamson's hand shot out, aiming a slap at my face. It stopped mid-air, an inch from my cheek.

"Don't." Trevor's voice was low with cold anger as his unseen arm restrained Williamson's hand.

How DARE you speak about her like that? Williamson's mental voice was blood-red and furious. I'd never seen him lose control like this. *You don't know what it was like to lose her!*

Thanks to you, today I almost found out. I tried unsuccessfully to rein in the tears that escaped down my cheeks. I'd been a sacrificial pawn in the chess game of someone I'd respected and trusted.

Williamson staggered back as though I'd been the one to slap him. His eyes widened and his mental shield slipped away. In that horrible moment, he saw all of his own flaws and weaknesses—and his own willful blindness. He recognized that, since he'd learned Isaiah was alive, he'd been playing Ahab to Isaiah's white whale. He looked at me, seeing me properly for the first time in months, realizing that his shield was gone, and that all of these flaws and faults were exposed to me.

"You nearly died." It finally registered with him, the awful realization that we'd almost been killed. He could've lost me—Maddie, the person, not just the G-positive telepath who might be able to stop Isaiah.

That's sort of the point we've been trying to make.

The edge of my anger evaporated with the intensity of his realization. Williamson was neither as good nor as strong as I'd hoped—as I'd needed him to be. But I understood him. He was trying, and that was a lot to ask of anyone who'd sustained the loss he had.

I'd been ready to raise the mental shield around my mind and Trevor's again. *I could shut him out—I could shut him out forever.* But now that impulse fell away. I remembered how terrible I'd felt back at the camp in Connecticut when I'd thought Williamson was dead. Despite my anger, I knew I didn't want him out of my life.

You're being pretty forgiving. Trevor had caught enough of Williamson's realization second-hand to understand why I felt that way, though. After the past week, Trevor could understand the dark places Williamson had gone to after Elise's death. He knew how it could take a good man down the wrong track. He respected the strength it took to keep going through all of that pain. Despite his flaws, Williamson did care about me—about all of us at Ganzfield. He was doing the best he could.

Isaiah knows where we are. He knows where my mom lives, because of this. What are you going to do about it?

Williamson realized that he'd lost a big chunk of my trust in him today. It hurt him more than he'd imagined it would. I really was like family to him, and he'd put me in danger. He'd let me down. *I'll never do something like this to her again.* With his shield still down, I felt his sincerity.

"I'm going back to Ganzfield. I hope you and Trevor will come. Nina, as well."

Next to me, Trevor radiated discontent. *Will we be safe there? Does Williamson really have Maddie's best interests at heart? Can I still respect him after this? Does this mean that I'm no longer bound to the promise I made him?*

I heard that, I whispered into his mind, realizing what that meant for our relationship. *Sounds like a silver lining to me.* Red energy began to tingle along my skin.

Trevor flicked his eyes across me. *Isn't your mom right here?*

Curses! Foiled again!

Trevor smiled. *Better than a cold shower.*

I sent him a mental splash of cold water and he gasped.

What do you think? I said, turning serious. *Should we go back? We can't stay here.*

A stray, loud thought from one of the sparks interrupted us. *Geez, minders are creepy!* Apparently, from his point of view, we'd just been staring at each other, giving random emotional responses from time to time.

I think they need us. And there's safety in numbers.

Across from me, I felt Williamson's flickering hope flare up, white and clean, out of the twisting regrets in his thoughts.

*If he ever puts you in danger again...*Trevor's protective anger swelled.

I turned to Williamson, knowing he'd followed the silent conversation. *Fix the weaknesses in the security. No more using unsuspecting people as bait. No shielding important things from me.*

He nodded.

Trevor still felt wary, but he trusted my judgment. He nodded.

It's home. If you go, I go.

Mom, I think there's a bunch of people up at Ganzfield with a lot of posttraumatic stress. They could use your help. How about a sabbatical, away from the house where the psychotic killer knows you live?

"I don't know…"

C'mon, Mom. Your choice—psychotic killer or time with your daughter?

"Well, if you put it that way…" She smiled. She already knew a colleague who'd cover her patients, since she'd considered taking a leave of absence over the past week.

We all hit the road a half hour later, heading up to the camp in Connecticut for the night. My mom drove her car in the middle of the caravan. The van followed, while Greg took the lead with the town car. Williamson mentally scanned the area until we took the on-ramp onto Route 287. This road would take us around the city and avoid the worst of the mental congestion. It was a relief not to be on-duty, listening for the thoughts of people who wanted to kill us. I could just go along for the ride.

From the town car, Williamson's thoughts turned to me. He knew he hadn't been forgiven, but I was willing to give him another chance. He was determined not to blow it. *I'm glad you're coming back.*

I sat between the suitcases in the back seat of my mom's car, a tiny sedan where legroom went to die. Trevor was in the front passenger seat. He startled at the secondhand connection, and I reached a hand over the top of the seat to take his. *I've never spoken mind-to-mind between two moving cars. It's a little weird.*

Think of it as using cell phones, thought Williamson. Something sparked in his mind at the mention of phones. *That reminds me—*

what exactly did you do with Locus Two Systems? I got a call from Nick Coleman a few days ago.

A rock of trepidation lodged in my gut. *Did I do something wrong?*

The SEC seemed to think so. They were in his office asking about you last week.

Oh, my God in Heaven.

Nick took care of it, Williamson quickly reassured me. *He deals with that sort of thing from time to time for me, as well. They've already closed the inquiry. But seriously Maddie—six million dollars?*

What? Cold splashed through my heart and my jaw dropped. Trevor startled. "What?"

My mom jumped and the car swerved slightly before she corrected. "What's wrong?"

Six million? Really? I thought it would be about sixty thousand dollars. I felt sick. Where had this six million figure come from? And, most importantly, had I made that much or lost it?

Nick said the value of your trust was over six-point-two million on Friday, with the new price on the options. Where'd you get the tip?

Elevator. On the way to Nick Coleman's office. Six MILLION? Really? What the heck had happened?

I felt Williamson's laughter as he figured out why I was so shocked. *Contracts are for a hundred shares each, Maddie.*

I'd optioned a hundred times as much as I'd planned. I was now worth millions of dollars after my very first stock trade. No wonder the SEC was looking into me. The highway sped along outside the window. I felt dizzy.

Oops.

In the front seat, Trevor started to laugh. *By accident? Let me get this straight. You're worth millions of dollars right now, and it's because you made a mistake?*

It took a lot of the fun out of being rich—the fact that I'd screwed up and it wasn't done on purpose. I'd be reminded that I'd done something wrong every time I thought about the money—money that would re-build my mom's house, install a fairly indestructible bed frame in the church for Trevor, fix up Ganzfield...

That's it, my mom thought from the driver's seat. *I'm going to try that dodecamine stuff. I'm tired of not being part of the conversation.*

Mom, I began, *I don't think you need to worry anymore about whether your homeowner's insurance will cover repairing the bullet-holes...*

THE END OF BOOK TWO

Keep reading for a sneak preview of:

LEGACY

THE THIRD GANZFIELD NOVEL BY

KATE
KAYNAK

Coming in January 2011 from Spencer Hill Press

CHAPTER 1

Trevor and I had wanted to wait until dark to steal the car, but that would've been too late. As soon as the last of the dinner stragglers cleared the area around the old barn, Trevor telekinetically opened the large, double doors and we both winced as the old hinges creaked loudly. I listened telepathically for someone to notice the noise as I continued to shield our thoughts from the other minders.

The late-May, New Hampshire evening suddenly felt too warm, and the pinkish-gold cast of the protracted sunset made everything look like it'd been dipped in honey. The sun stayed up until nine this time of year, so it was later than it felt. Wiping my palm against my jeans, I tried to slow my heartbeat.

I cast a quick mental glance into the main building. Williamson was up on the third floor, his head filled with financial forecasts. I couldn't feel Seth, but that meant nothing—his telepathic range was so large, he'd sense me long before I felt him. And the newest minder at Ganzfield was the last person I wanted to explain myself to tonight.

Trevor grabbed the keys for the grey sedan from the rack by the door. I slid across the driver's seat to the passenger side, never letting go of his hand. In the three months since we'd returned to Ganzfield, we'd practiced this shared mental shield frequently. It'd saved our lives when Isaiah Lerner had tracked us to my mom's place in New Jersey.

Trevor eased the car out of the barn. The long driveway looped in front of the main building and wound through the trees to the front gate. He turned on the headlights once we'd entered the gloom beyond the treeline.

Where do you think you're going?

Crap—*Seth.* Trevor gave my hand a quick squeeze as a figure moved across the driveway in front of us. I focused on the shield, knowing that even Seth couldn't get through it now.

Of all the lousy luck.

I'd been hoping that he'd be at the power station or the back gate, out of range. If anyone else had been on-duty here tonight, we could've bluffed our way out with a mention of "minder business.'"

Trevor rolled the car to a stop. The headlights illuminated Seth as he stood in the middle of the gravel drive—blocking our way. I glanced at Trevor, meeting his warm, chocolate-brown eyes. He gave my hand another reassuring squeeze as I bit my lip. *Maddie, I'll talk to him. It'll be okay.*

Trevor slid the window down as Seth stepped into the shadowed space between the headlights. Shielding, I couldn't broadcast thoughts to anyone other than Trevor. We'd have to talk aloud to Seth, just like normal people.

Actually, since I could no longer talk, Trevor would have to speak for both of us.

Seth's annoyance came through loudly. Nothing kept out

other people's thoughts—except distance. I always heard what other people thought around me, even when I didn't want to.

Seth's appearance still didn't match his mental presence for me. I'd never pictured him with this mane of red-gold hair. He kept it pulled back in a ponytail because he hadn't had a haircut in years—having people in physical contact made them excruciatingly loud to him. It'd actually hurt Seth to get a haircut.

"Hey, Seth." Trevor spoke just like everything was normal.

Seth's thoughts flashed through all the things wrong with this situation. We were stealing a car and trying to sneak out. Beyond the walls of Ganzfield, Isaiah was killing G-positives like us—and I was almost certainly near the top of his killing "to-do" list, since I shared the same ability to lethally overload other people's minds. After what'd happened in Jersey, he now knew who I was.

"Rachel said he was down near Atlanta this afternoon." Trevor knew that Seth would understand who *he* was. "It's safe." Rachel could track Isaiah better than the other RVs could—we'd figured a way for me to share my memories of him to strengthen her remote viewing ability. Once she knew a person or object, she could locate them anywhere on the planet. I sometimes wondered how far into outer space she might be able to find things.

Isaiah's not the only problem out there. The Sons of Adam—

"You know I'd never let anyone hurt Maddie, right?" Trevor interrupted him. "We need to do this. It's important."

What's so important?

Trevor and I both flushed and I pulled the shield tighter. "Can't tell you. We'll be back soon."

Let me ask Williamson—

Tell Seth to get out of the way right now or I'm dropping the shield, I said to Trevor. We were busted—but we could still do what we needed to before dealing with Williamson.

"Seth, she's going to drop the shield if you don't stand back." Trevor's voice held a you-know-what-she's-like tone. He didn't enjoy being in the middle of our bickering, but Seth annoyed me like the older brother I'd never had—or wanted.

Seth's shock splashed over me, tinged with annoyance and several really bad words. Dropping the shield wouldn't physically injure him, but my minder-loud thoughts would hurt as though hell itself had set up shop between his ears. He quickly backed out of the car's way. His accusatory mental presence followed us as we drove away, and dark-yellow guilt seeped through me. *Crap*—Seth had enough pain in his head without my adding to it. Sensing everyone's final, terrified thoughts as they'd died in the massacre a few months ago had traumatized him.

We keyed in the code to open the front gate. It only took a few minutes to drive out to North Conway. I kept up a constant mental scan of the area, alert for ambushes, for people who hated us, or for traces of Isaiah's mental presence. Once we entered town, the mental babble increased and I flitted from mind to mind, listening for those who wanted to harm us.

—think he's cheating on me—

—MORE ketchup!

—sick of hearing about her boyfriend problems. She should just dump him and—

—kid whines one more time about the damn ketchup, I'm feeding him to the damn wolverines—

—this dress make me look fat? I feel—

—want to get home and have a beer—

—she looks kinda heavy in that dress—

Paranoid behavior? I wish. It's not paranoia if people really *do* want to kill you.

We found the Rite-Aid, relieved that it was still open. Trevor wrapped invisible arms around us as I slid out of the driver's door behind him. At five foot three, I could stand in front of him and not block his view. Someone might shoot at us from beyond my mental range so we had to be careful. The anxiety made our muscles hum with a twitchy, nervous energy as we walked together to the front door of the store.

At least we could do that now—my limp was finally gone. One of the strokes Isaiah had caused had damaged my motor cortex so I'd been through painfully boring physical therapy to re-train my brain to control my left leg. Williamson had paid the physical therapist double her rate and had Cecelia charm her to forget anything strange that she'd seen, particularly my less-than-traditional way of talking into people's heads. We didn't want other people to find out about all of the unusual stuff up at Ganzfield. If word got out that a bunch of teenagers with super-powers were training up here, it would be very bad.

Witch-hunt.

I felt Trevor's hand on my shoulder, warm and reassuring, as we stepped into the overly-bright fluorescent light and scanned the signs at the ends of the aisles. The Rite-Aid was nearly empty—it was almost 9 p.m. and they'd be closing soon.

We found the right aisle: "Family Planning." I looked at the various products, totally unsure which one we needed. Trevor had even less of a clue than I did. I finally grabbed a purple-and-white box and we silently headed up to the checkout.

The blue-aproned woman behind the counter was probably in her sixties, grandmotherly and stern with short, salt-and-pepper hair and narrow-lensed glasses. She looked at Trevor and me, two clearly-anxious teenagers, and down at the sole item we were purchasing.

A home-pregnancy test.

Her mind filled with the obvious conclusion and I felt my whole face flush crimson. She took the cash from my hand. I now had a credit card tied to my ridiculous new bank account, but I didn't want a paper trail for this particular purchase.

The cashier looked critically at Trevor, internally debated saying anything, and then let it out. "I hope you plan to marry her."

I closed my eyes and counted to ten slowly, trying to ignore this stranger's unspoken assumptions. This was *so* not-her-business.

Trevor's face was serious. "Absolutely."

In a different situation, I know he would've laughed.

I held the little plastic shopping bag close as we headed to the car, checking again for people trying to kill us. Driving back, I felt a twitchy tension, like little wild birds under my skin. My hands opened and closed on the little box under the thin skin of plastic. The gate closed behind us.

You are SO busted.

I dropped my shield to yell at Seth, annoyed that he'd prudently gotten far enough away that my thoughts wouldn't hurt him. *You are such a jerk! You know we wouldn't leave Ganzfield if it wasn't important!*

What did you think was so impor—

I still had the pregnancy test in my hands, and now Seth could hear my thoughts.

What? HOLY—

Just SHUT UP! It's not what you think. I pushed up the shield again, feeling a painful sinking in my gut. There really was only one thing that he didn't know now, but protecting that last secret was important.

* * *

Acknowledgements

I'd like to thank everyone who contributed to *Adversary*. Specifically—Mom & Olin, Beth Rosenheim, Heather Tessier, "Aunt Nancy" Schoeller, Peter Alton, Mitch Ross, and Alison Ross for their suggestions. Rich Storrs and Jessica Porteous deserve a special mention for their detailed feedback, which caught things I'd missed even after a dozen readings. Leah Sloan, for her character and her prayer. My editor, Deborah Britt-Hay and all the people at Spencer Hill Press. Jed Goldstone, for first introducing me to the celebration of Groundhog's Day Eve. Jack Noon, for his 11th hour rescue of my manuscript from the clutches of its typos, as well as his expertise with firearms. Amy Fowler Rufo, Rosa Burtt, and Cassandra Hogle. And always—Taner, Aliya, and Logan.

Ve eşim Osman—seni seviyorum, canım.
Sen benim Trevor'sın.

About Kate Kaynak

I was born and raised in New Jersey, but I managed to escape. My degree from Yale says I was a psych major, but I had *way* too much fun to have paid much attention in class.

After serving a five-year sentence in graduate school, I started teaching psychology around the world for the University of Maryland's Overseas Program.

While in Izmir, Turkey, I started up a conversation with a handsome stranger in an airport. I ended up marrying him. We now live in New Hampshire with our three preschool-aged kids, where I enjoy reading, writing, and fighting crime with my amazing superpowers.

Come find out more about *Minder, Adversary,* and the other books of the *Ganzfield* series at **www.Ganzfield.com.**

5812018R0

Made in the USA
Charleston, SC
06 August 2010